# THE CAPITOL CHASE

# Also by Cap Daniels

**The Chase Fulton Novels Series**

# THE
# CAPITOL
# CHASE

**CHASE FULTON NOVEL #31**

## CAP DANIELS

ANCHOR WATCH
PUBLISHING
** USA **

The Capitol Chase
Chase Fulton Novel #31
Cap Daniels

This is a work of fiction. Names, characters, places, historical events, and incidents
are the product of the author's imagination or have been used fictitiously. Although
many locations such as marinas, airports, hotels, restaurants, etc. used in this work
actually exist, they are used fictitiously and may have been relocated, exaggerated, or
otherwise modified by creative license for the purpose of this work. Although many
characters are based on personalities, physical attributes, skills, or intellect of actual
individuals, all the characters in this work are products of the author's imagination.

Published by:

ANCHOR WATCH
PUBLISHING
** USA **

13 Digit ISBN: 978-1-951021-69-6
Library of Congress Control Number: 2025935300
Copyright © 2025 Cap Daniels – All Rights Reserved

Cover Design: German Creative

Printed in the United States of America

# The Capitol Chase

## CAP DANIELS

# Chapter 1
## *D-Day*

June 6, 1944 — Off the coast of Normandy, France

*It's pretty bad, I'd say. They tell me I'm aboard a tub called the HNLMS Soemba. At least I think that's what they said.*

*When they hauled me over the rail, I wouldn't have cared if it was a Jap boat. I was just glad to be out of the water. The day started at 0130 hours back at RAF Bodney. The weather was shite, and the faces of them over me weren't much better. They set out some electric lights down the edge of the strip so we could see to hold our heading 'til we got off the ground. The rain and fog wouldn't allow for fires to stay lit, so the dim lights were all we had.*

*I was in the third flight behind one and two of the 486th Fighter Squadron. When the second flight lined up after the first was airborne, I remember thinking their tails weren't exactly right, but I held my tongue. I had enough to worry about trying to take off in that soup. I guess now, I wish I would've called out. I knew they weren't right. I just knew it. They were lined up a few degrees off. They should've laid out those electric lights on both sides of the strip, but I guess they only had enough for one side.*

*When that second flight took off, Bob Frascotti, Bud Fuhrman's wingman, hit a control tower the Sea Bees were building. He was heavy, full of gas and bullets, so he probably never felt a thing. I couldn't get that orange fireball out of my head all day. 'Course, I didn't know it was*

*Bob 'til up in the morning after we were all airborne. Frascotti was a good man. He was from Milford, Massachusetts. Milford Mass, he called it. If I live through this war, maybe I'll go call on his mother just to tell her how good a man she raised. Maybe.*

*After Bob's crash, the fire on one side and the electric lights on the other kept us from lining up askew, and the rest of the 352nd Fighter Group got off the ground without any more trouble, except that trouble every one of us carried in our hearts for Bob.*

*By the time we got to Normandy, the weather was getting better, and we could see the ground, most of the time. The Navy was blasting 'em pretty hard. Utah Beach was our target. The USS Nevada with her 14" guns was giving them the business at Utah. She was the only battleship shelling Utah. The rest were farther east at Omaha, Gold, Juno, and Sword. I'd seen a lot of war before today, but I'd never seen none like that. Every ship in the world was lobbing ordnance on those beaches. It seemed like every airplane the allies could throw into the sky was there, dropping everything from paratroopers to bombs. The 101st and the 82nd Airborne looked like a hundred thousand mushrooms floating to the ground out of those C-47s. Those were some brave boys to jump out of those airplanes and ride that parachute to the ground just so they could shuck it off and get to fighting. I guess the good Lord gave them a measure of courage the rest of us didn't get, and I'm sure glad they're on our side.*

*We strafed the machine gun nests over the beach to soften it up for the boys from the boats. I guess they got themselves a double helping of that courage, too. They were pouring ashore like ants, and it was up to us and the Navy to make it as easy as we could for them. There wasn't anything easy about it from where I sat. I was close enough to watch those boys fall and never get up again. I wonder if they'll ever be able to count how many of our boys will die on that beach. I've come to know that there ain't never been nothing worse that man can do than war. Sometimes winning hurts worse than losing, and everything inside me thinks this day will forever be a reminder to the country of just how much it costs to win. To most folks whose sons and husbands and fathers are down there on that beach, I don't suppose it'll ever feel like it's worth it.*

*I put a five-hundred-pounder in a hardened, heavy machine gun nest that must've had a dozen guns in it. I don't know if it was Krauts, Italians, or Japs in it, but they were laying down some serious fire on our boys. That five-hundred-pounder turned that nest into a little corner of Hell, but there must've been a thousand more just like it, and I only had one more bomb. I was hell-bent on making it count, and I was doing it for Bob Frascotti.*

*The five-hundred-pounders weren't the only favor I brought to the party today. Those Browning fifty-cals in the wings packed a pretty good punch of their own. The other blue-nosed bastards of Bodney and I must've spit out a million rounds. We plowed the ground with them and sent many a man to meet his maker.*

*Don't get me wrong. It wasn't a cakewalk. There was no shortage of anti-aircraft fire. I watched more than a few of the C-47s burn in with paratroopers streaming out of them like rats from a burning ship. Those boys are big and slow. They make easy targets for a half-good ground gunner, but our Mustangs were harder to pick off. We're small and fast and nimble. That didn't stop them from trying. I'm still not sure what hit me, but I hope my boys behind me fed them a bellyful of American lead for their trouble.*

*My counter said I had less than a hundred rounds of fifty-cal left in the wings, so I was going to put my last five-hundred-pounder right down the gullet of some Kraut cutting down Americans on the beach. I guess I got too one-eyed on that big ol' heavy gun nest. It was all I could see. It was just him and me, and I'd be the one still alive thirty seconds after I turned her loose.*

*I was counting down the seconds and staring right down the barrels of that nest. There must've been more than two dozen of them. That probably meant fifty or more men who were about to take their last breath. With two seconds to go before setting that ordnance free, the whole world turned black, and it felt like I'd flown into a mountain.*

*I was in the dark and dazed. I thought I might be blind until I saw streaks of light slicing through the black oil covering my canopy. I flipped on the instrument lights, and the artificial horizon and airspeed indicator told me I was still flying, but the manifold pressure down to thirty-five inches said I wasn't going to be flying for long. With more oil outside the engine than inside, I had to decide where I was going to crash.*

*I dumped the five-hundred-pounder and the drop tanks to get myself as light as possible. I was making over three hundred miles an hour, so I had plenty of speed to get myself back out over the water, but which direction was the water? I figured it had to be north, so I gave her a turn, just hoping and praying I still had some control over what was left of my Mustang. She came around, but she did it ugly. The manifold pressure, airspeed, and altitude were falling, and I was pointed straight for the Nevada and her fourteen-inchers. I hadn't seen the round that hit me right in the blue nose, and if the Nevada hit me, I wouldn't see it either, thanks to the face full of oil on the windscreen.*

*I finally got the canopy open and tried to remember how high I needed to be for my parachute to open. I didn't want to get out and float down to that beach or into one of the landing craft. My single pistol and I wouldn't last ten seconds down there. I needed to get beyond the troop carriers, where I had a decent chance at getting picked up by an allied boat. My Mustang and I were going into the water. I just hadn't decided if we were going together or apart.*

*That's when the big, beautiful Merlin engine gave up the ghost, and I was suddenly a glider pilot. The Mustang does a lot of things well, but gliding ain't one of them. Airspeed was 220 and falling. Altitude 780 and falling. I seemed to remember eight hundred feet being the minimum jump altitude to get a full parachute deployment, so that was out. The old girl and I were going to keep dancing 'til the band packed up for the night.*

*For the first time in hours, my world was quiet. The only sound was the wind rushing past the open cockpit. A thousand things went through my head. I had a hundred bullets left. They probably weighed half a pound each. I could pull the trigger and shuck off 50 pounds, giving me a little more gliding distance, but if I pulled the trigger while pointed north, I'd be shooting into the good guys. Since I couldn't get rid of my bullets, my mind set out on a crazy course that didn't make any sense, but I was in the middle of World War Two, in a dead airplane over the largest invasion in the history of man. Making sense went out the window a long time ago.*

*I threw everything out of the airplane I could grab—my boots, manuals, star charts, my parachute, seat cushion, and the two biscuits I'd wrapped in paper before taking off. The instant the parachute left my hand and flew overboard, I remembered the number: five hundred feet. It takes five hundred feet for it to open. My eyes shot to the altimeter that was rolling past six hundred ten feet. It didn't matter. The decision was made, and I was committed to a water landing.*

*With the parachute and seat cushion gone, my harness was hanging loosely across my shoulders, so I drew up the straps and pulled them as tight as I could get them. That's when I took my first look outside. I leaned to the left and saw the grey water beneath me. What I didn't see was the battleship I expected. A few smaller boats dotted the water, but nothing big. The smoke from the stacks of the ships was blowing to the southwest, so that put the wind out of the northeast. Ditching an airplane in heavy seas is a death trap. Landing in the trough between two swells is the only way to survive, so I positioned myself parallel to the swells and prepared for the first water landing of my life. Part of me believed it might be my last.*

*The closer I got to the water, the more I regretted my decision to toss my chute, but I didn't have time to punish myself for that bad decision. If I survived, I'd give myself the stern tongue-lashing I deserved. I'd never been taught to ditch a P-51, but I was seconds away from either learning how to do it, or learning how to do it wrong.*

*The belly hit, and I thought I'd hit a warship. I expected to slide across the water like a boat before stopping, but I was wrong. The Mustang and I shuddered from the impact and stopped in what felt like* inches. When I caught my breath, I couldn't tell if I was hurt, but I could definitely tell that I was sinking. The Mustang makes a terrible life raft, so I got out. The Mae West life jacket we all hated turned into my best friend. I blew into the pipe, and the horse collar inflated like a balloon around my neck.

I didn't think I was bleeding, but I was in a lot of pain. My arms didn't work so good, and I wasn't sure I could feel my legs. I don't know how long I was in the water, but it didn't really feel very long. A couple of sailors speaking a language I'd never heard hauled me over the rail of a ship and laid me on the deck.

I'm now on a cot somewhere on the smallest ship I've ever seen, with only one man who can speak a little English anywhere in sight. The ship is Dutch, he tells me. She's the HNLMS Soemba. His Netherlands Majesty's Ship Soemba

I fared better than the Mustang, with a few broken bones and no boots. If Operation Overlord doesn't bring the world to an end, maybe I'll find a way to get off this Rotterdam raft and back to my squadron in Bodney.

1LT Robert Richter, 486th FS, 352nd FG, RAF Bodney

## Chapter 2
# *Rainbows and Butterflies*

Summer 2015 — Bonaventure Plantation, St. Marys, GA

I closed Dr. Richter's journal and squeezed the leather-bound, first-hand-account history book between my palms. It would always be challenging for me to think of my mentor, Dr. Robert Rocket Richter, as anything other than the greatest psychology professor in the world, but there had been a time when he was young and fearless and far from home. Reading his journals from WWII is one of the greatest pleasures of my life. Seeing the world through the eyes of the man who would change my life forever gave me a window into the reality of a world in perpetual conflict that few had. I would always be grateful that he took the time to document those days over Europe some seventy years before.

I typically read Dr. Richter's journals aboard *Aegis*, my 50' sailing catamaran, or in the hangar overlooking the North American P-51D Mustang that had been his before he left it to my loving care. On that day, though, I was sitting in one of my favorite spots on Earth—the gazebo in my backyard on the bank of the North River, with the centerpiece of the eighteenth-century naval cannon standing guard against pirates, or the British, or just a flock of seagulls in search of an easy meal.

The cannon had descended from the deck of a burning, sinking warship in the Cumberland Sound during the War of 1812. Clark Johnson and I pulled it out of the mud and muck as a gift for my great-uncle, Judge Bernard Henry Huntsinger, who'd left me the property that had been in my mother's family since the Revolutionary War. I turned the plantation into a state-of-the art operational and training facility for Tactical Team 21—my gang of misfit toys who traveled the world righting wrongs and growing tighter as a family with every new mission.

Our most recent assignment dropped us right into the heart of the Amazon Rainforest and the biggest mess I'd ever seen. Stone W. Hunter, a former member of the team, had turned one of life's corners and dedicated his life to the toils and trials of a missionary in the deepest, darkest jungle. He found himself in a little trouble, so we hopped on down to South America to give him a hand. The mission turned into more than any of us imagined it could be and left me to pay a toll I wasn't prepared to pay.

My world came crashing down around me after the mission, leaving me in desperate need of some time off. The rest of the team felt it, too, so we took a couple of months to recuperate and recharge. I don't know where everyone went, but we all made an escape from the reality of our lives in our own separate directions.

As for me, I finally made good on my promise to take Penny on the honeymoon she deserved. We dived, flew, surfed, skied, lay in hammocks, and fell in love a thousand more times from St. Barts to St. Moritz. I learned to snow ski. Well, that's not entirely true. I learned how to fall down and slide face-first down a mountain while wearing snow skis. Penny learned to land a de Havilland Twin Otter on one of the shortest commercial runways in the world.

The honeymoon was over, and I had called in the troops. It was time to get our bodies back in shape, put a few hundred thousand rounds through our weapons, and push each other through the shoot house until we could predict each other's movements as if they were our own. We'd been out of the saddle too long, and there was little doubt in my mind that duty would call sooner rather than later.

The team was due back at Bonaventure in 48 hours, but they

weren't the only ones headed for coastal Georgia. I had a little post-honeymoon surprise for my wife that I'd been working on for years. Thanks to a few well-placed friends in Foggy Bottom, I was finally ready to tie a big red bow around the present and lay it at Penny's feet.

Since the murder of my parents in Panama when I was barely a teenager, I longed for just one more hour with them—just one more chance to play catch with my dad or hear my mother sing. I was blessed with financial success beyond anything I could've ever imagined, but no matter how many digits there were in my bank balance, I couldn't buy just one more afternoon with my parents.

Penny was in a similar but slightly different situation. Her parents were still alive but out of reach. Mitchel and Carla Thomas made their way onto the wrong side of the federal court system. Her father, Mitchel, found himself in the federal Witness Security Program, and her mother, Carla, was on extended, albeit interrupted, parole for a complex collection of what Penny liked to call "misunderstandings." Ultimately, the two chose self-exile on the island of Vanuatu in the South Pacific, some eight thousand miles away, that coincidently had no extradition treaty with the U.S.

My beautiful, wild-haired wife glided down the stairs from the back gallery of our home and across the lawn. "Whatcha doin' out here?"

I waggled Dr. Richter's journal in the air. "Just a little reading."

She stepped barefooted onto the cradle of the ancient cannon and planted herself on the barrel. "Anything interesting?"

"You might say that. It gave me an idea for a trip, but it'll have to wait."

She cocked her head and brushed the hair out of her face. "I thought you were finished postponing pleasure trips."

"I am, but this one is for a really good reason. I have something for you."

She narrowed her gaze, and I slipped an envelope into her hand.

She studied it and froze on the seal at the upper left corner. "The Office of the President of the United States. What is this?"

"It's part one of your surprise," I said. "Think of it as an overdue honeymoon gift."

"Can I open it?"

"It's yours. You can do anything you want with it."

She bounced the envelope against her palm. "What have you done, Chase Fulton?"

"Just open it. I think you'll like it."

She never took her eyes from mine as she ran a fingernail beneath the flap. "Should I be afraid?"

"Definitely not. It's something very good and extremely rare."

She hesitated before pulling the folded sheets from inside the envelope. "I've never gotten anything from the President before."

I shrugged but kept my silence.

She unfolded the two sheets and examined them line by line. I don't know what I expected, but it wasn't what happened. Penny lowered her head and sobbed without making a sound.

I panicked. "Should I not have done it?"

She bit her lip, dropped the papers, and leapt into my arms. "How? How did you ever get this done?"

She squeezed me until I thought I was going to burst, and I returned the affection. When we parted, she kissed me as if I were her knight in shining armor, and I liked it.

She wiped the tears from her face and shook me. "Is there anything you *can't* do?"

"Sure, there's plenty I can't do, but this is . . ."

She reached down for the papers. "Presidential pardons? For both of them? Chase, this is the best thing anyone has ever done for me. You just don't know. When?"

"When what?" I asked.

"When can they come home?"

I checked my watch. "We're picking them up in Jacksonville in two hours."

She slammed both hands onto my chest. "I'm going to kill you. I've gotta wash my hair, and you know how long it takes to deal with this mane. My God, Chase. I can't believe you." She slammed a kiss onto my lips almost as aggressively as she'd pounded my chest. "I love you, I love you, I love you. Don't leave without me!"

With that, she was gone, back up the steps, and inside the house like a tornado. The envelope and papers still lay at my feet. I'd never understand women, but I loved it when I got it right.

Forty-five minutes later, she emerged from the bathroom, ready for the red carpet.

"What did I ever do to deserve a woman like you?"

She giggled. "This old thing? Aw, shucks. I just threw something on."

I took a step toward her, and she waved a finger. "Nope! Don't touch. I know you, Chase Fulton, and it'll have to wait. Trust me, though, I'll make it well worth your wait. Now, let's go."

The drive to Jacksonville should've taken an hour, but thanks to the confidence in the Secret Service credentials in my pocket and the tactical look of our blacked-out Suburban, we made it in less than forty-five.

I love airports, but I loathe commercial airport terminals. Everyone is late or mad or both. I hoped the day would never come when it was necessary for me to cram my legs into a coach seat on anything with wings. I loved our ability to fly privately, but hauling two ex-pats halfway around the world is a challenge, regardless of who owns the airplane. The tickets cost five grand, but Mitchel and Carla Thomas were back on American soil for the first time in almost a decade, and Penny was seconds away from holding them in her arms for the first time in what had to feel like a lifetime.

The reunion was beautiful to behold. I kept my distance as the three of them hugged, kissed, cried, and screamed as if a thousand years had passed since their last moment together. When the celebration waned, Mitchel looked up, caught my eye, and offered the most sincere nod of appreciation I would ever see.

My relationship with the White House wasn't always rainbows and butterflies, but my team and I had pulled the President's butt out of the flames enough to warrant a stroke of his pen to reunite the woman I adored more than anything on Earth with her parents she missed so deeply. I envied the emotion they were experiencing, but I treasured the joy of seeing all of them completely absorbed by each other.

The coming weeks of my life would be consumed by training. That would get me out of Penny's hair and give her absolute freedom to spend every minute with her parents, doing whatever they wanted, wherever they wanted, whenever they wanted. When the next assignment came down, the team and I wouldn't have that luxury, and I had every reason to believe the President himself would call in a favor or two in exchange for his most recent courtesy.

# Chapter 3

## *Court Martial, Anyone?*

"I've got a crazy request," my father-in-law said as I pulled the key fob from my pocket in short-term parking.

I tossed him the keys. "I live with your daughter, Mitchel. There's no such thing as a crazy request in my world anymore."

We climbed aboard the Suburban with Mitchel behind the wheel and wound our way out of the Jacksonville International Airport parking area that would've made a pretty good corn maze.

"I've not driven anything besides a dinghy, a bicycle, and a sailboat for ten years, and I feel like a lab rat in a puzzle. There's got to be an exit and a piece of cheese around here somewhere."

I was no help, but Mitchel finally picked his way out of the lot and onto I-95.

Penny and Carla shared a swimming pool full of genes. The elder gave me a glimpse into the future of how my wife would look in a quarter century, and I was pleased. The same flawless skin, the same beautiful bright eyes, and the most gleaming smile imaginable were but three of their unmistakable similarities. The most obvious of their common genetics was their shared ability to talk nonstop and listen at the same time.

Mitchel leaned across the console. "I owe you about a hundred thousand thank-yous, but for now, I'm really grateful for you giving her somebody to talk to besides me."

I tried not to laugh, but I couldn't pull it off. After a quick glance across my shoulder, I said, "They're worth it, though, right?"

"Oh, yeah."

After a few dozen cars passed us, I pointed toward the speedometer. "It's gonna take a while to get to Bonaventure at forty-five miles an hour."

He chuckled. "Yeah, I guess life on a sailboat kind of takes the concept of speed out of an old guy's head. Sorry about that."

We made seventy, then sixty-four, then eighty-six, and I said, "The cruise control works, too."

By the time we made the exit to St. Marys, Mitchel was back in the saddle with refreshed driving skills, and I gave him turn-by-turn directions until we pulled onto the pecan-tree-lined, crushed shell driveway of our home.

"Welcome to Bonaventure Plantation."

He leaned forward and took in the three-story brick structure that was far more than just our home, then he let out a low whistle. "Well, this is nice."

"It's been in my mother's family since the seventeen hundreds. They grew pecans, cotton, and tea through the years."

"So, your family owned slaves," he said.

There was no condescension or judgment in the statement, but it opened the door for me to tell the story that made me proudest of my family.

"Only for a very short while," I began. "My great-grandfather, and those before him, bought slaves at the market in Charleston and brought them to Bonaventure, but immediately upon their arrival, every patriarch in my mother's family made the slaves he'd just purchased freemen with the option to stay and work the plantation for a share of the profit. Most turned down the option, took their papers, and left the plantation as freemen. A few stayed and raised families here. They and their families were provided a place to live, education, healthcare, a Christian church, and a fair share of the profits of the plantation. It wasn't a glamorous life, but it was far better than life on most of the other plantations throughout the South."

"That's amazing, Chase. It sounds like you come from pretty good stock, as we say in Texas."

I said, "I know one thing for sure. If a man relies on the goodness of his ancestors to carry him through life, he won't make it very far. A lot of people are extremely proud of their ancestors, but I try to live my life in a way that would make my ancestors proud of me."

"You know something? A fellow couldn't ask for a better man for his daughter. Thank you for everything . . . all of it."

"Thank you," I said. "Come on. Let's get you settled in."

Penny led us upstairs and motioned down the hallway. "Both sides are suites with their own bathrooms. Take either or both, and we'll meet you guys downstairs." She took each of them by the hand. "I'm really glad you're here. This is a special day."

Penny and I settled into the living room, and she said, "This really is special, Chase. I don't know how to thank you."

I motioned toward the airport. "You bought me a PBY Catalina. I'm not interested in keeping score, but I'd say we're even."

"That airplane is a material thing, but those are my parents. It's not the same."

"I'm glad they're here, and as far as I'm concerned, they can stay as long as they want."

She shook her head. "Oh, no. I love having them here, but my mom will drive me batty if we're in the same house for long. I'll find them a place of their own. She'll probably want to see Hollywood, as well, but Dad doesn't care about that stuff."

I chuckled. "Whatever you say. Listen, I want to talk to you about something."

"Sure, what is it?"

"The team will be back tomorrow, and I was planning to start our workup for the next mission—"

She cut me off. "You've got a mission?"

"No, but only because I told Clark we needed some downtime. I think it was good for all of us, but we do have responsibilities."

She twisted in her seat, and I asked, "What is it?"

"I don't know. I guess I was getting used to you being home. I thought you might be thinking about retiring."

"Is that what you want?" I asked.

"No. I don't know. Maybe."

"I'm not ready for that. I've still got a few good years left in these boots."

She sighed. "I get it. It's just that . . ."

"Before we take this any further, listen to my idea."

She sat up. "Okay, shoot."

"Like I said, I was planning to start the workup, but after reading Dr. Richter's journal this morning, I think I'd like to see Normandy."

"Normandy, France?"

"Is there another one?"

She laughed. "Not that I know of, but that's a pretty random place to want to go."

"It's not random. I was reading about Dr. Richter getting shot down on D-Day over Utah Beach."

"Oh, wow. I didn't know he got shot down."

"Neither did I, but that's what makes me want to see it. What do you think?"

She frowned. "What do you mean, what do I think? I think we should go."

I sucked a stream of air through my teeth. "Here's the thing. I was thinking about taking everybody. We all had separate vacations, and I thought it'd be nice to get back together with a group trip."

With one word from her lips, she quashed my excitement about a family trip to France. "Anya?"

Anastasia Anya Burinkova was a stumbling block. She had been a Russian SVR officer dispatched to seduce and flip me during my first real mission as an operator. She succeeded with the first part, but not the second. In fact, I did the flipping. Anya defected from Russia and ended up working for the good guys. The problem was, there had been a time when I thought I was in love with her, and she claimed to love me, as well. Penny wasn't Anya's biggest fan, but she had a skill set we lacked on the team. That made her a necessary evil in Penny's eyes, and the psychologist in me understood that, even if the man in me didn't always get it.

"No, Anya doesn't have to come. She probably won't even show up tomorrow anyway."

"What about my parents?" Penny asked.

"I'd love for them to come, but I was thinking about chartering a yacht. Do you think they've had enough boat life for a while?"

"What kind of yacht?"

"I don't know. Something nice with a crew and staff so we don't have to drive or cook."

She raised an eyebrow. "Sounds expensive, and I like it." My wife stood, slid a hand across her stomach, and stared down at me. "You know what? Go ahead and bring Anya. I've been working out every day, and I've got a brand-new bikini I've been saving for just such an occasion."

"It's not a competition."

She leaned down, kissed me, and whispered, "Oh, you naïve, beautiful man. You can bet your cute little butt it's a competition, and Mama's winning."

There was nothing appropriate for me to say in that moment, so I held my tongue.

She danced out of the living room and spun at the door. "Cocktail, Mr. Bond?"

"Old-fashioned, please. Stirred, not shaken."

The drink and the in-laws arrived in unison, and we settled in for the first night's session of getting to know each other. The brief time I'd spent with them wasn't exactly social, so I was essentially starting from scratch, but Penny had a little history with them.

We laughed, talked, drank, and even shed a few tears before the clock struck midnight and I excused myself for the evening.

*  *  *

The team, including Anya, arrived sporadically throughout the morning, and it was a homecoming to remember. Everyone had grand tales of adventure, and we found ourselves gathered around the enormous dinner table for a catered meal that would've qualified as five-star in any restaurant on the planet.

Introductions were made, and everyone immediately loved Mitchel and Carla. When dessert was finished and coffee was poured, I threw out my idea. "Have any of you been to Normandy?"

Kodiak, retired Green Beret and master survivalist, said, "Yeah. In ninety-four, me, Mongo, and Clark did a jump over there for the fiftieth anniversary of the D-Day invasion. We were all stationed at Bragg back then. It was a pretty cool thing. There were a couple hundred vets there who actually jumped into that Hell. It was something to see those hard dudes tear up."

Mongo, our resident redwood tree, leaned back, laughed, and pointed at Kodiak. "That's the closest we ever came to getting court-martialed."

I planted my coffee cup solidly on the table. "Oh, I've got to hear this story."

Kodiak pointed back at Mongo. "It was all your idea, Sergeant Grand Theft Airplane."

The big man threw up both hands. "You've got it all wrong. Clark stole the airplane. I nabbed the chutes."

"What are you guys talking about?" I said.

Kodiak said, "Okay, okay. Here's how it went down. We got to talking and hanging out with the old guys who jumped in there in forty-four, and they were pretty cool old dudes."

Mongo jumped in. "Yeah, they were, and a bunch of them said they'd give anything to jump it again."

I slammed my hand on the table. "You did not!"

Clark wasn't there to defend himself, but Mongo and Kodiak answered in perfect stereo. "Oh, yes, we did."

Kodiak kept talking. "A couple of the guys were old warrant officers who flew the C-Forty-Seven, and Clark just happened to know where the airplanes were."

Mongo was too excited to stay quiet, so he took over. "We strapped those guys up, threw 'em on that airplane, and we were in the sky before anybody knew we were missing. Clark was the jumpmaster, and I went out first so I could watch those guys land. I was an Eighteen Delta back then, so it made sense to have a medic on the ground when a bunch of seventy-year-olds hit the ground under a T-Ten round."

"Did anybody get hurt?" Penny belted out.

Kodiak said, "Yeah, me. Broke my ankle. I'll never forget it."

Mongo sighed. "Man, what a day."

Penny was still intrigued. "But you got in a lot of trouble, right?"

Mongo and Kodiak gave each other a wink, and the big man said, "Yeah, we got in a lot of trouble until Major General Calem Gentry, retired, said he organized the whole thing. It blew over after that."

"Who's Major General Calem Gentry?" I asked.

Kodiak burst into laughter. "I got no idea. I made him up, but it worked."

"You impersonated a retired general?" I asked.

"Just on the phone, so it doesn't really count."

I reclaimed my coffee cup. "You guys are insane."

Mongo said, "Yep. That's why you keep us around."

"How about anybody else?" I asked. "Are there any other airplane thieves in the room?" Heads shook, and I said, "I think we should go. I'm going to charter a nice boat for all of us, and we'll make a family trip out of it. What do you say?"

Our Russian contingent said, "I thought we were doing workup for mission, no?"

"That can wait," I said.

Mongo deferred to Irina, his wife and former Russian FSB officer. After a nod from her, he said, "We're in."

At the other end of the table, Skipper, our analyst and practically my little sister, sat interestingly close to Gator, the youngest member of our team.

"How about you two?" I asked. "You seem to be getting cozy down there."

Gator swallowed hard, but Skipper didn't react. She merely said, "Oh, yeah. France, yacht, summertime . . . we're definitely in."

Singer, one of the world's deadliest snipers and also the most devout believer I've ever known, gave me a smile and a gentle nod.

Disco, our chief pilot and the oldest member of the team, said, "Would you mind if I invited Ronda?"

Ronda No-H was the CPA for our corporation and the best helicopter door gunner I've ever met. She and Disco had been an item long enough to turn the relationship into something more permanent, but they hadn't made the leap yet.

"Of course not," I said. "She's always welcome."

That left only Shawn the SEAL, who was the newest member of the team. He said, "If it means I don't have to do cardio for three hours a day, count me in."

"There's plenty of cardio coming your way when we get back, so enjoy it while you can."

I clapped my hands. "That's everybody. I'll make the reservations in the morning."

Penny held up a finger. "Not so fast, Mr. Travel Agent. What about my folks?"

"I counted them in by default, unless of course they'd rather stay here and feed the horses."

Mitchel said, "You've already done too much for us. We couldn't . . ."

I waved him off. "Cut it out. You're family, and there are no limits when it comes to family around here. You're in. Now, enjoy your coffee. We're doing cigars in the gazebo next."

# Chapter 4
## *Neanderthals in the Loire Valley*

From a distance, we could've been accused of sending smoke signals from the gazebo. A couple thousand dollars' worth of Cuban tobacco became aromatic white smoke that evening, and my father-in-law proclaimed, "I've never had a Cuban before, but this won't be my last if I can find a way to afford another one."

I motioned toward the house. "The humidor is in the library, Pops. Just don't smoke 'em in the house, or your daughter will kill us both."

He touched the rim of his glass to mine, and we had a moment that needed no words.

The gazebo wasn't a boys' club. Irina, Anya, and Penny held cigars of their own beneath curved index fingers, and something about that was sexier than it should've been.

I kicked Gator's boot. "Where's your girlfriend?"

His eyes turned into saucers. "I, uh, she's not . . ."

"Relax, man. I'm messing with you. But where is she?"

"Have you met her?" he asked. "Nobody can keep track of her. She's everywhere and nowhere all at the same time."

"Well, go find her. She's missing all the fun."

He pressed his palms into the arms of his Adirondack but stopped halfway out of the chair. "There she comes."

I turned to see Skipper doing what she does—skipping down the stairs. She danced her way into the gazebo and handed me a slip of paper.

I took it from her hand. "What's this?"

"Your receipt."

"My receipt for what?"

"The deposit on the yacht in France."

I started to check the number at the bottom of the page, but instead, I touched the paper to the tip of my cigar and watched it go up in smoke. "Nice work."

She perched on the arm of my chair. "You're a great leader and a decent pilot, but you're a terrible travel agent, so I thought I'd take care of it."

"What's the name of the boat?" I asked.

She crinkled her nose. "That's the best part. It's *Victory Four*. Is that perfect or what?"

"How big?"

"Big, even in France."

"Expensive?"

She touched the tip of my nose. "What do you care? I heard you say there's no limits on family around here."

"When?"

She hopped to her feet and fell into a chair beside Gator. "Day after tomorrow."

I peered through the crowd and found our chief pilot. "Hey, Disco. How many cocktails have you had?"

He held up his glass. "Just this one, why?"

"Good. We're flying to France tomorrow, so cut it off at one."

He extended his half-full glass toward Mitchel, but Carla intercepted it. "Oh, no. I've got plans for that man later tonight. I'll take that glass. Thank you."

That got a good chuckle, and the party slowly wound its way to an end as cigar butts were snubbed out and glasses were emptied. As much as I enjoyed my time alone with Penny, it was nice having my family back home. Perhaps it was leftover separation anxiety from the loss of my parents and sister two decades before, but I treasured the moments I got to spend with the gang of misfits who'd somehow fallen together to make my life better than it could've ever been without them.

* * *

We were wheels up far earlier than I wanted to be awake, but the time zones made it necessary for us to leap across the Atlantic as early as possible so we wouldn't miss dinner in La Rochelle, where we'd meet our yacht the next day.

To my surprise, Clark and Maebelle climbed the stairs into the Gulfstream behind us.

"Well, look what the cat dragged in," I said. "And a lovely cat she is. Hello, Maebelle. Why'd you have to bring him?"

Clark slapped away my offered hand. "Nice try, College Boy. You didn't really think you could sneak off the French Riviera without your handler, did you?"

I laughed. "You slept through geography, didn't you? We're going to Normandy. The Riviera is on the Mediterranean."

"And just where do you think the cruise ends, Mr. Fancy Pants Geography Man?"

"Sit down. You're bothering the important people."

He gave Maebelle a peck and turned for the cockpit. "I think I'll sit up front, where the really important people sit. I could use a few hours at the controls. It's been a while."

I wanted to continue berating him, but if he took the copilot's seat, that meant that I didn't have to, and that was just fine with me.

Gator pulled the door closed and counted heads. "If anybody's not here, please raise your hand."

That scored a round of boos, but Disco cut through the drone. "Welcome aboard Grey Ghost Airways nonstop service to La Rochelle. I'm your captain this morning, and I'm joined in the cockpit by Captain Kangaroo. You'll understand when you feel him try to land later today. Sit back, enjoy the flight, and don't flirt with the flight attendant. He gets feisty when you get handsy."

"Who's he talking about?" Skipper asked.

Mongo grinned. "Me."

The flight was long, but not as long as the return flight would be. The eastbound jet stream added almost two hundred knots to our ground speed, and we made the four-thousand-mile trip across the pond in just over seven hours.

"Welcome to La Rochelle," Disco said as we taxied to the ramp. "By the way, that landing was mine, so don't give my copilot any props he didn't earn."

As we rolled to a stop, Clark's wife—my cousin—Maebelle said, "Hey, everybody. I hope you don't mind, but I did a thing."

"What kind of thing?" somebody asked.

She blushed. "Well, I kind of maybe overstepped my bounds a little."

I laid a hand on her shoulder. "Impossible. Please tell me you made reservations for us at some amazing place."

Maebelle was a graduate of the Culinary Institute of America and the owner of El Juez, the hottest Cuban-American restaurant on Miami's South Beach. If she had a restaurant recommendation in France, I was all in.

Her blush turned to a brilliant smile. "I did a little more than that. I bought out the whole restaurant, and the chef has two—count them —two Michelin Stars."

Gator leaned to Skipper and whispered, "Don't they make tires?"

She slapped his arm, and Maebelle continued. "It's going to be amazing. I promise. You'll never forget it."

It took three vehicles to carry our merry band from the airport to the restaurant, where the sign read "Christopher Coutanceau — Chef and Fisherman."

I didn't know how to pronounce his name, but I liked him already.

Dinner was an exercise in experimentation. No one inside spoke enough English to describe anything to us, but we ate for three hours and drank some of the best wine I've ever had. The evening started slowly for most of my knuckle-draggers, but the wine and the beautiful and encouraging French waitresses turned them into connoisseurs in no time.

The surprise of the night, at least for me, was watching Penny, Carla, and Anya whisper and share bites from their plates. I wanted to believe it was a good thing, but my Russian Spidey senses were tingling.

On second thought, that wasn't the most surprising happening of the evening. The real shocker came when the head waiter delivered the check and Clark Johnson reached for it. I'd never seen him buy so much as a cheeseburger for anybody else, and I had no way to guess the cost of the meal, but I'd make sure my handler knew how much I appreciated the gesture.

Sleep doesn't work after a four-thousand-mile, eastbound journey. My brain thought it was still on Eastern Daylight Time, but the clock said we were on Central European Standard Time. Despite the screwed-up clocks in our heads, Skipper hit another home run with the hotel accommodations. I'd never know how she pulled off such witchcraft on short notice, but she was the reigning world champion of reservations.

When the cars dropped us off at the marina, just after noon the following day, the glistening hull of *Freedom IV* shone in the midday sun as if polished just for us. She was a masterpiece of marine architecture and opulence.

Penny squeezed my arm. "Is this real, Chase? I feel like a little girl in a Disney movie right now."

To my enormous delight, everyone behaved . . . even Clark.

The tanned, fit young captain placed his hand in mine. "It's a pleasure to have you aboard, Dr. Fulton. I'm Captain Greenlee, but please call me Elliot."

"Nice to meet you, Captain. Please call me Chase, and I'd like to apologize in advance for the Neanderthals I brought with me."

He smiled. "Not to worry, Chase. Neanderthals have a long history here in France. There's even some evidence in the Loire Valley that they lived alongside modern humans and faired quite well."

I knew it was coming, and there was nothing I could do to stop it.

Singer said, "That didn't happen, but I'll keep this flock under control, even if we don't exactly qualify as modern humans."

Perhaps our captain was in for a primer on ancient history from our resident theologian during the cruise, and I wanted to sit in.

The clock finally caught up with our bodies before we made it through the first dinner aboard *Freedom IV*. Eyelids grew heavy, and some of us even passed on dessert, but I wasn't one of the quitters. I savored every bite of the chocolate dessert that had a name I'd never learn to spell, but I knew I wanted it after every meal for the next ten days.

When I finally folded my napkin and placed it on my empty plate, I took a stroll around the ship before turning in. I expected to find Penny already asleep in our stateroom, but to my surprise, she was on the bow doing yoga with her mother and Anya. It was getting weirder by the minute, but I was too tired to step into that nest of women. It would have to wait for another day after a very long nap.

Captain Greenlee caught me on the leeward breezeway. "Good evening."

"Hello, Captain. Your chef is spectacular. How does the weather look?"

He held up a hand. "Please, it's Elliot. Formality is for the crew when they've done something to earn my ire. The weather is improving, and we should be off the dock at daybreak. Rumor has it that you're a bit of a seaman yourself. If you'd like, you're welcome on the bridge during our departure."

"I'd be honored, but I'm not calling you Elliot on the bridge."

He laughed. "Don't talk to me on the bridge. I'll have a billion-dollar yacht in my hands, and the owner prefers that I not scratch her."

"In that case, I'll see you at dawn, and I promise not to make a sound."

"Good night, Chase. Sleep well, and enjoy *Freedom Four*."

I nodded. "Good night, Cap . . . I mean, Elliot. Enjoying is what freedom is for."

# Chapter 5
## *Flat-Bellied Bullies*

There's no sleep like boat sleep. Something about the fluidity of it all makes me feel as if I'm moving *with* the world instead of against it, and that soothes my mind and body like nothing else. Well, there is one thing that comes close, and she was breathing softly against my skin as her hair cascaded across my chest.

When Penny sleeps, it's like the sleep of an innocent child, and sometimes—on extremely rare occasions—she'll softly purr like a kitten. On those nights, my mind and body react very differently to her presence. That night wasn't a purring night, but all the world seemed to be at peace, and I drank it in like water from a mountain spring.

I was on the threshold of ten days of cruising on somebody else's boat, with somebody else responsible for everything from toilet paper to navigation. Times like those are rare in the life of an operator, but the collection of warriors scattered throughout the most luxurious yacht I've ever seen deserved an eternity filled with such moments. They had fought, bled, and toiled at every corner of the globe for the entirety of their adult lives, and they never asked for anything in return from the people they sacrificed themselves to protect and defend. Those were the men and women who deserved the opulence and luxury of the life we would live over the next few days before returning to the world of evil and strife.

Dawn broke through high streaks of clouds that offered nothing but a perfect day to come. I watched it happen with a cappuccino in my hand because plain old coffee didn't seem to be an option. If I couldn't get a cup of black, high-octane coffee, I wanted my money back.

As I stood watching the sun claim the sky over the city of La Rochelle, with its half-timbered medieval houses and Renaissance architecture still on display, I was taken by the thought of a city being five times older than my country. I wondered about the peasants and knights and artists and clergy who called the city their home, even temporarily. Could any of them have had the insight or foresight to know what the world around them would become? Could I? And to which of those clans did I belong, if any?

Clergy? Certainly not. Although, my heart longed to show God to the world, and I would spend my life on the edge of a sword rather than in the depth of the Word.

Artist? Never, although I would dream of turning the sunsets I've watched in awe into words on a page to inspire those who'd never beheld such beauty as the world falling asleep under her own blanket of darkness.

Peasant? Perhaps when compared to aristocracy who believed themselves to be above both the law of man and the timeless law of God. Although I would sometimes scoff at the one, I would never dare take a stand other than kneeling before the other.

Knight? At brief moments, perhaps, and often in my dreams.

With the cappuccino cup left with nothing but froth clinging to the interior, I made my way to the navigation bridge and almost committed the nautical cardinal sin. My boot was airborne over the threshold when I realized I wasn't aboard the *Lori Danielle*, and I froze. "Permission to come aboard the bridge?"

Captain Greenlee . . . Elliot . . . answered without looking over his shoulder. "Come aboard, and thank you for asking. We're just finishing up our systems checks before casting off the lines. Would you care to see the checklist?"

"Thank you, Captain. I'd love to."

He didn't correct me, because on the bridge, he was the captain and nothing else.

He slid a binder toward me, and I flipped through the laminated pages. There must've been two hundred items on the checklist. I'm sure the *Lori Danielle* had something similar, but I'd never been privy to her departure secrets.

The captain said, "You'll notice we don't have a harbor pilot on board. That's because I hold a local pilot's certificate, and our insurance permits me to manage the *Freedom Four* in and out of a few European ports such as this one."

"Impressive," I whispered.

I was uncertain when the pre-commanded silence on my part should begin. Just then, it became apparent the time had come.

The captain situated a microphone in front of his lips and put on his confidently calm demeanor. "All stations, report status."

The radio's volume was low, but I could make out the transmissions as each station checked in.

"Bow watch and bow lines are ready and standing by."

"Forward spring ready and standing by, sir."

"Aft spring ready and standing by."

"Stern watch and stern lines are ready and standing by, Captain. All clear to the rear for thirty-five meters."

Finally, one additional voice said, "Port watch ready and standing by. Channel is clear with harbor tugs standing to port quarter and port bow with lines fast."

I was instantly intrigued by the tugboats, but I didn't understand why an ultra-modern vessel like *Freedom IV* needed the assistance of tugs to depart a relatively simple port in docile water.

The captain sensed my question and answered without me asking out loud. "We had an electrical malfunction departing Ibiza last year, and I lost thrust control from the bridge. Thankfully, we had solid comms with engineering, and they made the thrust inputs on my commands, but we got too close to the rocks for my comfort, so now, if tugs are available for departure, I consider them a necessity. It's a small price to pay to save a vessel like this one from meeting her fate on the rocks. I get a little ridicule from other captains, but I'd much rather take a ribbing than explain to the owner how I wrecked his yacht with tugs tied up around the corner."

His wisdom belied his youthful appearance, and I was impressed by his lack of bravado and tendency toward what some may consider excess safety precautions.

Captain Greenlee ordered, "Main engines at forty-five percent. Cast off all lines. Sound the departure."

The ship's horn let out one prolonged blast, and all shorelines fell slack. A cacophony of radio calls filled the air.

"Clear of the dock to starboard. Fenders coming in."

"Well clear astern."

"Tugs on the move."

The captain walked the elegant ship with the grace she deserved as we sidestepped into the channel and clear of the other vessels docked ahead and astern. It was a perfectly orchestrated dance, and I wanted to offer a golf clap, but I kept my hands solidly in my pockets.

"All clear astern."

"All clear ahead."

The captain manipulated the controls as if he could do it in his sleep, and our sideward motion morphed into slow progression ahead. As we built forward speed, the captain lifted a second microphone from the console and said, "*Les remorqueurs sont licenciés. Merci, messieurs.*"

With that, the tugs cast off the lines and broke away to stern.

The captain said, "In case your French is rusty, I just dismissed the tugs."

I studied the situation and believed it was safe for me to speak. "My French isn't rusty. It's nonexistent. Thank you for giving me the best seat in the house for the departure. It was fascinating."

"You're more than welcome," he said. "Come up when we touch ashore. Arrival is even more exciting."

"I'd like that, and I have one enormous request."

"We never say no aboard the *Freedom Four*."

I motioned toward the basic Mr. Coffee on a credenza at the rear of the bridge. "Could I have a cup of that?"

He glanced down at my cute little cup of foam. "Of course. Help yourself. There are some real mugs in the cabinet below, and I'll make sure the galley knows you want an Americano."

"That'll make my guys very happy. Thanks again, Captain."

When I returned to my stateroom, I was reminded how much I love the man who invented yoga pants, and I am certain it was a man.

"More stretching with the girls this morning?" I asked.

Penny gave me a good morning kiss. "You can watch if you want, but those eyes better not stray from your wife."

"I don't know. Your mom is pretty hot."

She rolled her eyes. "The boys are having breakfast out back, and we're doing yoga on the bow. Decisions, decisions. Make a good one, sailor boy."

I chose breakfast because I'd much rather be in trouble for not watching than for watching the wrong pair of yoga pants.

The captain turned out to be a man of his word. Good old American black coffee and real cups were on the table when I arrived on the stern deck. Omelets made to order, and sausage links, bacon, smoked salmon, fresh fruit, orange juice, champagne, and a collection of French bread that would blow your mind adorned the table, and I was a happy boy.

Disco raised his coffee cup. "Thanks again for this, Chase. We need to get the galley crew hired on the *Lori Danielle*."

Ronda No-H gave him a playful shove. "We can't afford these guys on the L.D."

He took the shove with the love it was intended, and Ronda said, "Thank you for letting me tag along, Chase. This is spectacular."

I raised my mug. "Just figure out how we're going to pay for it, and you're always welcome."

Shawn stretched and took in the scenery as we left the port for the open water of the Atlantic. "What's on the schedule today, boss?"

I said, "I thought we'd do some calisthenics and maybe get in a few hundred laps around the deck. What do you say?"

He grinned. "I say, try to keep up, old man."

I lowered my chin. "Oh, so intimidation is the game, huh? I can play that one." I turned to our CPA. "Ronda, dock that sailor's pay one month's wages for insubordination."

She drew an imaginary pen from her imaginary pocket and made a note, but our SEAL changed his tack. "You must've heard me wrong. I said, I don't think I can keep up since *I'm* an old man."

"I thought that might've been what you meant. Belay that order, Ronda, but help me keep an eye on this guy. He's slippery and may need to be keelhauled before the cruise is over." With the silliness astern, I said, "The plan for the day is to relax and enjoy the scenery. We'll stay within sight of the French coast the whole trip north. After we get a good look at Guernsey once we make our turn into the English Channel, we'll put in at Cherbourg-en-Cotentin to pick up our guide."

"We get a guide?" Kodiak asked.

"We sure do. He's an ex-pat named Don Wood, and from what I hear, there's nobody better."

"Is that all you know about him?" Kodiak asked.

"That's it, but I suspect we're in for quite a treat."

We finished our breakfast, and I said, "Our wives missed this incredible meal because they're doing yoga on the bow."

Gator was first with the correction. "Skipper isn't one of our wives."

Mongo lowered his chin. "And whose wife is Anya? Poon Poon Boondy, maybe?"

Ronda pulled me from the fire. "I'll hit the StairMaster later, but I wasn't going to miss this meal to play inverted upward dog with a bunch of girls in some kind of hormone-induced competition." She squeezed Disco's arm. "I've got my man, so I've got nothing to prove to those flat-bellied bullies on the bow."

# Chapter 6

## *Hell on Earth*

We spent the day doing nothing, and it felt glorious. The weather was perfect, the sea was flat, and the yacht was breathtaking. Two more meals passed, proving that we only *thought* the previous meals were perfect. The yacht's helicopter took off an hour before we anchored off the coast of Cherbourg-en-Cotentin just after sunrise the next morning, and I assumed the pilot was on his way to collect our guide. The port was alive with container ships, ferries, fishing vessels, and an impressive array of mega-yachts, but few compared to *Freedom IV*.

Breakfast was once again served out back, and it was even better than the previous day's fare. The chopper returned, and the pilot made a flawless approach and landing.

I watched one of the crew help a gentleman from the helicopter, but our guest obviously wasn't interested in the young man's help. He whipped the crewman across the wrist and shin with his cane, making it perfectly clear that he could walk just fine without his assistance. I was impressed, and I liked the old man already. He took his time making his way down the ladders from the helipad, but he made it to the breakfast table without a single stumble.

Emerging from the interior of the yacht in perfect timing with the gentleman's arrival, the captain shook the man's hand and turned to the rest of us. "Good morning, everyone. I hope you slept well and enjoyed your breakfast. I'm pleased to introduce Mr. Don Wood. I don't want to waste your time by having you listen to me, so I'll leave you in Mr. Wood's capable hands."

I stood and pulled out a chair for him, and Don planted himself with his cane hanging from the arm of the chair.

A waiter materialized. "Good morning, sir. Would you care for some coffee and breakfast?"

Don looked up at the uniformed man. "How about a Beefeaters on the rocks with four olives? Do you think you can scare up one of those?"

Don Wood may have lived in France, but his accent was pure Richmond, Virginia, and I loved every word that dripped from his antebellum tongue.

I said, "Let me be the first to thank you for doing this for us, Mr. Wood."

Don looked me over, seemingly measuring me against some scale he possessed deep inside his head. He cast the same appraising eye across every member of the team, then took a breath and said, "I see you boys have stormed a few beaches of your own in your day."

"We've drawn a little fire over the years," I said.

He lifted his cane and tapped it against my prosthetic leg below my knee. "More than a little fire, I'd say."

His gin arrived, and he plucked an olive from the wooden spear. "The best olives in the world come from the south of France. I'll bet you didn't know that, did you?"

He didn't appear to be talking to anyone in particular, but he certainly seemed to enjoy the gin-soaked olive.

We weighed the anchor and motored out of the harbor as Don finished his first gin and rattled the glass for another.

While waiting for its arrival, he cleared his throat and began. "I suppose we best get started if we're ever going to get finished. My name is Don Wood, and I'm one of the few remaining survivors of those of us who stormed those beaches on that day back in forty-four. I'll start by giving you a little history about me, and then we'll have a little pop quiz. You remember those from school days, don't you?"

Heads nodded, and we were already captivated.

Don continued. "We've got about an hour and a half before Utah Beach comes into sight. That ought to be plenty of time to set the scene for you." He resituated his chair and made himself comfortable. "I turned eighteen on the twenty-ninth day of May, in nineteen forty-three, and my draft notice arrived the very same day. I knew it was coming, and when it did, I quickly threw it away."

A collective gasp rose from the table, but Don was not deterred. "I threw it away because I had already signed up for the Army the day before. They postdated my signature to make me a day older than I was. Our country was at war, you see, and men of strong back and mind like me owed that country our very lives if that should become necessary, and for a great many of us, it required exactly that . . . and a good bit more."

His second gin on the rocks arrived, and he took an appreciative sip at just past nine thirty in the morning, according to my watch.

"On my birthday, I kissed my mother goodbye, shook my father's hand, and walked into Richmond to catch the train to Fort Jackson, South Carolina, for my first taste of the Army. I did boot camp there with about ten thousand other boys just like me. By the time it was over, we knew we were expendable, but none of us believed we'd be among the many who never came home. At least half of us were wrong."

Another sip, and every ear at the table was trained on Don's words.

"I was assigned to the Big Red One. I'm sure you boys know what that is. It's the First Infantry Division. I was to become part of the Sixteenth Infantry Regiment. They put us on another train headed to the coast, where we boarded a troop transport ship to Dorchester, England, to train up for Operation Overlord. I had never been on a ship before that day, and about twenty-four hours into the trip, I knew I never wanted to be on another one."

He took us through the details of his training throughout the winter of 1943 and '44. By the time he'd finished, we were well inside the

English Channel, and Don had his hand stretched out toward the starboard rail.

"Remember that I warned you about a pop quiz. If you'll look over there, you'll get your first glimpse of Utah Beach. That was the westernmost point of the D-Day assault. The boys took that beach without much trouble. They only lost around three hundred men during the campaign, but the problem was the flooded fields inland. The One Hundred and First and the Eighty-Second Airborne jumped in about five miles inland to soften up the defenses, and that worked pretty good, or so they tell me. I wasn't there. I was at the other end, Omaha Beach."

He had another sip and seemed to relive the day some seventy-one years before. When he returned from his memory of that day in Hell, he said, "Oh, yes. The pop quiz. I almost forgot. Who can tell me the first territory to be liberated on June sixth, nineteen forty-four?"

My team glanced between themselves and finally at me as if I were supposed to spit out the answer. I said, "I'm ashamed to admit that I don't know, but based on what you told us about the ease with which the boys took Utah, I'm guessing that was the first."

He raised his glass. "You'd think that, wouldn't you? But if you'll take a look just over there, you'll see a couple of small islands. One of them is called Saint-Marcouf, L'île du Large. It was named after a monk who died in five fifty-eight and somehow became a saint. I'll never understand how men left on Earth, wearing robes and funny hats, get to declare somebody to be a saint, but that's what they say they did."

If he was waiting for an explanation, he wasn't going to get one from me, so I turned to Singer.

He said, "Don't look at me. I'm a Baptist."

That got a good laugh from Don, and even though we failed the pop quiz, I soon learned that story time was far from over.

Don pushed himself to his feet and reclaimed his cane. "If you'll excuse an old man, I have to make a WC call."

He found his footing and made his way inside the yacht.

As soon as he was out of earshot, Gator asked, "What's a WC call?"

Ronda No-H said, "Don't you boys know anything? It's a water closet call. You know, going to the bathroom."

Gator screwed up his face. "Why couldn't he just say that?"

Kodiak threw an ice cube at him. "He's a World War Two vet, dude. He can call it whatever he wants."

Don was soon back with a fresh cocktail and more olives. He settled back onto his throne and asked, "Have I bored you to death yet?"

"No, sir," came the chorus of responses.

That made him smile. "In that case, we'll get to the part everybody always wants to hear but none of us ever want to tell."

I wondered if that was his way of asking for a way out of telling the story of his time on Omaha Beach, so I gave him an avenue. "Mr. Wood, if this is too much for you, we completely understand if you'd rather not take us through the fight."

He leaned forward and laid his curled, liver-spotted hand on my shoulder. "Son, it won't be long until there won't be anybody left to tell the story, so I consider it an honor. This may be the last time I ever get to tell the tale, and it's a privilege to have yours be the ears that hear it."

I was flattered and flabbergasted, so I closed my mouth and leaned back.

Don turned to watch the beach slowly drift past the starboard rail. "There she is, boys and girls. Omaha Beach. You'd sure never know it by looking at it now, but there was a day—both so long ago and yet sometimes it feels like yesterday—when that beach was the closest thing to Hell on Earth any of us had ever seen, before or since."

He took a minute to gather himself and devour more olives. "It was dark that morning in more ways than one. Most of the ships had their lights off, so we couldn't see the thousands upon thousands of men lined up waiting to take that beach. I, for one, felt more alone that morning than I've ever felt since. Thousands of us were in the same shoes, but every man was absolutely and completely alone with his own thoughts. Standing in that landing craft was the first time I thought I was going to die. I'll tell you this . . . A bunch of men who'd been atheists when they went to bed the night before changed their tune in those boats. I sure enough got things right with the Man Upstairs, and I've done my best to keep things right with Him since then."

More olives . . . more gin.

"When that gate opened and that water rushed in, everything changed forever. The roaring diesel got quiet, but only for a second. An instant later, the black smoke was rolling out of the stacks, and the boat was backing up. The momentum threw the first half dozen men out the front and into the water. Those men disappeared, and we never saw any of them again. Some lieutenant gave the order to hit the beach, and we didn't have any choice. We were out of that boat and in the water as if we were tied together with twine."

He took a long breath and wiped a bead of sweat from his brow. "We'd practiced all that stuff before, a hundred times or more, but we didn't ever step out of a landing craft and into ten feet of water before. We had packs that weighed fifty or sixty pounds, plus a rifle and all the ammunition in the world strapped to us. The strongest swimmer in the world couldn't have survived that. I was in the middle of the pack, and eighty percent or more of the men who got out before me drowned before they ever took their first breath outside the boat. You've heard men give speeches about standing on the shoulders of giants. I've done it for real, boys. I did it that day. My boots never hit the sand under that water. I walked across the shoulders and backs of drowned American soldiers until I could touch bottom and walk on my own. Sometimes, I think those boys were the lucky ones."

He bowed his head and groaned, and the moment touched each of us as if we'd been run through with a flaming sword. I tried to imagine the chaos and terror of that moment, but I couldn't fathom how it must have felt.

"That's when things started getting bad," Don said, his energy restored. "That's when the Krauts opened up on us with heavy machine guns and artillery. I could see the tracer rounds racing past and striking the men around me. I heard an artillery round land dead center of the landing craft I'd just left. The brutality of war dug her poison claws into my flesh in that moment, and I was still two hundred yards from the beach and hadn't fired a single shot yet. All of that would change before the sun came up, but I doubted that I'd ever see it."

We held our collective breath as he rolled up his sleeve and pointed to a quarter-sized scar inside his right elbow. "That's where I took the first bullet of my life, but it wouldn't be the last. When that thing hit me, I thought my arm had been blown off. It felt like somebody tied my right arm to a bull and turned him loose. I dropped my rifle and held up my arm, trying to see how much of it was left. Would you believe it was barely bleeding? That tracer round cooked its way through my arm, cauterizing the wound as it went. My hand still worked, but I couldn't feel it. That's when I realized I had all the bullets I could carry but nothing to shoot them out of. I figured if I made it to the beach, there'd be more rifles lying on the ground than I could count, so I started fighting the water with every bit of strength and fear I had. I made it to ankle-deep water and collapsed to my knees, but somebody grabbed the strap from my pack and hauled me back to my feet. I didn't think my legs would carry me one more step, but whoever grabbed me shoved me forward so hard my legs didn't have a choice. I grabbed the first rifle I saw and started sending lead toward the top of that cliff overlooking the beach."

I tried to visualize the scene, but I was certain the horror of it in my imagination couldn't come close to the reality of that terrible day.

Don kept talking. "Men were falling all around me, and sand was flying like a million stinging bees from every machine gun bullet that hit the ground. That's when the mines started lighting off. It was a concussion like none other every time somebody stepped on one of those German landmines. The air was full of bloody body parts, arms, and legs, and even heads with their helmets still on. I've been on this Earth nearly a century, and I've never seen anything that's one percent as bad as that was. I wish I had the words to make you feel it for just an instant, but even if I did, I wouldn't use them. That's too much to put on any man."

I tasted blood from where I'd clamped down on the inside of my cheek, and my heart felt as if it were on the verge of collapsing inside itself. I was horrified and honored to be sitting in front of a man like Don Wood. It was one of the most impactful moments of my life, and I prayed I'd never forget how I felt on that morning aboard the aptly named *Freedom IV*.

He was far from finished.

"The sun was coming up by that time, and that made everything worse. The Krauts could see the landing craft, and they started cutting down whole boats full of men before they could step off the craft. The boats became enormous floating coffins for hundreds of men at a time, but I couldn't look back. Behind me was nothing but death. The enemy was in front of me, and if I was going to do the job that I swore to do the day before I turned eighteen years old, I had to get to it. The mines were invisible beneath the sand, but they were so close together that when one would cook off, it would sometimes unearth one or two beside it, and those unexploded mines and the dismembered bodies of boys just like me became the only trail any of us could survive. The razor wire was the next devil we had to face. It was like ribbon all over the beach with mines underneath, and barricades like giant jacks taller than me littered the ground. The artillery kept coming, but most of it was directed at the ships and boats sending boys ashore. The closer we got to the cliff, the safer we were from the big rounds, but not from the mines and wire. I saw men lose fingers, and they had open lacerations in their flesh big enough to put your hand through. As terrifying as the mines and bullets were, that razor wire cut us deeper than just our flesh. It cut us clean to our will to keep moving forward. Every step sliced another piece of cloth from our uniforms, and every inch I moved felt like forcing my way through hot coals."

From the look on his face, I wasn't certain Don was going to be able to continue the story, but he soldiered on, just like he'd done on that day in 1944.

"We finally cut our way through most of the wire and got ourselves tight to the bottom of that cliff. I watched men around me reach for their canteens, only to find they didn't have any fingers. I heard men screaming the most unearthly screech you could imagine. I'd made it across the beach, but a hundred-foot-tall cliff stood between me and more fighting. Those of us who could, scratched and clawed our way up a trail that would scare a billy goat. It wasn't wide enough for two men side by side, but it was our only way up that cliff, so we took it."

The waiter abandoned waiting for Don to call for another and delivered drinks without being asked.

"When we made it to the top, I found myself surrounded by boys I'd never seen before. Our platoons had been shredded like trash paper, and we were the scraps that happened to land together on top of that wall. It didn't matter what anybody's name was. We were all Yankee Doodle Dandy that day, and that's exactly how we fought, I tell you. We took that plateau like the lives of everybody we loved depended on it, and maybe it did. We threw too many grenades to count and fired more rounds through our M-Ones than they were ever built to fire. We picked up ammo off every dead body we crossed, and the longer we fought, the harder we fought. I wish I could tell you what drove us, but I'll never know. Maybe we knew we had to fight to stay alive, but I'll tell you the truth—I wasn't sure I was still alive. I was afraid I'd been killed the second I stepped from the landing craft, and now I was doomed to spend all eternity fighting a battle that could never be won."

The old soldier's shoulders drooped, and a look of physical exhaustion overtook him. "I'm sorry, boys. I'm afraid that's all this old man's got in him for today. We won the war—or at least that's what they tell me. I'm not sure anybody ever wins a war. Somebody just stops fighting before the other guys. Maybe the world would be a better place if we all stopped fighting before we ever got started."

The wisdom in his words weighed more than any of us could bear alone, and I was proud to be surrounded by men of similar spirit to Don Wood. His was, without question, the greatest generation, and we owed it to him, and those like him, to give every breath in our chest in defense of what he and his brothers-in-arms gave so much to win.

# Chapter 7
## *Duty Calls*

We sat in silent awe of Don Wood's story as if none of us had any idea what to say. He seemed to understand our situation. I thought it was very likely that his audiences were always left with such wonder in their eyes.

He threw us a lifeline. "Judging by the sun and the temperature, I'd say it's after noon, and even young sprouts like all of you can have a drink after noon, can't you?"

We ordered a round of the best spirits on the boat, and the questions began.

Ronda asked, "If you don't mind saying, Mr. Wood, what made you move to France after the war?"

He smiled for the first time in hours. "A beautiful young nurse named Patricia. I managed to storm the beach with only one hole in me, but the rest of the battle wasn't so kind. I would've died in the mud if that angel hadn't found me and nursed me back to health. I married her and took her home with me, but Virginia didn't suit my little French country girl. I promised her I'd take her back to France the day I retired, and that's exactly what I did. Now, we live on a little piece of land outside Saint-Lô, and I'll probably die there, less than a mile from the battlefield where I should've died seventy-one years ago."

"You should've brought her with you," I said. "It would've been nice to meet the lady who kept you alive so you could spend the morning with us and share your story."

He waved me off. "She's heard the story so many times she can tell it herself. She'd rather prune her plants and bake her bread than come out here, even on a boat like this."

I caught sight of Clark pulling his sat-phone from his pocket and staring at the screen as it vibrated in his palm. He closed his eyes and slowly shook his head. "Go for Clark." He listened for half a minute before saying, "Give me five minutes, and I'll call you back." He shoved the phone back into his pocket and said, "I hate to cut this short, but duty calls."

We stood as one, but Don took my arm. "What is it you boys do?"

I gave his question some thought and said, "We solve problems before the rest of the world knows they're problems."

He gave me a sharp salute and glanced down at my prosthetic. "Come home with all your pieces this time, won't you?"

I returned the salute. "I'll do my best, sir."

We reconvened in the closest thing the yacht had to a conference room, and Clark took his seat at the head of the table. "Ladies and gentlemen, we've got a situation. This time it's pirates, and they've taken a cruise ship from the Mediterranean."

He instantly had our full attention, and I asked, "Numbers?"

"Not yet. We're in the very early stages, but there's a hitch. And I mean a serious hitch."

Everyone leaned in, and he said, "I assume you've all heard of Congressman Landon Herd, one of the junior congressmen from the great state of Colorado."

I let the name roll through my head, and it rang a small bell, but not a big one.

Mongo said, "Yeah, I've heard of him. He's making a lot of noise about throwing his hat into the ring for a run at the White House. That's the guy, right?"

Clark nodded. "That's the one."

"What does he have to do with a pirated cruise ship?" I asked.

Clark drummed his fingers on the table. "He's on board the ship."

The air left the room, and I asked the most obvious question. "Why us?"

My handler said, "I don't know, but we're about to find out. Skipper, can you—"

She said, "Way ahead of you." She plugged her satellite phone into a port on her laptop and typed a long string of commands. "We're calling the Board, right?"

Clark nodded, and she hit the enter key.

Seconds later, a man's disembodied voice asked, "Is that you, Clark?"

"Yes, sir, and the team is all here. We're level two secure. That's the best we can do from here."

"Exactly where are you?" the voice asked.

Clark sighed. "We're aboard the *Freedom Four*, a private yacht off the coast of Normandy."

"That's what I thought, and that's why you were our first call. Here's the abbreviated briefing."

Skipper produced a notepad and pen and gave Clark a nod.

He said, "Send it."

"A satellite distress call came from the cruise liner *Desert Star* at just past midnight last night. She was steaming from Monaco to Palermo by way of Algiers, but her whereabouts are currently unknown."

"Unknown," Clark barked. "How can the whereabouts of a giant cruise ship be unknown twelve hours after a distress call?"

The voice said, "It's possible the pirates scuttled the ship."

"Do you mean they sank it?" Skipper asked.

"That's correct. We believe that may be the case, but we have a team conducting satellite surveillance in the Central Med. There's another problem."

Clark moaned. "Oh, good. There's more."

"The *Desert Star* isn't a traditional cruise ship. She's an ultra-luxury cruise liner of the Ocean Star line. She's just under four hundred feet in length."

I said, "So, we're looking for a tiny ship somewhere between Monaco and Algiers. Is the Navy joining the search?"

"Not yet," he said.

"And why not?" Skipper asked.

"That's reason number two that we called you first. The President says you owe him a favor. Is that true?"

I palmed my forehead. "I didn't expect him to call in the marker so soon, but yes, he did something very kind for my family recently."

"I see," the voice said. "That would no doubt be the presidential pardons for Mitchel and Carla Thomas."

"Yes, sir."

He said, "It should go without saying that the President of the United States doesn't want the whole world to know that a serious potential political rival has vanished aboard a cruise ship in the Med. It's safe to say he'd like to keep that under wraps if possible. Therefore, discretion is of utmost importance on this."

"I get it," I said, "but we're on a chartered yacht, a long way from home, essentially unarmed, and we have our entire family with us. What is it you expect us to do?"

His voice turned stern. "I expect you to recall your ship from her little marine biology distraction in the Persian Gulf, rendezvous with her, and go find the congressman. Is that clear enough, Mr. Fulton?"

I avoid conflict when I can, but posturing is a game I play well, so I couldn't resist. "It's *Doctor* Fulton, and the Research Vessel *Lori Danielle* is on a fully sanctioned, privately funded operation in the Persian Gulf with the full knowledge and approval of your board. I'll find your congressman for you, but it's not going to be easy or cheap. Fund the account with ten million initially, and our CFO will call for more when necessary."

"Thank you, *Doctor* Fulton, and we apologize for interrupting your vacation."

Skipper took over. "Send us the full briefing package, including everything you have on the ship, the congressman, the precise coordinates of where the distress call was made, the pirates, officers and crew, complete passenger manifest, and absolutely anything you're considering holding back. Keeping things from us only delays successful completion of the mission and dramatically increases the expenses. Do you have any more questions for us?"

"We do not, and the data packet is on its way via secure satellite communications system."

She disconnected the phone and said, "Looks like we've got a new course to plot. Are you telling the captain, or shall I?"

"I'll take care of it," I said. "In the meantime, download the packet and start combing through it with a microscope. I want the whole team on it, not just you. If they sank that ship, they had to have a way to get a bunch of people off of it in a hurry and in the middle of the night."

"Consider it done," she said, and I headed for the bridge.

I didn't ask for permission and instead marched onto the bridge as if I owned the billion-dollar yacht. "Captain, we've got a change of plans. I need you to make for La Rochelle at full speed."

"Is everything all right?" he asked.

"I'll tell you more when I'm authorized to do so, but for now, just turn this thing south and open the throttles."

He turned to a younger officer. "Set a course for La Rochelle, all ahead full. You have the bridge."

The younger officer said, "Aye, sir. I have the bridge."

Caption Greenlee followed me from the bridge and stopped me in the corridor. "I need to know if you're putting my vessel in danger."

I checked my watch. "I am not. We just have to get back to La Rochelle as quickly as possible."

"Chase, I need to know what you're doing with my ship."

"We're not your typical charter guests."

He huffed. "I figured that out on day one."

"We're a team of contractors who do things around the world that you'll never see on television, and we've been activated. Your only role from this point on is to get us back to our airplane so we can meet our ship. She's steaming from the coast of Kuwait in the Persian Gulf."

I could see his wheels turning.

He said, "Where are you planning to meet your ship?"

"Probably Cairo."

His wheels continued turning. "Kuwait to Cairo is four thousand miles. I'll have you back in La Rochelle in twenty-four hours, but there's no ship in the world that can make four thousand miles in that length of time."

"The *Lori Danielle* is no ordinary ship, Elliot. If we don't hurry, she'll beat us to Cairo."

"If you say so."

I said, "We're in the very early stages of this thing, and it could resolve itself before we truly get involved, but for now, just get us back to our plane as fast as possible."

"No problem, but what are we going to do with Mr. Wood?"

I slapped him on the shoulder. "You just head south. I'll take care of Don."

I jogged back to the conference room, where the team was poring over the packet from the Board. "We're turning south for La Rochelle and the Gulfstream. We'll rendezvous with the *Lori Danielle* in Cairo. What do you have for me."

Skipper said, "Nothing yet, but what are we going to do with Don Wood?"

I said, "Hey, Kodiak. Remember taking those old guys parachuting over Normandy in ninety-four?"

He looked up with a full-sized Green Beret grin. "Please let me tell him."

"Nope, but you can come with me while I tell him."

We left the interior and found Don still telling stories to Ronda and two waiters.

He looked up as we approached. "I guess that's my cue to head back for the chopper, huh?"

I said, "That's up to you. If you're up for a little adventure, you're welcome to come with us."

Kodiak said, "We promise not to get you shot . . . probably."

He stood without his cane. "Hell yeah, boys. Count me in. But you've got to give me something better than an M-One this time. That bolt tried to cut my thumb off a hundred times."

"We can handle that," I said. "You'd better call Madame Patricia and let her know you'll be late for dinner."

"She'll be delighted," he said. "Where's the phone?"

# Chapter 8
## *How Do We Know?*

With the bow pointed southwest, we steamed out of the English Channel at the yacht's top speed of twenty-four knots, and I made the call to our wolf in sheep's clothing. The RV *Lori Danielle* was our five-hundred-eighty-eight-foot warship that trolled the world's oceans wearing the disguise of a world-class scientific and environmental research vessel. Beneath the skin of a humble research ship beat the heart of an ultra-modern warship with capabilities well beyond those of most of the world's naval vessels.

When the team wasn't operational aboard the *L.D.*, the ship was in the loving hands of Dr. Masha Turner, a marine biologist working to save the vaquitas, one of the ocean's most endangered species. The ship had recently been refitted to relocate three mating pairs of vaquitas from the Gulf of California, where they were dying in fishing nets far too often. One pair went to the Scripps Institution of Oceanography at UC San Diego, while two were relocated to the Persian Gulf off the coast of Kuwait, where the oceanographic conditions were extremely similar to those in the vaquitas' native waters off Mexico. For several weeks, Dr. Turner had studied and recorded the vaquitas in their new environs, closely monitoring for adaptation to the new region. Pulling the ship from the project wouldn't sit well with her, but we made it crystal clear that the primary purpose of the *Lori Danielle* was covert operation for the good of mankind. The biological and oceanographic research efforts would fall into a very distant second place.

My first call was to Captain Barry Sprayberry, the master of the *Lori Danielle* and a dear friend.

"Bridge, Captain."

His tone when he answered the phone was always one-hundred-percent business, and that's exactly how he ran his ship. His was a military style of leadership with a pinch of a pirate's bravado beneath his hat. The officers under his command respected and admired him, and those of us who worked in his periphery came to know him as an absolutely stalwart man of the sea with a devotion to duty, ship, and crew that was unparalleled aboard any vessel on any of the world's oceans.

"Barry, it's Chase. How are things in the research business?"

He sighed. "Please either tell me I get to sink a Russian ship this afternoon or shoot me in the head. I'm bored out of my mind watching twelve-year-old PhDs stare at baby dolphins. You have to get me out of here."

"How about something in between? I don't have a Russian for you to shoot at, but I do have a mission."

"Thank God. When and where?"

I said, "The Med, ASAP."

He turned away from the phone and gave the order. "Recall the ROV and make ready for high-speed operations for the Med."

"Wait!" I said. "I need to talk to Dr. Turner first."

He said, "Belay that order and stand by." He returned to the phone. "Do you want me to connect you with Dr. Turner?"

"Yes, if you can."

"Sure, stand by."

The line clicked twice, and a much more pleasant voice with only the slightest of Hungarian accents filled my ear. "Hello, this is Masha."

"Masha, it's Chase. How are the vaquitas?"

"They're so good. You can't imagine how beautifully they're settling into their new home. They've even begun bumping and playing. Those are the first signs of mating, so we're very hopeful."

THE CAPITOL CHASE · 61

THE CAPITOL CHASE · 61

"That's great news," I said. "Unfortunately, though, I have some bad news. We need the ship."

"Oh, no. Can't it wait a few more days?"

I said, "It cannot. There are lives at stake, and you know the priorities of the ship."

Although I couldn't see her tears, I could hear them. "Okay, how soon?"

"Now."

She sighed. "I'll recall the ROV. Does the captain know?"

"He does, but I wanted to be the one to tell you."

"Thank you, Chase. That means a lot. I guess you need to talk to him again, yes?"

Her accent thickened when she was emotional, but I couldn't let her love for the vaquitas outweigh my responsibility to the lives aboard the *Desert Star*, even if they were at the bottom of the Med.

"Yes. Recall the rover, and send the call back to the bridge. Oh, and just so you know, I am sorry."

She sobbed for a moment and collected herself. "I know, and thank you. As much as it hurts, I understand what it means when duty calls."

Two more clicks came, and Barry said, "Bridge, Captain."

"Masha is recalling the ROV, but she's not happy about it."

He said, "I'm sure she's not, but when duty calls . . ."

"That's exactly what she said. So, here's what's going to happen."

"Stand by one, Chase." He turned away from the phone again. "Make ready for high-speed operations the second that ROV is dry. Set a course for the Suez with all haste." He returned. "All right, Chase. I'm all yours."

I said, "I'll have Skipper transmit the target package for command staff and Weps only."

The ship's weapons systems officer was third-in-command, but I wanted Barry to understand that we might have to pull a trigger before this thing ended.

"Got it," he said. "We'll be underway in less than half an hour, but we need gas."

"There's no place on Earth where fuel is cheaper than the Persian Gulf, so top her off."

He said, "You've got our financial officer, and we kind of need her when we're buying a million dollars' worth of MGD. It's not like I can stick my credit card in the pump at self-serve."

"Oh, yeah. Sorry about that. I'll put her on the phone when you and I finish. The Board should've just transferred ten million into the ops account, but Ronda will take care of all that. What else do you need from me?"

"I'm solid from here," he said. "I'll have the armorer service your weapons. They're still working out the kinks with the new helo and the hangar deck. That thing's a lot bigger than the Huey, but they'll figure it out."

"That's all I've got," I said. "Here's Ronda."

I handed the phone to the CPA and stepped away. She was more than capable of handling anything Captain Sprayberry needed without me tagging along.

The team was still gathered around the table with their heads buried in their tablets as they read and reread the mission packet.

I knocked on the table as if gaveling the meeting to order. "We've got a couple of decisions to make. We can take everybody with us, or we can leave the civilians behind. They can stay aboard the yacht and continue their vacation, but there's no way to know how long we'll be gone. Any thoughts?"

Skipper spoke up first. "I say we bring them, but brief them up so they know they have to stay out of the way."

Mongo, always the voice of reason, said, "Why don't you let them decide? If they want to stay on the yacht, let 'em stay. If they want to come with us, there's plenty of room on the *L.D.*"

"Good call," I said. "Now, give me the down and dirty on the *Desert Star*."

Skipper took the reins. "She's small at a hundred and twenty meters, so it's another needle-in-a-haystack situation. If she's still afloat, all of her electronics are down. There are—or were—sixty-five passengers, twelve crew, and forty staff for a total of one seventeen. Captain Yannis Aetos and senior crew are Greek. The staff is mostly Italian."

I committed everything I could to memory and said, "Give me the rundown on the congressman."

She scanned through her notes. "Landon David Herd, age thirty-nine, born Landon David Montgomery on December ninth, nineteen seventy-five, undergrad from . . ."

I held up a hand. "Whoa. He changed his name?"

Skipper said, "I'm working on figuring out why. The most common reason is adoption after the mother remarried, but I'll figure it out. May I continue?"

I nodded, and she picked up where she'd left off.

"Undergrad at USC—that's Southern Cal, not South Carolina—in political science, did a stint in the Navy before Northwestern Pritzker School of Law in Chicago, graduated middle of his class, nothing special."

"Stop there," I said. "Tell me about his Naval service."

She ground her teeth. "That's a little tricky. He likes to throw the word SEAL around on the campaign trail and when he's making public appearances, but he's never directly come out and claimed to have been a SEAL."

Shawn said, "That's easy. I can make one phone call and tell you if the guy was a SEAL."

"Do it," I said. "I need to know what we're working with. If the dude's a SEAL, he's the best asset we've got on this thing and the best chance the people on that ship have to make it out alive."

Shawn made a few notes, grabbed his sat-phone, and stepped to the edge of the room while Skipper continued.

"Practiced corporate law with a big firm in Denver, elected to city council, and ran a small campaign for governor but couldn't raise enough money to be a serious player, so he dropped out. Finally got himself elected to Congress, and now he's in his second term as the congressman from Colorado's first congressional district. That's the Denver area. He seems to be a bit of a rising star in the party, and there's a lot of talk about him announcing his bid for the presidential nomination in twenty sixteen."

I said, "Sorry to interrupt again, but *who* doesn't like him?"

Skipper shrugged. "Everybody on the other side. His platform is right down the party line. There's nothing surprising there."

"No, I mean, who *really* doesn't like him?"

She huffed. "I'll dig deeper, but nobody jumps out. He's never done enough of anything to collect any real enemies. Honestly, he seems like a decent guy."

"Who backed him?"

She cocked her head. "What do you mean?"

"You said he couldn't raise enough money to run for governor, but he got elected to Congress. Somebody had to back him."

She said, "That's not in the brief, but I've done a little background, and it appears to have been a grassroots campaign."

I leaned back in my chair. "We're missing something. If we assume the ship was taken because of the congressman, there are only two reasons that would happen. One, somebody's afraid of him and they want to take him out. Two, the pirates want a congressional-sized bargaining chip."

Gator leaned in. "What do you mean by bargaining chip? America doesn't negotiate with terrorists."

Everyone got a good chuckle out of that, and Kodiak slapped the youngster on the back. "Grow up, kid. Of course we do. That's the main reason for piracy. These strung-out wannabe warlords take a ship and offer it back for a handsome ransom. By the way, Handsome Ransom used to be my nickname on the street."

Groans rose, and Gator said, "I'm not talking about shipping companies or insurance carriers. I mean the U.S. Government. Hasn't it always been our policy not to negotiate with terrorists? Taking a U.S. congressman isn't a very good way to get paid."

I said, "Yes, that's been our public position, but Kodiak's right. Be-

THE CAPITOL CHASE · 65

hind the scenes, the U.S. writes a lot of checks to keep potentially noisy things quiet—like the abduction of a ship carrying a prominent American politician."

Mongo motioned toward a television in the corner of the room. "Why isn't this thing on every news channel in the world?"

Skipper said, "Just like the Board said, the President himself wants to keep it quiet."

Mongo shook his head. "I'm not buying it. Sure, the White House is powerful, but how do you cover up a missing cruise ship in the Mediterranean from Washington, D.C.? How many people heard the distress call? Somebody's looking for that ship. If no one else, the company wants to know where it is. What did you say the name of the cruise line is? Star Line?"

Skipper said, "That's right, and you've got a good point. Why isn't the CEO of Star Line losing his mind on BBC and CNN?"

Gator asked. "Is it possible the company doesn't know their ship is missing?"

Kodiak groaned. "They have to track their ships, right?"

"We're getting ahead of ourselves," I said. "Let's do a balance sheet. Assets, let's go."

Skipper started the list. "We *may* have a SEAL on a hijacked ship. That has to be our biggest asset, right?"

Everyone nodded, and Shawn returned to the table. "He's not a SEAL, but he's almost a SEAL."

Skipper frowned. "What does that mean?"

"He made it through BUD/S after getting washed back once. That's Basic Underwater Demolition/SEAL training. And it's not rare to get washed back. It happened to me. I got hurt pretty badly, but I recovered and graduated with the next cycle. Anyway, that's probably what happened to him, but it doesn't really matter. The problem is that he never went to SQT."

Gator raised an eyebrow. "Throw me a bone here. I'm a civilian, remember?"

Shawn said, "Seal Qualification Training. It's a four-week advanced tactics course. You have to make it through BUD/S and SQT to wear the trident and qualify as a SEAL. Ensign Herd didn't do that, and the people I talked to don't know why."

"How common is that?" I asked.

Shawn shook his head. "The only time I've ever heard of it happening is when somebody loses his mind in SQT. I mean, it happens. There are some wackos who make it through BUD/S partially because they're crazy, but the Navy figures it out, and they don't make it through SQT."

"So, is that what happened to Herd?" I asked.

Shawn said, "Nope. He just never started SQT. It's weird. Who would go through BUD/S and then quit?"

I stared through the glass table and tried to wrap my head around Landon David Montgomery Herd. "So, where did he go?"

Shawn looked at Skipper.

She threw up her hands. "I don't know, but I'll find out. Can we continue with the balance sheet?"

I said, "Yes, sorry. We got derailed. I think we still have to consider the congressman as our greatest asset. He may have never worn the SEAL trident, but he made it through BUD/S, so he's got the stones, right?"

My question was primarily directed at Shawn, but he didn't give me the nod I wanted. Instead, he said, "Maybe. Like I said, there are some real wackos who make it through BUD/S. Maybe he knew he was going to flip out, and he saved his career by walking away. At best, he's a wildcard."

I said, "Okay, what's next on the asset list?"

Skipper motioned around the table. "You guys."

"And you," I said. "You're high on the list."

She said, "Not from here. I'm muzzled without my computers. I need to be in the CIC or the op center. I don't have the computing power to accomplish much of anything from here."

I said, "That means our greatest liability is you being here. Where do you want to be? On the ship or back at Bonaventure in the op center?"

"There's no difference. Either is as good as the other, but I'd prefer to stay with the team. These round tables are more valuable in person."

I said, "Good, the ship it is. It feels like our balance sheet doesn't balance very well right now. We've got a missing ship with no electronics. Nobody else is looking for it. It's probably on the bottom. And the White House wants to keep it quiet."

Singer had been silent until that moment. "How do we know it was pirates and not an inside job?"

# Chapter 9
## *Rooty Tooty*

Singer's question froze each of us in our seats until I asked, "What kind of inside job?"

Our sniper said, "Maybe we're looking at this from the outside in instead of the other way around. How much research does a congressman's staff do before they put him on a cruise ship? Do they run background checks on the staff and crew? Do they send personal security with him? You're the one with Secret Service credentials, so what's the protocol?"

I pulled my cred pack from my pocket. "These aren't worth the material they're made of. I won this throwing baseballs at the carnival. I don't think congressmen get Secret Service protection, do they?"

Gator said, "Finally, I know something you don't. Believe it or not, I was a Congressional Page my junior year in high school."

Kodiak ruffled Gator's hair. "Aww, how cute. I thought you were a jock, but you were a nerd. You were probably on the Scholars Bowl team, too, huh?"

Gator swatted his hand away. "Keep it up, and I'll show you how a nerd kicks an old man's butt. Now, as I was saying, I know a little about Congress."

I knew every detail of Gator's life before joining the team, so I wasn't surprised, but I was anxious to hear his version of what he observed as a sixteen-year-old high schooler in D.C.

He said, "The Capitol Police, not the Secret Service, are responsible for the protection of the Capitol and the members of Congress on Capitol grounds. Sometimes, they offer personal protection for members of Congress when they travel, and there are a few specially trained officers who are qualified to provide security during overseas travel. Most of the time, though, congressmen don't have a protection detail."

I asked, "Who would be left behind to run Herd's office while he was on this cruise?"

Gator said, "It's not like he's the speaker of the house, so there would probably be a couple of aides left behind. But for a junior congressman, there's not a very big staff to begin with."

I turned to Skipper. "Add that to your list. Find out if we can talk with anyone in Herd's office. The more we know about who he's with, the better. Is he married? Kids?"

"Got it. Yes, he's married with two teenagers—a boy and a girl."

"Are they on the ship?"

"I don't know yet. I haven't seen the ship's manifest."

I said, "What? You don't have the manifest?"

"If we do, I haven't found it yet. Has anyone else seen it?"

Everyone flipped through their packet, but we came up with a room full of shaking heads.

"What are they hiding?" I asked.

"That's the wrong question again," Singer said. "The right questions are *who* are they hiding, and *who* is doing the hiding?"

I leaned back in my chair. "I need to talk to the President."

Skipper said, "On the record or back channel?"

"I don't want to be on the White House switchboard call log, if that's what you're asking."

"You know what I'm asking."

"I know, but I'm not ready to dial that number yet—not without at least letting the Board know I'm doing it. I've done enough to get under their skin, and I'd rather not push them any further."

"Good thinking," she said, and then cast a thumb toward Clark.

"You know, your handler is right here, and he's your direct link to the Board."

I raised an eyebrow. "What do you think, boss?"

Clark steepled his fingers. "If we don't tell them you're going to do it, I'm afraid we'll be up the creek without a pickle, but I don't think they'll authorize a call."

I squeezed my eyelids closed. "Up the creek without a pickle?"

Clark waved a hand. "You know what I mean."

"No, I really don't. Could you spell it out for me?"

"You call the President. I'll call the Board."

"Seriously?"

He said, "Sure. We need to know what he knows and what he expects, and if the Board says no, we can't get around that. If we make the calls at the same time, we're not technically disobeying . . . yet."

"That's why you're the handler."

He laughed. "No, I'm the handler because you got me shot up so bad I'm no good in the field anymore."

"There is that," I said.

I bounced the sat-phone in my palm several times while staring into space. Every eye in the room was trained on me, so I dialed the number from memory and pressed send.

The next voice I heard was one I still couldn't believe I had access to. The President of the United States said, "I've been expecting your call. I guess you've got some questions."

"Yes, sir, I do. Is now a good time?"

He laughed. "There's no such thing as a good time for a call like this, Chase. You know that. But I've got thirty seconds for you, so go."

My brain turned backflips trying to prioritize my questions before my thirty seconds ran out. "Does Herd have a protection detail?"

"No."

"Is his family aboard the ship with him?"

"Yes."

"Does Star Lines know their ship is missing?"

The President hesitated. "I don't know, but I hope not. We're working on that."

An entirely new collection of questions poured into my head, but I stayed the course. "Is the ship still afloat?"

His voice cracked. "God, I hope so."

"Can I call the cruise line?"

"No."

I swallowed hard. "Mr. President, forgive me, but am I looking for a ship, or am I covering up a steaming pile you don't want the world to see?"

He didn't hesitate. "For now, you're looking for a ship. If it turns into the other, I'll let you know. I've got time for one more question, and then I'm hanging up, so make it a good one."

The cranial backflips turned into a freefall, and I said, "I need the manifest."

The President said, "I'll see that you have it."

The line clicked, and the screen turned dark.

I looked up at Clark, and he said, "They authorized the call."

I chuckled. "That's because they knew I was going to call either way."

"You're probably right," he said. "Did you get the answers you wanted?"

"Some of them."

I ran down the list of answers, and Clark said, "Interesting. What do you think he's afraid of?"

I chewed my lip for a moment. "I don't know yet, but he's definitely uneasy about something."

As the pressure built inside the room, I was pleased to see Penny peeking around the door. I said, "Come on in. You need to know what's going on."

She slinked through the door. "I'm sorry to interrupt, but I thought you guys might be hungry, and they're ready to serve lunch. Do you want it in here?"

Skipper said, "Yes, thank you. I'll take mine in here, but you can take the rest of these guys with you. I need the privacy."

We followed Penny from the conference room and into the main dining area. At the yacht's speed, dining outside might've made our napkins a little hard to catch.

A pair of waiters appeared and served the table. One of them said, "For today's lunch, we have grilled salmon over wild rice with apricot and honey chutney and steamed vegetables. Please enjoy."

And enjoy we did, although the meal was far quieter than our typical gathering. Too many thoughts were running through too many heads for conversation.

When the dishes were cleared, I said, "It's time I let everyone know what's going on. We have a mission. You probably figured out that much already. The assignment requires the use of *Lori Danielle*. That's why we're racing back to La Rochelle. We'll take the Gulfstream to Cairo, where we'll meet the ship. If anyone wants to remain aboard the yacht for the rest of the cruise, you're welcome to stay. It's ours for ten days. If you'd like to join us on the ship, you're welcome there, as well, but just know that it won't be a pleasure cruise."

The decisions were made in an instant. Penny and her parents chose to remain aboard the yacht, as did Irina and Maebelle.

Don Wood said, "If the invitation is still open, I'd rather have one last adventure before it's too late."

I said, "Of course it's still open, my friend. If I remember correctly, you want a better rifle this time."

He laughed and wiped his chin before tossing his napkin onto the table.

"Then it's settled," I said. "I'll tell the captain who's staying, and I'm sure he'll want to discuss the itinerary with you. The yacht is yours for nine more days. Enjoy."

Skipper stepped from the conference room. "I've got the manifest."

Clark glanced over his shoulder. "Anybody interesting on the list?"

"I don't know yet. I'm running background checks on everyone, but with only my laptop, it's going to take a while. There is one curiosity on the manifest."

She had my full attention. "What is it?"

"The congressman's birth name of Montgomery is listed on the manifest instead of Herd."

"That's probably for security reasons," I said.

Skipper nodded. "Maybe, but I can't find any other times he's used that name. I'll be able to dig a little more when I get inside the CIC, but I'm doing the best I can for now."

"Did you eat?" I asked.

"Yes, and it was delicious."

She vanished back into her temporary lair, and the waiting game began.

I visited the bridge, and Elliot seemed pleased to see me. "Come on in, Chase. Is everything all right?"

"It will be. I'd like to bring you up to speed."

He said, "I'd like that. Captains aren't good at not knowing what's going on."

"As you already know, we've been called away for professional reasons, but what you don't know is exactly what those reasons are. I wish I could tell you everything, but suffice it to say that we're in the security business, and it would appear that a person of some importance has gotten himself into a . . . well, let's say a pickle, for lack of a better term at the moment."

Elliot said, "Interesting. And you're going to pull this important individual out of that pickle. Is that a fair assessment?"

"It is, but there's a catch. We have some civilians with us who would rather stay behind and finish the cruise with you since we paid for ten days."

"Of course. I was hoping that would happen. There will be a fuel assessment fee, I'm afraid. We burn a lot of fuel at this speed."

"I understand, and we'll take care of it."

"Thank you for understanding. Is there anything else you need from me?"

"That covers it," I said. "Will we be able to keep up this speed overnight?"

"Of course. I'll have you back in La Rochelle before lunch tomorrow."

\* \* \*

The night passed with very little sleep for me, and I imagined the same was true for most of the team. I doubted if Skipper ever left her laptop. Just as promised, we pulled into La Rochelle just before noon and wasted no time hitting the ground.

The Gulfstream was fueled and waiting on the tarmac when we pulled up, and Disco and I made quick work of the flight plan and pre-flight inspection.

Don stood on the tarmac, staring up at the *Grey Ghost*. "You boys travel well. I wasn't expecting this."

"We do all right," I said. "Come on. Let's get you aboard and settled in. We'll be in Cairo before you know it."

Three hours into the flight, I ran the fuel calculations, and Disco said, "What's the matter? Don't you trust the mice on the wheel?"

"I trust them, but I've got an idea."

"Let's hear it," he said.

"We've got the fuel to make Djibouti. That puts us aboard the ship at least eighteen hours earlier. What do you think?"

He said, "I think you should call Captain Sprayberry and tell him, 'Rooty tooty, meet me in Djibouti.'"

# Chapter 10

## *Hell's Outhouse*

We stepped off the plane, and Clark Johnson stuck his nose in the air. "This don't smell like Cairo. There's no Kentucky Fried Chicken."

I stepped by him. "The only American colonel you'll find here is Disco. Welcome to Djibouti."

Anya giggled. "This is fun word to say, yes?"

That ignited a chorus of voices calling the name of both the city and country on the horn of Africa, where the Gulf of Aden meets the Red Sea.

Our colonel without a white suit and bow tie rolled his eyes. "We're a sleeping mat and a cup of raisins away from being a daycare center. Would you guys grow up?"

Singer laughed. "Probably not, but I'd love a cup of raisins."

Skipper finally cut through the revelry. "Do you guys want to know where we're going to sleep, or would you rather dance in a circle and sing the Djibouti song all night?"

I expected the wrong answer, but my crew showed a little respect and perhaps a measure of fear for Skipper since she had the power to stick them in a North African Motel 6.

"That's what I thought. I booked us in the Djibouti Palace Kempinski. It's the closest thing to a luxury resort I could find."

Kodiak did a pirouette. "Did you say we're booked in the Ja-Booty Palace?"

Gator gave him a shove and tipped his cap to Skipper. "Thank you for always taking such good care of us."

She blew him off. "It's not for you knuckle-draggers. I'm the one who needs the peace and quiet . . . and maybe a spa day. You just happen to get to tag along."

With the arrangements made for a hangar for the *Grey Ghost*, we scored a couple of SUVs for the ride to the resort. Skipper hit it out of the park again. The Palace couldn't compete with Dubai, but it certainly wasn't bad.

The team wasted no time cramming calories down their throats and hitting the sack. We would need both the fuel and rest if the coming assignment proved to be half as challenging as I expected.

After breakfast the following morning, Skipper stood from the table and took Anya's and Ronda's hands. "Excuse us, boys. We've got a date with the spa this morning."

Mongo groaned. "And you didn't invite me? My nails could use a little buffing, and I could go for a shave."

Skipper huffed. "You need a grinding wheel and a bushhog, not a spa. Enjoying the morning, boys."

As they turned away, I called, "Don't forget that we've got a ship to catch."

Skipper held up a pair of fingers. "Two p.m."

Later, the ladies returned looking well cared for, and a second set of SUVs returned us to the airport.

"How was the spa?" I asked no one in particular.

Anya extended a leg and pulled up her pants. "Feel of leg. It is wonderful."

Without a thought, I reached for Anya's calf, but Skipper slapped my hand away with far more force than necessary. "No! You know better. You can feel mine."

I declined but said, "I'll take it you had a good time."

Anya giggled. "We should have spa installed on ship."

I shook my head. "We? Is that what we're doing now? Is it *our* ship?"

Ronda grimaced. "Yeah, it kind of is, and I agree with Anya. A spa next to my office would be perfect. I'll get to work on that."

I hoped she wasn't serious, but I had no way to know.

The Boeing Vertol came into sight over the coast, and Barbie—call sign Gun Bunny—kissed the tarmac with the tires as if she were touching down on glass. The new helicopter increased our capability in both gross weight and volume of materiel we could move. I missed the Huey, but the Vertol was an excellent upgrade since we left the old one in pieces somewhere in the Amazon.

Without any gear to load, it took only seconds for all eleven of us to pile ourselves onto the helo, and Barbie had us airborne and seabound.

I watched closely as we touched down on the helipad aboard the *Lori Danielle*. "Wow, that's tight."

Shawn said, "It sure is. Have you tried it yet?"

"No, this is the first time I've seen the new helipad and hangar deck."

He gave me a slug on the shoulder. "You might want to get some reps in, brother. You can't let a woman show you up."

I laughed. "At best, I'm the fourth-best pilot on this chopper. Barbie shows me up every time I fly with her."

He stood. "We're blessed with some real talent around us."

"You're not wrong, brother, and you bring a basketful of it yourself."

He flexed a bicep. "I just move heavy things when they get in the way."

We unloaded, and I waited for Barbie to shut down and climb out. I said, "Show me around, would you?"

She pulled off her helmet and gloves. "Sure. As you can see, it's still pretty tight up here. There's just not enough room to build a bigger pad."

"I noticed. Have you done any landings in heavy weather yet?"

She pointed beneath the Vertol. "I have, and that's why we've got this little gadget." She lay down and pointed toward a covered opening in the center of the pad. "That's a winch cable. If you can get the chopper close enough to the ship for the deck crew to hook that cable to the sling load hook on the belly of the Vertol, they can winch you in while you're holding tension on the cable."

"Nice," I said. "How strong is the winch?"

She patted the deck. "Fifty thousand pounds."

"Are you serious?"

She hopped to her feet and slid a palm across the skin of the Vertol. "This baby can pull hard, too. I didn't want to risk snapping a cable in high wind. Hopefully, we'll never need the cable system, but we've got it just in case."

"How about the hangar?" I asked.

"It's tight, too, but it works. The Vertol is actually easier to handle on deck than the Huey was. The wheels make the difference, but that also means we have to tie her down a little stronger for those nights when the ocean doesn't want to behave."

"So, you're happy with it?"

She shrugged. "Yeah, it's good. I wish the ship was two feet wider or the Vertol was four feet shorter, but I'm not complaining. It's a great upgrade."

"I'm glad it's working out."

She shoved her gloves into her helmet and tossed it to a deckhand. "When do you want to get some takeoffs and landings in?"

"We're going to run hard for the Med, but when we slow down, I'd love to get in some hours."

"I'm ready when you are. Oh, and it's probably a good idea to get Disco and Clark up to speed, as well."

I said, "Definitely Disco, and I'll talk to Clark and see if he's interested."

She turned for the hangar bay. "Whatever you say. You're the boss."

My next stop was the bridge as a courtesy to shake Barry's hand, but I didn't stay long. I found the rest of the team in the armory, inspecting their kits.

"How's everything look?" I asked.

"Looks good," Mongo said. "You hired a first-rate armorer."

Shawn inspected a rifle. "We need to verify zero on everything before we step off into Hell's outhouse."

"What's that?" Gator asked as he adjusted the sling on his M4.

Shawn feigned surprise. "Hell's outhouse?" Gator nodded, and Shawn said, "That's what we used to call the Red Sea when I was with the Teams. If you're going to encounter serious pirates anywhere on Earth, it's going to be right up there."

He pointed north, and Gator's eyes followed. "It's that bad, huh?"

"Put it this way," Shawn said. "I've worked eight piracy missions in my life, and seven of them were in the Red Sea."

"Where was the eighth?"

Shawn laughed. "I had to knock some porch pirates off my front doorstep while they were trying to steal an Amazon delivery."

Gator shook his head. "Are you ever going to stop messing with me?"

Shawn grabbed Gator's shirt with both hands. "If I do, kid, something's gone very wrong, and I need you to shoot whoever's behind me."

"Consider it done, brother."

Underway and making fifty knots, we dragged our bullet-trap deck targets to the stern of the ship and zeroed our weapons. It took only a handful of shots, and Singer said, "That new armorer is on his game."

I holstered my Glock. "It's nice to have good support."

"It sure is," the sniper said. "The hardest-hitting team in the world is no good without a powerful home team."

"Let's get these bullet traps put away," I said. "It'll be dark soon."

"You got it."

The deck was clear in fifteen minutes, and all that remained was waiting for Captain Sprayberry to get us through the Suez Canal and into the Mediterranean.

I checked my watch and the sun before heading for the CIC, where

I hoped Skipper was neck-deep in data she couldn't gather on the yacht. I made it three strides up the ladder when the ship's claxon sounded and the speaker system came to life.

"Attention on deck. General quarters. All hands man battle stations and prepare to repel boarders from astern. This is not a drill."

Captain Sprayberry's words froze me in my tracks, and I turned to see three vessels approaching from astern. We had slowed as we steamed through the busy shipping lanes of the Bab al-Mandab Strait and approached the Hanish Islands. The Red Sea is a narrow band of water less than two hundred miles wide, but it had a backbone of shallow water and islands running most of its length that divided the sea into two navigable waterways. Somewhere near the northern end, where the sea became the Gulf of Suez, a gaggle of fleeing Israelites ran through the parted waters to escape the pursuing Egyptians a few thousand years ago, but Egyptians weren't our problem. There was little doubt about the identity of the Houthis chasing the innocent-looking research vessel as the sun nestled herself against the western horizon over Eritrea and Sudan.

Although the team and I didn't technically have assigned battle stations, the pirates had chosen the worst possible time to approach the *Lori Danielle*.

There were nine battle-hardened, world-class commandos armed to the teeth on deck, with one of the most combat-ready warships on Earth beneath their boots. The day was not going to end well for the pirates, but we were going to have a lot of fun welcoming them aboard the American-flagged vessel.

## Chapter 11

## *I Am Captain Now*

I descended the ladder and took my position on the starboard side away from the rail and pulled my radio from my belt. "Bridge, Sierra One."

"Go for bridge."

I said, "Captain, we're nine strong on deck with rifles and sidearms. Do you plan to outrun these guys?"

Captain Sprayberry asked, "Body armor?"

"Negative."

He said, "We don't have the space to get up on the foils, but we can probably still give these guys a pretty good run. At the very least, we can match their speed and keep them from catching up. They'll run out of gas before we do."

I said, "I've got a better idea. Let's use this as a learning opportunity. Run until we can get fully kitted out and then slow enough for them to catch up."

Barry said, "Are you seriously going to intentionally allow Yemeni pirates aboard my ship?"

I tried not to laugh. "You said you were bored, so here's your opportunity to get unbored."

We sped up, but barely noticeably, and I rounded up the team behind the superstructure. "Get to the armory and get your full kits on, including comms. I'm inviting some friends over to play."

No one hesitated or asked any questions. None of us would turn down the opportunity to shoot it out with a gang of pirates, especially if we had a chance to rid the region of one more band of bad guys. We suited up, tested our comms, and tripled our ammo loadout. Singer exchanged his M4 for his trusty .338 Lapua Magnum and headed for high ground.

In full battle rattle, I sprinted to the combat information center and thumbed in my code to enter. Skipper looked up when I stepped through the hatch, but the weapons systems officer did not.

As I slid by Skipper, I whispered, "Exciting, huh?"

She grinned up at me. "Not yet."

Stepping behind Weps, I said, "Let's spray the first pair and see how they react."

"Roger."

The captain slowed just enough to allow two of the three pirate vessels to come alongside. The ship's perimeter security cameras displayed the action in real time and high definition. I was impressed. Their boats were bigger than I expected, and they seemed well organized and not poorly equipped.

As the largest of the pirate's vessels came alongside, someone fired a hook across our starboard rail amidships and hauled a rope ladder behind the hook.

"Not bad," I said. "Let them think they're doing well before we get them wet."

Weps nodded and kept his face buried in the monitors in front of him. Two tall, thin men with AK-47 variants over their shoulders stepped from the boat and onto the rope ladder. Our video system could almost read their minds. They climbed in practiced coordination, never missing a footing. This wasn't their first time, but I planned to make it their last.

The *Lori Danielle* was equipped with a state-of-the-art, near-boiling water system arranged in her exterior surfaces. The system came in handy in cold environments to keep ice from forming on the ship, but it was specifically designed to discourage unwanted guests from coming over the rail. Weps had full command of the high-pressure system from his station.

I watched the two men climb until they were high enough above the water to risk breaking their spines if they fell.

"Hit 'em!" I ordered, and Weps activated the localized sprayers only inches from the two pirates. The two-hundred-degree water exploded from the jets under enough pressure to slice into a man's flesh.

The blast lasted less than a second before the two men tumbled from the ladder and landed on their backs on top of the vessel they'd ridden to the party. Neither man moved after striking the deck, but I couldn't tell if they were dead or just unconscious.

As quickly as the two men landed back aboard their boat, the driver maneuvered away to starboard, and a team of gunmen lined the vessel's portside rail.

Weps said, "Oh, how cute. They're going to shoot at us. Shall I return fire?"

The ship's armored glass bridge windows could withstand anything short of a meteor strike, and her skin wouldn't notice the AK rounds ricocheting like pinballs when the pirates opened fire.

"I've got a better idea," I said. I called the bridge. "Are you watching the video, Captain?"

"Affirmative. It's pretty clear they're going to open fire. What's your grand plan now, Cowboy?"

"When they open fire, let's pretend to be cooperative. Pull the speed back, but keep the engines making full power."

It was almost time to unleash our giant, but not quite.

Through our open-channel comms, I said, "Mongo, stand by to heave that ladder."

He said, "Roger," with a little humor in his tone.

I said, "Kodiak and Gator, I want you to deal with the two goons Mongo hauls aboard. Can you do it?"

Both answered, "Affirmative," and our initial plan was underway.

The line of gunmen opened fire on our starboard side but accomplished nothing besides wasting bullets.

The captain took my plan one step further than I expected. Instead of immediately slowing to a stop, he began a zig-zag pattern through the water as if trying to evade the gunfire. It was a reasonable tactic that lent credibility to our charade. Finally, he dialed back the Azipods and allowed the ship to settle into the water.

A raucous cheer erupted from the largest of the three pirate boats, and all three of them motored alongside the ship as fast as they could move through the water.

Weps asked, "More water?"

I asked, "Can you fake a system failure in one spot?"

"Oh, yeah."

"Do it. Knock everybody down except the two coming up the original ladder when they come."

"No problem."

They fired two more hooks and deployed two more ladders. This time, six pirates climbed the three rope ladders in pairs, and Weps blasted two of the pairs back into the sea, but he fed low-pressure water to the jets near the original ladder. The water was still hot, but it wasn't slicing into the men's flesh. I hoped they would battle through the scorching water to claim their coveted prize.

They didn't disappoint. They flinched at the heat but kept climbing, so I gave the order, "Haul them in, Mongo."

Our three-hundred-pound stack of muscle gripped the rope ladder and yanked, hand over hand, hauling the climbing pirates toward the rail at over twice their original speed. I expected them to abandon their ladder-turned-escalator and dive back into the sea below, but they kept climbing as if oblivious to the coming peril.

As soon as the muzzle of the first man's rifle rose above the rail, Kodiak leapt from cover, circled his man's neck with an arm, and dragged him over the rail. Gator provided the same service for the second man, and soon, we had our first two prisoners of the raid.

"Truss 'em up and stack 'em," I said. "We've got more to come."

The unconscious pirates were cuffed and stacked against the super-structure in seconds.

We allowed four more of them to climb aboard to the same welcoming party as the original two, and I made the call. "All right, Weps, warn them off."

He asked, "Arabic?"

"Sure. They're hanging out in Yemen, so even if it's not their first choice, they'll understand."

Weps opened the speakers and leaned toward his microphone. After a deep breath, he declared, *"Abtaeid ean alsafinat wa'iilaa sanatliq alnaar ealayk."*

My Arabic was weak, but even I knew he said something close to "Move away or we'll shoot."

They didn't pull away, so I said, "Give them one more chance."

He repeated the Arabic warning both louder and harsher the second time.

"We've done all we can do, Weps. Give 'em the SEE-Wiz."

The Phalanx Close-In Weapon System was a marvel of modern weaponry. It was a radar-guided 20 mm Vulcan cannon mounted on a rotating base and was capable of dispensing 4500 rounds per minute. The weapon could reduce pirate boats to kindling in seconds.

Weps entered the commands, and three of the *Lori Danielle*'s four CWIS systems rose from hidden compartments near the starboard and port rails.

An instant later, the air erupted with roaring fire pouring from each Vulcan at 75 rounds per second. The smaller of the two pirate boats splintered into hundreds of thousands of slivers of wood and fiberglass glistening on water's surface. The largest of the three boats remained intact only a second longer than the other two. What had been a fifty-footer with thirty armed men aboard was reduced to flotsam, and if any of the men aboard survived, it was unlikely they'd make it back ashore before a school of patrolling sharks enjoyed their evening meal.

The attack was over, but our learning experience was yet to begin.

I said, "Weps, I recommend we secure from general quarters."

He relayed my suggestion to the captain, and the announcement came over the speaker system.

With the direct line to the bridge, I asked Captain Sprayberry if he'd launch a RHIB in search of survivors, and he agreed.

My second call was to the team. "All Sierra elements to the stern."

By the time I made it from the CIC to the deck, the team had the cuffed pirates spread out on the deck as if ready for inspection. I strolled the line of bone-thin pirates until I found one who appeared to be at least partially awake. I took a knee by his feet and asked, "Do you speak English?"

His answer came in the form of a mouthful of airborne spittle. I dodged the attack and folded him in half, pinning his knees to his chest in an instant. "That wasn't very nice, and if you do it again, I'll cut out your tongue. Now, let's start over. Do you speak English?"

He glared back at me with hatred in his eyes, and I glanced up at Shawn. "Send him over the rail."

Our SEAL didn't hesitate. He grabbed the semiconscious man from the deck and hurled him across the starboard rail with his hands and feet still bound.

The recovery team in the RHIB below picked him up immediately, but his fellow pirates didn't know that, and I had just earned a little respect from the other pirates who were conscious enough to witness the exchange.

"Wake 'em up," I ordered, and the team produced packs of ammonia and waved them beneath the pirates' noses.

Soon, all five of the remaining bad boys were wide awake.

I said, "Does anybody speak English?" Empty faces stared back, so I turned to the team. "Who wants a little translation practice?"

Mongo said, "My Arabic isn't bad, but Clark's is better than anybody's."

I said, "How about you, Shawn? You're conversational, right?"

He shrugged his powerful shoulders. "Yeah, conversational or maybe a little better."

"Good. Here's what I want. Shawn, Mongo, and Clark each take one man and have that man explain every step of the piracy process. I want to know how they pick vessels, how they decide what to do with the ship and crew, and what their plan is if nobody pays the ransom. Get every detail."

Shawn grabbed a man by the foot and dragged him across the deck until they were out of earshot of the other pirate. Mongo pulled his man by the arm, and Clark jerked the third man to his feet and forced him to hop across the deck. The remainder of the team guarded the remaining two men while I tried to decide who was in charge.

The younger of the two men at my feet appeared to wear a gaze that was a bit more distant and ominous than anyone else, so I kicked his foot. "Are you in charge? *Hal 'ant almaswuwli?*"

I knew fewer than two dozen words in Arabic, so I wasn't going to understand whatever he said, but I wanted him to understand that even if he had been in command a few minutes earlier, I was captain now.

When the interrogations were finished, I asked Shawn to translate for me.

"Tell them they have three choices. I can turn them loose and they can swim back to Yemen, I can turn them over to the U.S. Navy, or I can put a bullet in each of their heads."

Shawn rattled off the options in Arabic, and Clark stepped beside me. "He's not just speaking Arabic. He's speaking Yemeni Arabic. He's good."

The five remaining pirates spat outbursts of gibberish until Shawn got them calmed down. He turned to me and said, "These three want to swim, but the other two want the bullet."

I stared at the two who wanted to die. "I guess it's too bad for these two that this is a democracy. Three votes for a nice swim, two votes for bullets in the head. Put life jackets and lights on them, cut them free, and throw them in the water. Al-Hanish Island is a hundred yards to port. Point them in that direction."

# Chapter 12
## *Just Plain Sexy*

With the attack thwarted and the ship secured from general quarters, I assembled the team in the CIC. The weapons systems officer was lingering and reviewing the video of the incident. I peered over his shoulder. "See anything interesting?"

He froze the video and pointed toward the screen. "See that?"

I studied the low-light shot. "It looks like a banner of some kind, but I can't read Arabic."

He sighed. "This wasn't a ship- or crew-for-ransom event."

"What was it, then?"

"The flag says 'Death to America. Death to Israel.'"

"That's interesting."

"It gets better," he said. "Take a look inside the boat. The light isn't good, but I can brighten it up."

I leaned in and studied the screen. "Are those LAWs?"

"Maybe some of them," he said, "but the two in the front are A-T-Fours."

I looked up to see the whole team surrounding me and trying to get a glimpse.

Skipper said, "Here, guys. It's up on the big monitor."

The images from the small weapons video screen appeared on the massive overhead monitor.

Clark said, "Those are definitely anti-tank weapons. Look at the ones on the side. I can't remember the name of them, but they're old German tubes left over from World War Two."

Mongo said, "They're called Panzerfaust, but I can't believe there are any of those left on Earth. They were serious weapons back then, but not like the LAW and A-T-Four."

"They were planning to sink us," I whispered.

Shawn said, "No doubt. That's what I got from the interrogation. They saw the American flag and couldn't resist."

"Why did they try to come on board?" I asked. "Why wouldn't they just open up with the rockets?"

Clark said, "My guy said they were looking for valuables and cash."

I leaned against the console. "This didn't turn out like I expected. I wanted to learn their tactics and procedures, but they had no intention of taking us hostage, did they?"

Clark shook his head. "No. We were targets, not hostages."

"I don't love the way that feels in my gut. Have they sunk any American-flagged vessels?"

Skipper said, "I'm on it." It only took seconds for her search to yield results, and she said, "It's so nice to have my computers. I felt useless without them."

"What did you come up with?" I asked.

She scanned the screen. "There have been three attempts in the past four months on American-flagged ships. The Navy handled two of them, and it looks like the third got a little hairy." She continued reading and said, "Ouch. Three crewmen on a research vessel were killed and five wounded, but the crew overpowered the pirates and stopped the attack. That happened just six weeks ago. I can't believe it wasn't all over the news."

I let the new information simmer in my head for a moment. "So, that means the Navy is already aware of the situation, right?"

Skipper said, "They handled two of the three reported incidents, so I'd say they know."

"Put a briefing together and get it to the Board anyway. They need to know about the rocket launchers, and they need to know I let six Houthis aboard. I don't want them hearing it secondhand."

"I'm already on it," she said. "I'll have a draft for you within the hour."

I turned my attention back to the team. "Did we learn anything from the interrogations other than the fact that they wanted to sink us?"

Everyone turned to Shawn since he seemed to have the strongest grasp on the language, and he said, "I got a lot of rhetoric and ideological garbage, but nothing tactical."

"So, we wasted half an hour."

Mongo jumped in. "No, not exactly. We sent a cache of anti-tank weapons to the bottom and reduced the number of pirate boats in the area by three. It was time and energy well spent. It's not like we would've been on the foils in this area anyway, so we didn't really lose any time."

I said, "Get the captain, please."

A few seconds later, Barry's voice fell from the speakers. "I guess you guys had a little fun with that adventure, huh?"

"Hey, Captain," I said. "We were just doing the debrief, and I wanted to know how soon we can fly."

"We're back in open water and well clear of the islands. We can deploy the foils anytime."

I said, "Make it happen when you're ready. I don't want to waste any more time. Have you checked traffic in the Suez Canal?"

He said, "If we fly now, we'll get there during a lull in traffic."

"Let's do it," I said. "The decks are clear of bandits and bullets."

The captain said, "Here we go. Oh, and Chase . . . one more thing."

"What is it?"

"Don't let any more pirates on my ship."

"Aye-aye, Captain."

The *Lori Danielle* shuddered and roared beneath us. The carefully choreographed ballet of converting the ship from a massive displacement hull and into a flying machine on her foils wasn't easy on the vessel, and it wasn't particularly comfortable for her occupants. Once the foils were deployed and the hull rose from the water, the ride became the smoothest at sea. Making over fifty knots in a vessel the size of the *L.D.* was a marvel of modern naval architecture and engineering, but to me, it was just plain sexy.

Skipper completed the briefing and sent it to the Board before we headed to the mess for dinner and then to our cabins for one more night of peaceful sleep before we went to work in the Med.

We were twenty-four hours away from tasting the waters of the Mediterranean if everything went smoothly, but my mind was a galaxy away from coming up with an approach that would give us any advantage over pure luck. The Med was too big for us to be the successful hunter in a game of hide-and-seek, and without electronics, the *Desert Star* was but a single grain of sand on the endless Sahara.

* * *

The Suez Canal is a much simpler arrangement than the incredibly complex system of lochs and lakes in her Panamanian sister. The canal is merely a sea-level trench through the desert connecting the Red Sea to the Med. Captain Sprayberry was no stranger to the waterway and navigated the long, narrow gap as if he were cruising up his own driveway.

Our first morning in the new sea found my team working on assault drills under our SEAL's direction in case we had to board the *Desert Star*, if we ever found her. While they honed their skills in the steel corridors of the ship, I huddled with Skipper in the CIC and stared at overlapping satellite courses until my eyes crossed.

"I don't know how anybody does this without losing his mind."

She laughed. "It takes all kinds. Since we seem to have at least some support from your well-seated friends in D.C., I've been given a lot more latitude than usual."

"How many birds did they give you?"

She said, "Technically, none, but I got part of several. It's not like satellites just float around out there with nothing to do. They are all fully tasked most of the time, but there are priorities, which means when there's a waiting list for time, the higher priorities—like those sanctioned by the President—get first dibs."

"It's nice to have friends."

She laughed. "Yeah, but in this case, the satellites, even the ones with the best cameras, are just another set of eyes looking for the same white dot on a giant blue ocean."

"Every little bit helps."

She pulled her hands from the keyboard and relaxed. "This is a wild goose chase at best, but I've put some parameters in place."

"Let's hear it."

She said, "I took the coordinates from the position of the brief distress call. It only broadcast for eight seconds, by the way."

"That's interesting. Ships don't sink in eight seconds."

"No, they don't, and that's the one reason I think she's still afloat, or at least she *was* still afloat when the distress signal failed."

"Or was shut off intentionally," I said.

"Exactly. So, anyway, I plotted the position of the distress call against previous positions from AIS histories. The histories don't stay in the system long because it would take an enormous amount of storage, but I've got about nine hours of course and speed information for the *Star*."

"Show me."

She brought up the screen. "Here's the point of the signal, a hundred seventy-seven miles from Monaco and three hundred fifty miles from Algiers. And these blue markers are nine hours of position data pointing straight back to Monaco."

I traced the course with a fingertip. "So, there's nothing unusual leading up to the signal."

"That's right. She didn't change course or speed."

"Can you pull Automatic Identification System data from other vessels in the area at the time of the report?"

Skipper said, "Sure." Yellow triangles dotted the screen. "This is every vessel with AIS at the time of the distress call."

"What was the closest vessel?"

She clicked on the nearest symbol to the *Desert Star*. "That would be the *Bella Mattina*, an Italian-registered private yacht that was forty-four miles away."

I huffed. "That's no help."

"No, but I'm putting together a database of all satellite-observed vessels greater than two hundred fifty feet within the designated search area I outlined from the *Star*'s original course."

"How many do you have so far?"

"Almost two hundred, but only twenty of them aren't broadcasting AIS, so I've isolated those, and I'm having the computer compare the footprint of the *Desert Star* with the unidentified boats the satellites picked up."

"That sounds like a good plan, but the search area expands exponentially with every passing hour. If she's afloat, we have no way to know which direction she's headed."

"It's worse than that," she said. "Because of the gag order, we can't ask for other ships to help spot her."

I rolled my chair beside Skipper so I could see her face. "I wanna try something, but I need you to trust me."

"Okay. Just don't do anything weird."

"I promise. Now, put your hands on your lap and close your eyes."

She did as I asked, and I said, "Now, don't think. Just tell me the first thing that pops into your head. Can you do that?"

"I can try."

I said, "Tell me what happened aboard the *Desert Star*."

Her eyes flew open. "Are you serious? How should I know?"

"Close your eyes and relax. Just tell me the first thing you thought of."

She closed her eyes again and said, "Something bad happened and she started taking on water. The pumps and engines were overwhelmed too quickly to deal with, and she sank quickly, eliminating any electrical power." She opened her eyes. "I know that's stupid. It can't be what happened, but it's the first thing that came to me."

"That's all right," I said. "I plan to play that same game with everybody. The captain's next. I believe all of us will get it wrong, but we might be able to pluck bits and pieces from everyone's answers and put the puzzle together."

"That's not a very scientific method."

"No, but we've got a lot of people with a lot of experience dealing with crazy stuff all over the world. Our minds aren't like average noggins on Earth."

She laughed. "I'll help compile the data, and we can let the computer do the sorting."

She twirled a pen between her fingers. "Wait a minute. The engines and generators could've failed in a catastrophic influx of water, but the AIS and sat-coms have batteries. Even if she took on water rapidly, that wouldn't account for the transmitters failing."

"Of course. Don't pick it apart. I just want gut reactions to start. We'll weed out the impossibilities later."

Captain Sprayberry's answer was exactly the opposite of Skipper's. He said, "Pirates stormed the boat with an overwhelming force of maybe thirty or forty well-trained men. They killed the electricity and destroyed everything with batteries that wasn't their own gear."

"I like it," I said, "but why?"

He opened his eyes. "The *why* is the only part that makes sense. It's obviously a political opponent who wants Congressman Herd dead. In the big scheme of things, it wouldn't cost that much to hire a hit team to take him out at sea. I'd say less than a million bucks could get it done."

His theory wasn't bad, but I was trying to stay neutral during my little experiment.

He scratched his chin. "They'd have to either sink the boat or have a serious exit strategy, though. I don't know. I'm second-guessing myself now."

"That's okay," I said. "Nobody's going to guess correctly, but together, we might hit on something."

He grimaced. "I don't like guessing."

"We're not guessing. We're brainstorming."

He laughed. "If you say so. Let me know what the rest of the guys spit out of their wild imaginations."

I played the same game with every member of the team, and the overwhelming response said the *Desert Star* was on the bottom.

I dropped off each session's notes with Skipper, and she asked, "Is this everybody?"

"I've just got one more to go, and I thought you'd like to come with me to get it."

Five minutes later, I found my final participant sitting on a chair by the starboard rail with the wind blowing through what remained of his grey hair. "It's a pretty night out here, isn't it?"

Don Wood looked up and grinned. "It sure is, and when you get to be my age, young fellow, you don't want to miss nights like this."

I took a seat on the deck beside his chair, and Skipper knelt.

I said, "If you don't mind, I'd like to get your take on something."

"I don't mind a bit. What would you like to know?"

I spent a few minutes telling him the story of the missing luxury cruise ship and the congressman, and he listened intently.

When I was finished, he said, "You've got quite the mess on your hands, don't you?"

"It's what we do, but this one is a little unique in that we don't have any easily identifiable bad guys to target yet."

"Sure, you do," he said. "It's easy to see what's going on."

With those seven simple words, he had my undivided attention.

"It's obviously a blatant publicity stunt by that politician to get his name up in lights. The only thing those kinds of people like better than a kickback in their pocket is seeing themselves on TV."

# Chapter 13
## *Men Are Pigs*

I wished it could be as simple as Don seemed to believe, but having the ship completely gone for two days, without any signs of life, made me believe it couldn't be a publicity stunt like he thought. If it was, it was the worst one in the history of the world. Not only was Congressman Herd's face not on TV, but nobody was talking about the missing ship. In my book, that constitutes the *opposite* of a publicity stunt.

By the time Skipper and I made it back to the CIC, her supercomputer had chewed on the team's ideas and spit out a probability report.

I said, "Let's hear the computer's opinion."

Skipper planted her hands on her hips. "Computers don't have opinions. They only have data. Creativity isn't what drives a computer. It's purely logic and nothing else."

"In that case, let's hear the computer's logic."

After a little coaxing, the big brain inside the box declared, with eighty-four-percent probability, that the *Desert Star* had suffered a catastrophic breakup and sunk quickly.

"I was hoping for something a little more exciting," I said.

Skipper slid the report into a folder. "It was probably pretty exciting for the people on board when that ship came apart."

I stood, silently staring into space.

She said, "You're not convinced, are you?"

"Not yet. I just know she's still out there and that there's a logical explanation for everything."

She said, "It's not logical that the President of the United States is working so hard to keep a missing congressman a secret from the whole world."

"I'm trying to see my way through the political angle and find a path toward something that makes sense. What did you say you were using as search parameters for the satellite imagery?"

"Everything longer than two fifty and less than five fifty with no AIS signal."

"How about debris?"

Skipper said, "That's hard to program."

"But if a ship breaks up, there's always a debris field, and the currents in the Med are like clockwork. If she broke up and sank, it should be a simple matter to track where the debris field would've drifted. If we do that math, we'll either find a bunch of junk floating, or we won't. If we don't, she didn't sink."

She stuck her head back into her computer. "I'm on it."

While I sat drowning inside my head, Skipper worked feverishly at the keyboard until she threw up her hands. "Done. The bird is on its way."

"How long?"

She said, "It'll take twenty to thirty minutes for the satellite to reposition, and we'll have our answer within minutes of it arriving on station."

"It's a high-resolution cam, right?"

"One of the best in orbit."

The twenty minutes felt like two decades, but the bar on the left of the screen finally stopped flashing.

She said, "The bird's in place, and we'll be live in thirty seconds."

I rolled as close as I could without forcing her out of the way. That's when she did the last thing I could've expected her to do. She held a hand over the screen and said, "Tell me what you're hoping to see."

I recoiled. "What?"

"Do you want to see a debris field or an empty ocean?"

"What I want has nothing to do with what's out there."

She said, "I played your silly game, so now you can play mine."

I took a deep breath. "The optimist in me hopes to see nothing but blue water. That means there's at least a chance that a hundred seventeen missing people are still alive, but my gut tells me we're going to see trash everywhere."

Skipper moved her hand, and I leaned in. She panned and zoomed until her pointer stopped. "Nothing."

I asked, "How big is the area we're looking at?"

"It's about fifty by fifty miles, but I plan to broaden the parameters to compensate for any calculation errors in the wind and current numbers. Don't get freaked out when we get a hit. There's going to be something out there. I programmed the computer with very loose standards. It'll pick up everything, but that'll give us the chance to put eyes on it ourselves instead of relying wholly on the machine."

"I like it," I said. "How long?"

"Be patient. It'll only take a couple of minutes."

She was right. The scan was quick, and the computer came back with a long list of possible hits. Most of them turned out to be white-caps the computer misinterpreted as floating material. A few flocks of birds caught the machine's attention, and even some small boats rang the bell. Ultimately, after the exhaustive search of the expanded drift area, we still had nothing, and I considered that to be the best possible news we could receive.

I said, "She didn't sink."

Skipper said, "Hold on. We're pretty sure she didn't sink in the spot where she set off the alarm. That's all we know, and there's still a possibility the current or wind didn't behave exactly as the models predicted."

I shook my head. "She's not on the bottom. She's still out there, and the people on that ship are in grave danger. Stop looking for debris, and start looking for ships without AIS again. She's out there, Skipper, and we're going to find her."

I headed for the door, but she stopped me. "Hey! Where are you going?"

I spun on a heel. "I'm going to see the captain. Why?"

"You've got that look, so promise me you'll go straight to the bridge and back here. Don't bump into Anya along the way."

"Why? What's going on with you?"

"It's a girl thing. Just trust me on this one. Go straight to see the captain, and come back here."

I couldn't make myself turn around. "What kind of girl thing?"

She blushed, and I was doubly intrigued.

"Okay, you have to tell me now."

She giggled and covered her mouth. "It's not me, okay? So don't get that idea. You're like my big brother, so, no. When you get that look . . ."

"What look?"

She pointed at me. "The one you got when you decided the *Desert Star* hadn't sunk and we were going to find her no matter what. That look is irresistible to women who aren't me. It's something in our genes, okay? Women love men who know they're going to kill a sabertoothed tiger and drag it home. Anya doesn't need to see you with that look."

I shook my finger at her. "I knew it. You've been digging on me for twenty years."

She threw one of her shoes at me, but I artfully dodged the missile. "Get out of here, you filthy pig. Go ahead. Go straight to Anya's room. See if I care."

I tossed the shoe back to her. "I'm sexy and I know it."

"Get out!"

I didn't even think of Anya on the way to see the captain, but I couldn't get that stupid song out of my head.

When I made it to the bridge, I was surprised to find the first officer in command. "Where's Barry?"

"He's taking a break. He'd been awake for way too long. What can I do for you?"

I said, "I need to ask him a question, but you'll do for now. If you were going to hide a ship, where would you put it?"

"What kind of ship?"

"A four-hundred-footer."

He furrowed his brow. "What part of the world?"

"Right here."

A mischievous look came over him. "Am I a research vessel skipper or a pirate?"

"You're enjoying this far too much, but give me both answers."

He said, "In this uniform, I'd duck behind some island high enough to block shipboard radar and shut off the AIS."

"Now, let's have the pirate's answer."

I'd shut everything down and run for the Atlantic. The only place better than the Atlantic to hide a small ship is the Pacific, but we're a long way from that pond."

"You're my favorite pirate. Keep it up. Oh, and when Barry comes back, ask him the same question, and if his answers are different, let me know."

"They won't be," he said. "He's the one who taught me both tricks."

"Don't be so sure. And don't ever expect Captain Barry Sprayberry to teach you everything he knows."

I made it back to the CIC without an Anya encounter, and I caught Skipper mid-bite. She was munching on a sandwich that looked amazing.

"What is that?"

She swallowed. "It's a sandwich. Maybe you've heard of them."

"No, I mean, what kind of sandwich?"

She hugged the sandwich to her chest. "Uh, pastrami, and it's mine. You've still got your clothes on, so I take it you didn't run into Anya."

"That whole thing was ridiculous, but I've got a new set of search parameters for you."

She laid down the sandwich. "Send it."

I said, "Look for anything headed to the Atlantic without AIS. The pirate who's masquerading as our first officer thinks that's where they're headed."

"The first officer? That's who we're trusting to direct our searches now?"

"For now, yes."

She spun to her keyboard and went to work.

"This is my favorite part," I said.

She huffed. "What? Ordering me to conduct ridiculous searches because of the first officer's hunch?"

"No. The part when we know our target and the chase is on."

"Okay, Ridley Scott, we don't have any idea who our target is, and we're not chasing anybody yet."

"Yeah, but it's getting close. I can feel it."

"What are you, a treasure hunter now? Calm down."

I parked myself in a rolling chair and snuggled up to my favorite analyst. "Is this the look you like? Huh? Is this the one?"

She shoved me away. "You're an idiot, and I already told you it doesn't work on me."

"Gator seems to be working on you." I said it before I realized it was out of my mouth, so I backpedaled. "I'm sorry. That was out of line. I didn't mean to—"

She said, "He's sweet and respectful."

"Are you two . . ."

"We're friends," she said. "And it's nice to have somebody to talk to who isn't you."

I said, "I'll never interfere. I promise. He's one of the good guys, and he's getting better every day, but you know what this life does to a man."

She said, "Yeah, it gets him dead. I know that better than anybody, but I'm not willing to live my life alone just because something bad *might* happen to somebody I care about."

The big brother in me was concerned, but the psychologist in me was pleased to hear her refusal to live in fear.

She said, "It's not serious yet. We haven't even kissed or anything. He's just nice. Did you know he writes poetry?"

I tried to contain my laughter. "Do *not* let any member of this team know he writes poetry. You don't understand what kind of heat that would bring down on that boy. Keep that one to yourself, for his sake."

"You guys are such animals."

"Men are pigs," I said, "and I'm the chief boar. Trust me. Keep the poetry thing quiet."

A tone reverberated from the console, and Skipper directed her attention to the screen. She typed furiously, and I watched, having no idea what I was seeing.

A few seconds later, she threw both hands into the air and screamed. "I'm going to kiss the first officer right on the mouth. I found it! I found the *Desert Star*!"

# Chapter 14
## *Nobility*

My eyes darted to Skipper's monitor. "Show me!"

Instead of pointing with her mouse, the analyst jabbed a finger onto the screen. "Right there. That's her."

"How tight can you zoom in?"

She went to work, and the oblong dot became a cigar-shaped white spot, and finally, the outline of a small cruise ship.

My heart pounded like a jackhammer. "What's her position?"

Skipper zoomed out to display Europe to the north and Africa to the south. "She's ninety miles east of Gibraltar and heading west."

"Tag her so we don't lose her. We need to do some math."

Skipper scoffed. "Oh, don't you worry. I'm not losing her. What's the math?"

"Plot a back course to the position of the distress call."

She followed my instructions, and a course line appeared across the Med. Skipper said, "She's eight hundred thirty miles from the position of her distress call. Give me a minute for the computer to plot her speed."

We waited until the ship on the screen covered enough water to permit the supercomputer to calculate her speed across the water. When the gerbils stopped running, she said. "Eighteen knots."

I waited while she worked, but I didn't have to wait long.

She leaned back in her chair. "Chase, it's perfect. The math is spot-on. That's her."

Everything about our mission had just changed, and my saber-toothed tiger was in my sights.

I said, "I promise not to tell Gator."

Skipper spun and screwed up her face. "What are you talking about."

I laughed. "I promise not to tell him you're planning to make out with the first officer."

She rolled her eyes. "You're good at what you do, Chase Fulton, but you're still an idiot. I love you, though. Let's go get the *Desert Star*."

"Are you coming with me to the bridge?"

She said, "No, not now that you've screwed up my thing with the first officer. I'll just stay down here in my little cave while you get all the glory."

"That's noble of you," I said. "I'll be back soon. Can you send that video to the navigation bridge?"

"I can, but I don't want to send it before you're up there. They won't have any clue what's going on if it just pops up on their monitor."

"I'll let you know when I get there."

I pushed through the hatch from the CIC and thumbed my radio. "Clark, Mongo, meet me on the bridge ASAP."

Both answered almost instantly, but I beat them to the helm by a minute.

When they showed up, I called Skipper. "Send the video feed."

I pointed toward the monitor. "Gentlemen, we found her. She's headed for open water ninety miles from Gibraltar."

Captain Sprayberry tapped the console in front of a young officer I didn't recognize. "Plot a course to intercept at maximum speed."

"Aye, sir."

The captain then turned to me. "How certain are we?"

"High nineties," I said. "She's in perfect position for her speed based on the location of the distress call. She's the right size and shape and she's running silent."

The captain turned back to the officer still plotting the course. "Find the nearest ship to the target that's likely to have a crew who speaks a language I know."

The young officer's eyes turned to moons. "I don't know which languages you speak, sir."

Barry eyed me, Mongo, and Clark. "Just find me the closest ship and get me on the sat-com with them. Surely, one of us will speak their language."

Thirty seconds later, the young man asked, "How about English, sir?"

Barry chuckled. "We should be able to muddle through it. Put it on speaker."

The crystal-clear voice of a New Englander wafted from the speaker above our head. "Ahoy, *Lori Danielle,* this is Motor Vessel *Downeaster.*"

Barry said, "Ahoy, *Downeaster.* I need a favor if you've got the time."

"Sure, what do you need?"

Barry gave me a wink. "There's a cruise liner off your port beam, the *Desert Star.* The skipper is an old Academy chum of mine, and the company's having trouble reaching them. Can you give them a look?"

"Yeah, sure, we can do that. We've got the long eyes on her now. Want us to try and raise her if we can?"

Barry raised his eyebrows at me, and I wrestled with the decision before giving him a nod.

He said, "Affirmative. See if she'll come up on the VHF."

A few seconds later, the other captain said, "We can't get her on the radio, and she's not pushing AIS, but the young kids with good eyes say she's definitely your boat. Should I crowd her a little and get her attention?"

"That's not necessary, Captain, but thank you. We're just happy to know she's all right. She'll put in at Tangier. Thanks again, and have a good crossing."

Captain Sprayberry made a slicing motion across his throat, and the line went silent. He said, "I'd say we just moved from the high nineties to a hundred percent. When the boy-wonder over there figures out how to get us to Gibraltar, I'll let you know how long it'll take to catch her." He took a step closer to us and whispered. "I'll catch her in forty hours, but don't tell him. He's still learning."

* * *

The next two days of our lives were spent studying deck plans of the *Desert Star*, running assault drills, and digging through every inch of Congressman Landon David Herd's life that we could find.

As valuable and crucial as those tasks were, the one event I enjoyed most was an hour spent with Don Wood. I drew an extra rifle and gun belt from the armory and found Don on the aft deck, enjoying the sun on his face.

I said, "Good afternoon. Do you have some time in your busy schedule for a little marksmanship training?"

He poked me with his cane. "Sure, young fellow. I'll be happy to teach you to shoot."

I liked Don more with every passing minute, and I prayed I'd have his wit and vigor when I reached my nineties.

I handed him the belt, and he adjusted it to fit his waist and strapped it on. Next, I put the M4 rifle in his hands and showed him how to adjust the sling to fit his shoulders and arms.

He studied the weapon carefully. "This sure isn't an M-One Garand like we had in the war."

"No, sir, it's not. This one is an M-Four. It's built off the same model as the M-Sixteen the military used in Vietnam. There are two major differences between the two. First is the barrel. The M-Sixteen used a twenty-inch barrel while this one is fourteen and a half. The stock on the M-Four is also adjustable and collapsible. Those factors make it significantly better for close-quarters battle inside restrictive spaces."

"I can see that," he said. "I don't expect you'll want me to clear any rooms, though."

"No, sir. We'll leave that to the young bulletproof guys."

"I used to be one of those," he said.

"Me, too."

I took him on a tour of the rifle and showed him the function of every switch and control. "This one is capable of full-auto fire by switching the safety selector all the way around, but let's stick with semi-auto for now."

We loaded and unloaded the rifle several times and practiced switching magazines until it was second nature for him.

"Are you ready to send a few downrange?" I asked.

He grinned. "I thought you'd never ask."

The bullet trap targets we used for training on the ship were still in place at the stern rail, so it was time to have the red dot discussion.

"Have you ever used a red dot sight?"

He said, "I've used a few on pistols over the years, but never on a rifle."

"It's exactly the same concept. Just put the dot on what you want to kill and press the trigger."

"I think I can manage that."

We donned our hearing protection, and Don fired the M4 for the first time in his life.

After half a magazine, he pulled the rifle from his shoulder, moved the selector switch back to safe, and said, "I can see why those boys in 'Nam liked these things. It doesn't feel as substantial as the old M-One, but it's sure lighter."

"Let's go see how you did," I said.

We strolled across the deck to the target. The fifteen rounds he fired punctured the target in a shot group that I would've been pleased to shoot.

I said, "You're holding out on me. You didn't tell us you were a sniper."

He laughed. "Oh, that's funny. I'm no sniper, son. I just know how to shoot a little."

With Don's marksmanship fundamentals firmly in place, we had a little fun with some full-auto bursts that never failed to leave him grinning like a happy child.

We spent a few minutes covering remedial action in case the rifle malfunctioned, and he mastered the techniques in seconds.

After we'd burned through a few hundred rounds of ammo, Don said, "I believe I'll need one of these for myself."

I said, "I don't know how the French government will feel about you having an M-Four, but as long as you're on the ship, you can consider that one to be yours."

He said, "To hell with the French government. If it weren't for us, they'd be eating sauerkraut and speaking German."

I didn't necessarily share his sentiment toward the French, but he earned the privilege of saying whatever he wants at Omaha Beach in 1944.

* * *

One other minor event took place around midnight on our second night in hot pursuit.

My phone vibrated and chirped on the metal nightstand beside my bunk. Fresh out of a dead sleep, I couldn't focus well enough to read the caller ID, so I thumbed the button and stuck it to my ear. "Yeah, it's Chase."

A voice I should've recognized said, "I hear you're inside the twelve-hour window."

Nothing about the statement registered in any part of my brain that was capable of cognitive performance at that hour. "I'm sorry, what? And who is this?"

The caller cleared his throat. "It's the guy who signed the pardon for your in-laws."

I was suddenly wide awake. "Mr. President, I'm sorry. I was—"

"Yes, sleeping. I figured that would be the case. You're a few hours ahead of us here on the East Coast."

"Yes, sir. It's around one in the morning here. What were you saying about a twelve-hour window?"

"Your friends who fund your little adventures tell me you're within twelve hours of catching the *Desert Star*. Have I been wrongly informed?"

I checked my watch. "No, sir. We'll intercept them around noon tomorrow. I mean, today."

"That's good. And what do you plan to do when you make the intercept?"

I wasn't prepared to discuss our battle plan with the President in the middle of the night, but in that moment, I didn't believe I had any choice. I sat up, wiped my eyes, and turned on the bedside lamp.

"Well, sir, our plan is to get them in sight, attempt to make radio contact—"

He cut me off. "And when that fails?"

"We do expect it to fail," I said. "And when it does, we'll fly a drone as close as we can get it and gather as much intel as we can capture."

I expected a question or comment, but it didn't come, so I kept talking. "If it becomes necessary, we'll board the vessel, identify the threat, and neutralize it."

He said, "In international waters, I assume."

"Well, Mr. President, we don't have the luxury of putting the ship where we want her. We're left with chasing her wherever she goes. I've not seen the track in a few hours, but she was northbound off the coast of Portugal when I went to bed."

"How far off the coast?"

"I don't know, but I can get you that information in a few minutes."

The line was silent for a long moment before he said, "Listen to me, Chase. If you assault that ship, do it well out of anybody's jurisdiction. Whatever's happening on board that vessel should never see the light of day. Is that understood?"

I said, "I knew we were keeping this as quiet as possible, but again, sir, I don't have any control over where the *Desert Star* goes. Are you instructing me to leave her alone if she's running within twelve miles of the coast?"

His tone turned ominous. "What I'm instructing you to do, Chase, is keep everyone other than the men you control out of this business."

What I was about to do tied my gut into a knot that I was afraid could never be undone. We were way outside the bounds of protocol, and I was about to drag the President of the United States even deeper into a hole with me. "Forgive me, but if I knew exactly what you were concerned about protecting, sir, it would make my job a great deal easier. My family is in your debt, so it's important to me that you understand that I'm an honorable man who pays his debts. Just tell me what you want done, and if it's within my power, you can sleep well knowing it's as good as done."

He let my statement hang in the air a moment longer than I was comfortable, but I kept my mouth shut and waited.

Finally, he said, "I'm trying to decide if you're sucking up or accusing me of some sort of conspiracy. I'll be honest. It sounds like both to me, so even though I don't owe you an explanation of any kind, I'll give you this."

He paused, but I didn't bite. It felt good believing I had the upper hand, if only for an instant.

When he spoke again, he demolished any resistance I could've had about the operation.

"Here's what's going to happen, Chase. When you rescue Congressman Herd and put down the people who put him and his family in danger, I'm going to take the credit. I'll go on national television and tell the world how I authorized a covert mission to save the life of the only real competition the other side can put on the ticket to challenge me in twenty sixteen. That's the political angle you've been trying to pry out of me, so now you have it."

I felt like a jerk, and nothing I could say would undo the offense of me questioning the motives of the leader of the free world. So, instead of groveling, I became the sword the President believed me to be.

"Mr. President, if the congressman is alive when I put boots on that ship, I'll deliver him to your doorstep better than I found him. And the animals who took him will never draw another breath to tell their stories or anyone else's."

I glanced down to see the call had ended, but I didn't know if the President cut me off before or after my attempt at recovery.

Falling back asleep was a wasted endeavor, so I showered, dressed, and made coffee. The chair my favorite WWII veteran had enjoyed on deck was empty when I got there, so I took advantage of the vacancy and solitude. The sound of the wind and waves around the *Lori Danielle* gave me a sense of home I'd never felt before that moment. It wasn't as if I were suddenly a child of the sea. I was at home with myself with the decisions I made and the intentions of my heart. I would do the right thing by saving the lives I could and taking the lives I had to. And I would always do it cloaked in the belief that I was grounded in the same ideals of freedom, liberty, and nobility as the men before me who fought not only with their muskets, but also with their mighty pen, to stare tyranny in the eye and trample it beneath their boots. I could never be a founding father, but I was their son—a man driven and determined to preserve the nation they birthed and gently laid in my hands to enjoy, treasure, and protect as long as mortally possible.

# Chapter 15

## *Tallyho!*

Having drilled ourselves until we could predict each other's movement three steps ahead, we were as prepared as any team could be to assault a ship at sea. I knew every corridor, hatch, and ladder aboard the *Desert Star*, and every member of my team knew them just as well. If any team could be ready, mine was, and the wait was finally over.

The fully fueled Vertol was crouched on the helipad with her twin turbines warm and her pilot poised inside the hangar bay. The drones were programmed and fully charged. Every box was checked, and the *Desert Star* lay just beyond the horizon.

The team and I sat in a semicircle around our analyst as she skillfully kept the target vessel centered on the overhead monitor. The *Star* had made a dramatic turn to sea in the early morning hours when she came abeam the city of Porto, Portugal. She'd run the due west course for over three hours, putting her well outside the territorial waters of the country. She was in open, international water, and I had made a vow to the President that we'd bring Congressman Herd home . . . if he were still alive.

Captain Sprayberry slowed the *Lori Danielle*, allowing her to settle into the ocean from her foils. We gave up twenty-five knots of speed but gained the advantage of looking like every other ship on the water. Launching the Vertol while the *L.D.* flew on her foils was far too dangerous, but that wasn't the primary reason for the speed reduction. We wanted to approach the *Desert Star* as inconspicuously as possible without raising an alarm. It took three minutes to rerig the ship for conventional operations after the foils were stowed and system checks were complete. We were, once again, a ship like any other—as far as the unknowing observer would believe.

Skipper adjusted the volume of the direct line we shared with the navigation bridge as we closed on the target vessel at ten knots of overtake speed. She then turned and pressed a finger to her lips while simultaneously pointing to the second monitor. The feed was from a camera mounted at the highest possible point on the ship and focused directly ahead.

A tiny speck appeared on the screen where sky met ocean, and Skipper whispered, "Tallyho."

A few seconds later, a voice from the bridge rang over the speaker, echoing the call he hadn't heard Skipper make. "Tallyho!"

Captain Sprayberry's calm voice replaced the excited tone of the officer with binoculars pressed to his eyes. "We've got her, folks. I'll keep closing until you tell me to heave to."

"Is she running radar?" I asked.

Skipper pointed to a yellow arrow at the bottom of her screen. "She is, but we're running both radar-absorbing and active jamming systems, so she won't see us until we want her to."

"She won't see us on radar," I said, "but if they're looking out the window, we'll be hard to miss."

The captain said, "You haven't been briefed on our newest piece of spy gear, have you?"

"Apparently not," I said. "Let's hear it."

He said, "During the refit, we made a few modifications to improve some of the systems on board. One of those modifications allows us to take on water from the ocean around us and spray it as a fine mist ahead of the ship."

"What does that accomplish?"

He said, "From three miles away, it makes us practically invisible. We'll just look like an apparition on the horizon instead of another ship.

I've had the system up and running since just before we came into visual range."

"Isn't that nifty?"

"It is nifty, indeed, but it looks like we're going to get a helping hand from the heavens. You must've had Singer on the line to topside. We'll be in a moderate rain shower in fifteen minutes, so that'll help with our desire to appear invisible."

"Every little bit helps," I said. "Can you put us in the rain three miles dead astern of the *Star*?"

"Consider it done. I'll have you in position in twenty-six minutes."

I asked, "How much zoom capability do you have with the superstructure camera?"

Skipper slid an odd-looking mouse toward me. "Plenty. See for yourself."

It took me a few seconds to learn to operate the mouse, but I was soon looking across the stern rail of the *Desert Star* with astonishing clarity and definition. Her name was emblazoned across the stern, leaving absolutely no doubt she was our target. I panned and zoomed until I'd seen every inch of the back of the vessel.

I glanced over my shoulder. "Does anybody see anything I don't?"

"A bunch of nothing," Mongo said. "From here, that thing looks like a ghostship."

I said, "Somebody commanded that westerly turn off Porto, so she's under someone's control. We just don't know whose."

Skipper said, "We'll know soon. Are you ready to give them a shout?"

"Tune up the VHF. It's definitely time to say hello."

She slid the microphone toward me. "It's on sixteen at full power."

I leaned forward and pressed the bar along the base of the mic. "*Desert Star . . . Desert Star*, sixty miles west of Porto, this is the Research Vessel *Lori Danielle* on one six. Over."

Some irrational part of me thought they'd answer, but the logical portion of my brain wrote it off as a wasted transmission. Nevertheless, I made the call twice more with the same absence of any reply.

Skipper stowed the VHF microphone. "We had to try. What's next?"

I said, "I wish it was dark. That would give us an idea which compartments of the ship were occupied."

Mongo said, "We know they're making power because the radar's operating. That means they're intentionally avoiding the radio and AIS."

"I don't think they're avoiding the radio," I said. "I suspect they're listening but not responding. If whoever has that ship is smart, they'll have every available system up and running to warn them of approaching vessels."

Kodiak said, "I'm not a squid, but surely some of you guys can come up with every possible way they could know we were coming. How many ways can there be?"

"The list is actually pretty short," I said. "Radar, AIS, satellite tracking, and looking out the window."

"How many of those can we defeat?"

Skipper said, "We're jamming their radar, and we have our radar-absorbing system running, so we're invisible on their scope. The captain shut down the AIS last night. Having live satellite tracking is pretty rare, and they'd have to have some well-placed officials in their pocket to get access to the satellites. If they do have access, we're powerless to shut that down."

Kodiak said, "So that covers radar, AIS, and probably satellites. We obviously can't stop them from looking out the window, but if we're dead astern, we're not so easy to pick out, especially since we know there's no one on the back of the ship. We can see that on the camera monitor."

I said, "I like where your head's at, and there's one more weakness. Radar jamming and absorbing is only good for so long. If we get close enough, we'll appear as a void on their radar scope. A void is just as telling as a return, so we're gonna get busted when we get too close."

"What's that distance?" he asked.

I turned to Skipper, and she said, "Don't ask me. That's a question for the bridge crew."

Captain Sprayberry said, "I'm sorry. I missed the question. What was it?"

I said, "How close can we get without them realizing we're a void on their radar?"

"About a mile, if they're paying attention," he said. "If they're only glancing at the scope every so often, maybe a half to three quarters of a mile."

Singer leaned to look around Mongo. "I can take out their radar from a mile, or maybe a mile and a quarter."

I couldn't contain my excitement. "Yes, you can, you great big beautiful man. But can you do it in the rain?"

"Depends on the wind speed and direction, but probably."

I turned to Skipper, and she already had the weather screen up. "The wind is two ninety at twelve, gusting to eighteen."

The sniper studied the ceiling for a moment. "The vector is within a few degrees of due west, so two ninety is just twenty degrees of crosswind. When that's combined with the relative wind of the ship's westerly course at twenty-five knots, the resultant apparent wind is less than ten degrees. Even Clark could make that shot."

Every eye turned to Clark in expectation of a little healthy retaliation, but he said, "You're giving me way too much credit. I could botch that shot a dozen times before getting it right."

I met Singer's gaze. "How close do you need to be to guarantee a kill shot with three rounds?"

"If the sea stays flat like it is, I can do it with two shots from eighteen hundred."

"Yards?" I asked, and he nodded. I said, "Go get your rifle."

Gator and I met Singer on top of the hangar bay. That was the highest platform on the ship that was large enough for a sniper and a spotter side by side. I didn't qualify as either one, but I didn't want to miss the action.

Singer laid down his mat and nestled himself behind his M107 fifty-caliber rifle, and Gator spread the short legs of the tripod to support his spotter's scope. When both men were in position, I knelt behind them with binoculars pressed to my face.

Gator asked, "Are you shooting cold bore?"

Singer swung the massive rifle a few degrees north of the *Desert Star*. "No. I'm going to send one to warm it up."

"Why not shoot at the tip of an antenna?" Gator asked. "I'll be able to see the round. That'll warm up the barrel and give me a wind read."

Singer moved back into his original position. "Call the antenna."

Gator said, "Look right of the radar dome four mils for a cluster of three."

"Got 'em," Singer said.

"Tallest of the three."

"Got it. Call the range."

Gator said, "Seventeen sixty."

Singer asked, "One-seven-six-zero?"

"Affirmative. Hold one-four point six over and left point five."

Singer took a long, slow breath. "One-four point six and left point five."

Gator double-checked his calculation. "Send it."

The massive rifle bucked, and the concussion of the fifty-caliber round felt like a kick in the chest, but I watched the vapor trail of the bullet as it screamed toward the *Desert Star* at two and a half times the speed of sound. The optics of Gator's spotting scope were significantly better than my binoculars, so he could see the slightest variation in the flight of the heavy round.

Both Gator and Singer let out a guttural sound simultaneously, and I asked, "What?"

Singer didn't lift his head from the rifle, but he said, "We almost hit a pencil with a cold bore shot at a mile. I think I grazed the left edge."

Gator said, "You didn't graze it. You missed by less than half the bullet width, but that ain't bad for a beginner."

Singer chuckled. "I'll work on it. Call the target."

They were suddenly all business again, and Gator said, "Radar dome four mils left of the antenna cluster."

"Got it."

Gator ran the numbers again. "Same hold."

"Same hold," Singer breathed.

"Send it."

The weapon thundered again, and two and a half seconds later, the radar dome mounted high on the superstructure of the *Desert Star* exploded in flames.

I couldn't believe my eyes. "Why did it burn?"

Singer capped his scope and pulled the magazine from the rifle. When he held the mag up for me to see, the light blue tips of the rounds left in the magazine told me he'd fired incendiary rounds. As he stood, Singer said, "I wanted it to burn so when they send a guy up there to check it out, he'll think it was an electrical issue and not a rookie sniper like me."

# Chapter 16
## *A Covert Option*

"How big are the smallest drones we have?" I asked.

Skipper said, "I'm not sure you're asking the right question. The smallest drones we have are about the size of your fist, but we can't fly those in this weather. The rain would destroy them in no time. The smallest drones we have that can fly in this weather are PB-Sixty-Fives. They're about two feet square."

"What's the range on them?"

"Line of sight," she said. "As long as the antenna can see the drone, we can fly it, and it has a thirty-minute battery life."

"Excellent. Let's go take a look."

Skipper called the hangar deck. "Stand by to launch a pair of PB-Sixty-Fives."

The deckhand said, "Standing by and ready to launch."

Skipper spun a monitor so she could see the video feed from each of the drone cameras. "Spinning up. Stand clear."

"Clear," came the deckhand's reply.

The monitor in front of her showed the screen split horizontally with the feed from drone number one on top and number two on the bottom.

The screen showed the hangar deck and helipad as the drones lifted off and banked away toward the *Desert Star*. The resolution was good, but rain collected on the lens a few seconds after takeoff.

I asked, "Will we get any good footage with a wet lens?"

Skipper smiled and sent a command to the drones. An instant later, a blast of pressurized air blew the lens clear. Dr. Celeste Mankiller, our technical services officer, was a genius and one of the most valuable members of the team. James Bond has his Q, but we had a Mankiller.

The silhouette of the target ship came into view, and the drones split their formation. The first drone accelerated and took up a stable position a hundred feet above the highest point on the *Star*. The second drone moved to within three hundred feet of the target and matched the ship's speed.

"How can you fly both drones at the same time?" I asked.

She said, "It's easy during the trip to the ship, but it would be impossible once we start the search. Drone number one is fully autonomous now. It'll fly high cover, constantly searching for movement on deck. If it detects anybody moving around, it'll send a tone to notify me that somebody could be watching, and I'll fly drone number two away from the prying eyes."

"Well, that qualifies as cool."

She nodded. "Cool is what we do, baby." She motioned to the lower half of the screen. "There's your melted radar antennas."

I gave Singer and Gator a thumbs-up, and they nodded in unison.

Just then, a tone sounded, and Skipper's hands moved like lightning. "There comes the radar tech. He's in for quite a treat."

Drone two followed her commands and moved away from the ship, positing itself out of sight behind one of the stacks. Drone one kept a watchful eye on the radar tech as he inspected what was left of the pair of formerly rotating antennas. Another blast of air cleared the lens again, just as the look on the man's face turned from curious to frustrated.

Mongo laughed. "That's right, buddy. There's no repairing that thing."

The tech finished his inspection and headed back down the ladder without looking up at either drone.

"They must be pretty quiet," I said.

Skipper shook her head. "Not really, but it's raining hard enough to hide most of their acoustic signature."

Gator elbowed Shawn. "Acoustic signature. Those are fancy words for *noise*."

"Thanks," the SEAL mumbled.

Gator said, "No problem. If I get some time next week, I'll see if I can teach you to read a few simple words and eat with utensils."

"You're a real pal, you know that?"

Gator offered an animated nod of agreement. "That's me."

With the radar tech gone, Skipper resumed her snooping. Drone two flew back toward the starboard bridge wing, and Skipper said, "Let's take a peek in here and see who's home."

I leaned to my right as if I were riding the drone and trying to see around the corner. As she crept forward, more real estate inside the bridge became visible. Two men appeared, both facing forward as if standing routine watch.

"Can you take us any farther forward so we can see the whole bridge?" I asked.

"I could," she said, "but I'd like to keep as much steel between the eyes on the bridge and my drone. I'll fly over the top and approach from the port side."

She flew the maneuver and approached from the other side just as she'd done from the right. A third person appeared near the port side bridge wing, but she didn't have the same look as the two men. She held a pair of binoculars in her hands, just below her chin.

I said, "Something has her attention. I need to see what she's looking at."

Skipper elbowed the oddly shaped mouse toward me, and I took control of the camera mounted high on our ship. I zoomed and panned the horizon ahead of the *Star*, but there was nothing to see, so I scanned the radar scope and AIS, but nobody was there.

I turned to the team. "There's nothing out there. The visibility through the rain isn't great, but the radar and AIS both say it's an empty ocean."

"How about the satellites?" Gator asked.

"They're useless in this cloud cover, but it's just a squall line, so it'll blow out in another half hour."

With my attention back on the drone video, the woman raised and lowered the binoculars several times and swept the horizon in what appeared to be a forty-five-degree arc. I said, "She's not looking *at* something. She's looking *for* something."

Mongo said, "Of course! They're going to rendezvous with another ship. That explains the turn at Porto."

I closed my eyes and forced everything I knew through my skull, but nothing of value came out the other side. "Let's hear it. Any ideas on what's going on?"

Groans returned, but nobody offered any ideas.

Of all the sounds the combat information center was capable of making, the least common is a ringing telephone, but that's exactly what I heard.

Skipper pressed a flashing red button. "Go for CIC."

I never expected to hear the voice that flowed from the speaker, but she said, "Skipper, it's Ronda. Are you watching the news?"

Skipper glanced up at me and then back at the phone. "No, we're in the middle of an op."

"I know," Ronda said, "but you have to see it."

Skipper pointed to an overhead monitor, and the screen came alive with a close-up shot of Congressman Landon David Herd.

A newscaster spoke in a somber tone:

"We have only moments ago learned that a private yacht carrying Congressman Landon Herd of the first congressional district of Colorado has likely sunk off the southern coast of France in the Mediterranean Sea. Early reports indicate the yacht sank quickly, with likely no survivors escaping the horrific catastrophe. Authorities responding to the presumed location of the private yacht report that no debris field has been discovered. Our own sources close to the investigation tell us the absence of a debris field could only mean that a catastrophic structural failure of the vessel resulted in an extremely rapid sinking. Again, Congressman Landon Herd from the first congressional district of Colorado is presumed to have perished in the sinking of his chartered yacht off the French Riviera. Stay tuned for more details as they become available."

Clark extended a hand, and Skipper placed the receiver of the secure satellite communication system in his palm.

A few seconds later, he said, "Yes, sir, we have, and I need to provide a sitrep. We're eighteen hundred yards astern of the *Desert Star*, approximately ninety miles west of Porto, Portugal, and steaming westward at eighteen knots." He listened and then said, "Absolutely certain. I have live drone footage as well as onboard camera footage if you'd like for us to deliver it to you."

Skipper's fingers were poised above the keyboard, awaiting Clark's order to pipe the footage to the Board, but he shook her off.

After more listening, he said, "Stand by. I'm going to bring our analyst and Chase into the conversation." He pointed to Skipper, and she brought the speaker to life.

Clark said, "Say that again, please."

The same voice that briefed us prior to the start of the mission filled the room. "Can you board the vessel and ascertain the status of the congressman without a physical confrontation?"

Clark looked at me, and in turn, I looked at Shawn.

The SEAL shrugged and mouthed, "Fifty-fifty."

Clark sat in silence, so I took that to mean the ball had fallen into my lap.

I said, "Good morning, sir. I believe we're capable of boarding the *Desert Star* and ascertaining the congressman's condition, but we have no way to offer any assurance it can be done without meeting resistance."

The line was silent for a long moment until he said, "Is there a covert option?"

I was immediately a fat kid with keys to a candy store. "Yes, sir, there most certainly is. Are you authorizing the hostile covert boarding of a civilian vessel in international water?"

A second voice came on the line. "Dr. Fulton, you are authorized to proceed with any prudent course of action to rescue or recover Congressman Herd. Precautions should be taken to avoid the unnecessary loss of life or injury to any noncombatant encountered during the operation."

I sifted the authorization through my head, and what remained in the sieve was nothing short of piracy, but it was also nothing short of what I'd been planning to do for days. "Understood, sir. Expect a sitrep from our end within twelve hours."

He said, "I expected no less. Now listen closely, Chase. Do not waste the lives of your operators. There is clearly a sinister element at work here, and by all indications, the crew of the *Desert Star* may be involved."

"Thank you for the concern," I said, "but we knowingly and fully accept the risks associated with our service."

I tried to hide my concern over his most recent revelation, but I feared the hesitation was evident in my voice.

He said, "Send the video feed."

Skipper nodded, and I said, "Wilco."

The line fell silent, and Skipper stowed the handset. "I guess our timetable just got moved up, huh?"

I said, "Yes, but not necessarily by the Board. Whoever the *Desert Star* is scheduled to rendezvous with is the accelerator. I don't want to be aboard the *Star* when a whole ship full of reinforcements show up."

Skipper asked, "Do you think they're reinforcements or a getaway car?"

"Either way, it's bad news for anybody left alive on the *Star*. If it's a getaway car, they'll scuttle the *Star* out here in deep water. If it's reinforcements, the bad guys will be on a power play and we'll be badly outnumbered."

Kodiak chuckled. "When was the last time we *weren't* outnumbered?"

I took a moment to piece together a plan to board, search, and escape the *Desert Star*. When I had the skeleton of a plan assembled in my mind, I said, "I'm going, and I need one volunteer."

Everybody in the room rose to their feet, and in that moment, the reality of my condition poured over me like a massive wave.

I was in command of the finest group of fearless patriots in existence. They devoted the bulk of their adult lives to the preservation of freedom and liberty and stood beside me against the greatest of odds. There was likely a limit to what we could accomplish together, but no one in that room would admit to accepting limits upon each of them individually, and they'd absolutely never be convinced we were anything short of invincible as a team.

When I swallowed the pride in my throat, I stood with my team. "Shawn, you're with me. Disco, you're at the helm. We'll insert via the RHIB with the pirate's ladder over the stern rail. The rest of you will stand by aboard the chopper as a quick-response force ready to fast-rope aboard if Shawn and I get pinned down. We're going soft and quiet until we get busted. If and when that happens, we take the ship by overwhelming force."

# Chapter 17
## *Dead Calm*

The squall line turned into two lines, but the rain finally stopped falling. That was a double-edged sword for us. While I liked the idea of being able to board the *Desert Star* and remain dry enough to avoid tracking water into the interior and leaving a trail leading straight to us, I didn't like the fact that we lost the rain as an element of camouflage. We'd never be able to control the weather, but with patience, we could use the never-ceasing clock to our advantage.

The clearing skies offered one decided advantage in our favor—our ability to access and exploit the satellites overhead would allow us to find and identify ships approaching the *Star* from the open Atlantic. I couldn't get the woman from the bridge with binoculars out of my head. She had to be searching for a rendezvous vessel. There was simply no other reasonable explanation.

With the *Desert Star* well identified on both the radar and satellite feeds, we backed off eight miles as the sun traversed the sky. We had the speed and might to intercept any ship that appeared to be steaming to rendezvous with the *Star*, so the eight miles wasn't a hurdle for us. Keeping her alone and unaided was my primary goal until the advantage of darkness consumed both her decks and ours and opened the door for our covert advance on the ship.

The afternoon and evening passed without any signs of a rendezvous ship, so we closed the distance between us and the *Desert Star* and put the drones back in the air. The second Peeping Tom mission gave us less information than the first. No lights appeared anywhere on the vessel except the soft glow from the bridge windows. Only two crewmen appeared through the windows, and neither held binoculars. The one significant difference over the noon mission was the speed of the ship. They slowed to nine knots but continued on their due west track. The darkened corridors of the ship played beautifully into our capabilities. With some of the highest quality night-vision devices in existence, we could move at will and completely unseen inside the darkness with the ship's layout burned into our minds from hours of study.

"Why do you think they slowed down?" Skipper asked.

"I suspect it has something to do with the fact that their radar antennas melted down, so they don't have any way to prevent a collision other than looking out the windows."

"I should've thought of that," she said. "I think I'd turn on every light I had to make myself as visible as possible."

"I still think they're trying to hide. They obviously want to escape detection, but running dark isn't a great idea on the open ocean."

As the clock reported eleven p.m., I gave the order to launch the insertion. Shawn and I geared up in full black with sidearms, MP-5s, and our trusted helmet-mounted night-vision devices. The rest of the team suited up and headed for the helipad, but instead of the small, lightweight MP-5s Shawn and I carried, they armored up with M4s and SR-25s in case they had to fight their way onto and into the *Desert Star* to pull us out.

I checked Shawn's gear, and he checked mine. Aside from our size, we were practically identically suited. After Disco examined the rigid hull inflatable boat and declared it ready for war, a pair of deckhands unlocked the RHIB from its cradle, and we climbed aboard. The three of us wore water-activated flotation devices in case we found ourselves out of the boat and in the water. The weight of our gear would make staying afloat almost impossible if we went overboard, but we wouldn't carry the flotation devices aboard the target vessel. There was too great a chance of tangling in a critical piece of gear if we stumbled into—or started—a gunfight. Once we left the RHIB, we'd take our chances with a water encounter.

The crane operator lifted us from the cradle and swung us over the side. Being suspended thirty feet above the water while making almost ten knots was a bizarre feeling, especially when there was no discernable difference between the sea and sky. We didn't hang suspended between heaven and Earth very long, and the keel of the boat sliced into the water seconds after crossing the rail. Disco started both engines and waited for them to come up to operating temperature before shucking off the bridles connecting the RHIB to the crane.

We motored away from the ship's wake and conducted another comms check. Failed comms killed far more operators than any other threat. If we had no way to communicate with CIC and the team, we would be truly alone in what was likely an extremely hostile environment. Knowing the QRF was only minutes away was an insurance policy that gave both Shawn and me the comfort to conduct our insertion without fear of being alone, outgunned, and pinned down.

The pitch-black night felt like swimming in an obsidian pool as we crossed the distance between the *Lori Danielle* and the *Desert Star*. Her absence of lights made the ship invisible until we lowered our NODs and the world came alive. Tiny specks of starlight twinkled in the eternal distance, and the movement of the *Star* through the water left an eerie glow in her wake. The ocean seemed to know we needed her cooperation, and she lay dead calm beneath our fiberglass hull. The rare glassy conditions allowed us to make forty knots and close on our slow-moving objective in just three minutes after hitting the water.

Disco brought us dead astern of the ship and matched her speed precisely. We set our sat-coms for open-channel operations and checked in.

"CIC, Sierra One. We are astern and prepared to board. Say status of QRF."

Skipper said, "Roger, Sierra One. Stand by for QRF status."

Mongo said, "Quick reaction force is staged inside the chopper with blades turning. Happy hunting, Sierra One. We're thirty seconds away if you need us."

"It's nice to know you're there," I said. "Start the clock, CIC. We're going over the rail."

Since the Houthi pirates had been generous enough to leave their rope ladder aboard our ship when they came over for tea and scones, we used theirs instead of ours. If the mission fell apart, I liked the idea of a ladder from Yemen hanging off the back of the *Desert Star* instead of one of ours made in the U.S.A.

Shawn twirled the hook in an underhand motion and launched it skyward. It topped the stern rail as if he'd measured and calibrated the throw. The hook crossed the rail and caught its own line in one fluid motion.

Shawn glanced back at me, and I gave the nod. He scaled the rope ladder like a circus performer and cleared the rail in seconds. Although I couldn't see him, I knew the posture he would assume and every movement he would make in the coming seconds. Just as expected, a single hand appeared between the deck and the rail, signaling it was safe for me to board. I climbed the ladder a bit less skillfully than the younger SEAL, but I didn't stumble. We were soon side by side on the deck with no one in sight.

I fell in line behind Shawn, and we advanced on the portside hatch that was marked on our deck plans as Point A.

We pressed through the opening and into the interior. Once we were confident the corridor was clear, I reported, "Point Alpha."

Skipper said, "Roger."

We slowly advanced through the corridor, stepping as lightly as our boots would allow and listening for any signs of life. The gentle hum of the engines droned on, but nothing else made a sound.

When we reached the first collection of doors, Shawn gripped a handle and carefully pressed it downward. The handle moved smoothly through ninety degrees, but the door didn't open. The electronic key reader stared back at us as if asking for our ID, so I produced a wallet-sized electronic device—designed and built by Dr. Mankiller—and pressed it against the card reader. A series of tiny white lights illuminated, and one by one, slowly changed color. When all seven lights glowed a dim green, Shawn tried the handle again, and the bolt receded into the mechanism. We were in.

Staying low, he moved through the door and into the first room with his NODs at maximum illumination while I stood guard just outside the door. If anyone appeared in the corridor, I would duck into the room, and we'd wait until the hallway was clear to continue our search.

Time flows at an impossible rate during moments like those. We had a large ship to search, but we also needed to maintain silence as we moved. The perfect operation would be not only silent, but also undetected. If we could find Congressman Herd and get him off the ship without anyone knowing we'd been there, our mission would be an overwhelming success.

Shawn backed from the room and shook his head, so I slowly allowed the door to close without making a sound.

He moved close to my ear and whispered, "Two. Man and woman asleep. Not Herd."

We continued through the bank of four doors until we'd made the same discovery in each of the compartments. It took twenty minutes to clear the first deck, and we moved up a stairwell to the deck above.

The rooms on the second deck were slightly larger than those on the previous level, but just like below, none of the sleeping couples or singles was the congressman.

The third deck offered wider corridors and elegant carpeting, and the doors were farther apart. The first door opened easily on our first attempt with the electronic lockpick, and a sliver of light escaped when Shawn pushed the door inward. The room proved to be empty, but our luck was about to change.

Just like the ocean had been, the interior of the ship was dead calm.

No music, televisions, dancing, drinking, or revelry of any kind. Nothing about it felt like a ship under siege, but we had to press onward under that assumption.

The next opening we approached was an ornately carved double door with both an electronic lock and a keyed deadbolt. Since the electronic lock was time sensitive, I picked the deadbolt first. Unlike its electronic partner, once it was open, it wouldn't automatically relock itself. It wasn't an easy pick. There were nine pins in an extremely tight configuration. Picking five, or even seven pins, is a relatively simple task after hundreds of hours of practice, but a precise lock such as the nine-pin deadbolt in my hands required smaller tools and limitless patience.

I worked on the lock for two minutes before closing my eyes and taking a deep breath. "This one's tough."

Shawn whispered, "Want me to try?"

I shook him off and continued my work. A bead of sweat ran down my face, and another forty-five seconds passed before I had nine pins depressed and the tension rod turned. The deadbolt was finally open. I stowed my pick kit and laid the electronic key against the pad. The lights cycled from white to yellow and back to white. I ran the sequence four times before we finally got the open signal from the device.

Shawn gripped the door handle, and the second he did, I dropped the small electronic skeleton key. I watched it fall and extended my leg to allow it to hit my boot instead of the floor. About halfway through the fall, I remembered the plush carpet and relaxed.

The key hit my boot and then skittered across the deck, and Shawn bumped the door handle far more aggressively than he meant to. The door sprang open with a click and a tone inside the room. We both froze in place, holding our breath and praying no one heard the sound of the door being opened.

Just as our heart rates returned to normal, a man's voice boomed from inside the room. "Who's out there? Honey, did you forget to lock the door?"

A female voice mumbled, "Huh?"

I played the voice from inside the room against the memory of hearing Landon Herd speak on video.

*Are the voices the same? Could that be him?"*

Shawn and I remained motionless until footsteps moved toward us, and we retreated, pulling the door closed as we moved. Diagonally across the corridor was a heavy metal door, and Shawn grabbed the knob in a desperate effort to find someplace, any place, to hide.

Thankfully the knob turned, and the door swung inward. We were through it in an instant and bathed in white, fluorescent light. I slammed my NODs upward and away from my eyes as I tried to adjust to the light. To the left was a steep ladder leading both up and down, and to the right was a small elevator with the sliding door standing open.

From beyond the door, an angry voice roared. "Hey! Who's out there?"

I shot a glance at the doorknob and thumbed the lock button. The move didn't make us safe, but it might have bought us thirty seconds. Shawn took a step toward the downward ladder, but I hooked his arm and leaned toward the elevator. He followed me inside and thumbed the button to close the door. I reached overhead and pressed the access panel upward until the small, square opening was free, then I took a knee directly beneath the hole. Shawn planted one boot on my knee and the other on my shoulder. He was through the opening and reaching back down for my hand before I could get to my feet. Shawn pulled the instant we clasped wrists, and I leapt upward, hoping to do it silently. The elevator car rattled back and forth but came to rest as I shimmied through the whole.

Shawn slid the plate back in place, closing the opening, and we caught our breath in the darkened elevator shaft. We were well and truly trapped in a steel box, and for the first time during the mission, I doubted our comms were capable of overcoming the predicament we were in. I listened for voices from below, but I didn't hear anything yet.

"CIC, Sierra One."

Nothing.

"CIC, Sierra One."

Still nothing.

Shawn whispered, "This ain't good."

"It's worse than not good," I said. "We've gotta get out of here."

At that instant, the elevator door slid open, and the cables oscillated as at least two people walked into the car. They spoke in what sounded like Italian, but I couldn't be sure. A series of electronic tones sounded, and we descended with the cables between us gliding smoothly through the well-greased pullies. I knew absolutely nothing about how elevators worked, so I was afraid to touch anything. We balanced on the balls of our feet, absorbing the movement of the elevator car and trying to avoid falling against the moving cables or the walls of the shaft.

We stopped abruptly, and I fought to maintain my balance. More heated discussion wafted through the ceiling of the elevator, but I couldn't understand any of it. The nature of the Italian language makes it sound exciting even when they're discussing the most boring subject imaginable. The two or three men could've been yapping about intruders, or they could've been discussing their favorite sauce recipe, but there was no way to know.

The elevator stayed on the second deck for only a few seconds before dinging again and moving upward. It climbed at what felt like breakneck speed, and we both watched the ceiling of the shaft grow closer with every passing second. I studied the design with the weights, pulleys, cables, and tracks, but none of it made enough sense to give me any degree of comfort that we wouldn't be crushed when the elevator reached the top.

As we drew nearer to the top of the shaft, we instinctually ducked until we were lying facedown on top of the elevator car. When it came to a stop, there were perhaps eighteen inches of open space above us, but between the bulk of our gun belts and rigs, coupled with Shawn's massive arms and shoulders, we had almost no room to move. The door opened, and the men who'd ridden the car to the top exited, still talking with great excitement.

They walked away, opened and closed a heavy metal door, and left us stranded in what could become our mausoleum if we were discovered.

Shawn said, "What now?"

"We could go back through the hatch and take our chances on the top deck, or we could wait for the elevator to move again."

A crackling, garbled sound resonated inside my ear. "Sierra . . . Sierra . . . CIC."

I called, "CIC, Sierra One. How do you hear?"

More crackling.

"It's no use," I said, "but we must be close to an opening of some kind. I hear Skipper a little."

Shawn said, "Can you reach my sat-phone?"

"Maybe. What do you have in mind?"

"We might be able to get off a text."

I squirmed and extended my arm around his waist, feeling for his phone. "Almost got it. Roll toward me if you can."

He groaned. "I'm trying, but my shoulders are pinned."

We fought our confinement until exhaustion and frustration overtook us.

I said, "Hang on. Let me catch my breath."

We calmed our breathing, and Shawn said, "Try to slide toward me. I might be able to reach your phone."

The crackling continued in my ear, but I tried to ignore it. Getting our hands on one of our sat-phones was the immediate goal, and everything else could wait. The more we wrestled, the farther away our phones felt, so I relaxed and gave my brain permission to work on another way out.

"I'll try to open the hatch and get back into the car."

Shawn said, "Okay. I'll stay out of your way the best I can."

I squirmed until I was on my elbows and knees with my back pressed against the top of the shaft. As I struggled to find the hatch, I felt something pop against my back.

I froze, and Shawn said, "What was that?"

"I'm not sure, but something moved by my left shoulder."

He said, "I'm facedown, so I can't see anything."

"Me, too."

After I convinced myself the pop must've been a piece of my gear rubbing against the ceiling, I jumped back into my fight to get at the hatch. Then, the pop happened again . . . and again.

I said, "It's a topside hatch."

Shawn sighed. "If you're right, all we have to do is force it open."

"Okay. Here goes nothing."

I pressed my body upward with all my strength. The popping continued, and the hatch gave an inch, then two, then six.

The relief of a cool salty breeze made its way into the shaft, and freedom felt closer than ever.

"Try the radio again," Shawn said.

"CIC, Sierra One."

Skipper's reply was scratchy but readable. "Go for CIC."

"We're pinned in the elevator shaft and breaking our way through the topside hatch. Get eyes on the top of the ship. If we make it out, we're going into the water on the closest side."

It sounded like she said, "Roger," but I couldn't be sure.

I pressed until every muscle in my body spasmed, and just before I collapsed back to the top of the elevator car, the hatch broke away and flew open.

My head was still pinned in the tiny space, but my hips and lower back were free. I contorted my body until I got one of my feet through the hatch and prayed I wouldn't be looking down the barrel of a rifle when I finally emerged from the opening.

Having no feeling in my prosthetic made it challenging to work my fake foot through the hole, but it finally happened, and I was upside

136 · CAP DANIELS

down with my bottom half sticking out of the top of what I believed to be a hijacked luxury cruise ship somewhere off the coast of Portugal. The seriousness of the situation lost its grasp on my consciousness, and I laughed.

My relief was contagious. Shawn laughed with me and said, "From the outside, I bet you look like a jackass stuck through a fence."

I caught my breath and squirmed until I was free. The monumental task of pulling Shawn through the same small opening lay ahead, and I wished for a blowtorch. Fortunately, his head was near the opening, so I grabbed the collar of his vest and dug my heels into the deck. He pushed as I pulled, and together, we got him through the hole without ripping off an appendage.

When he got to his feet, he said, "Where's your helmet?"

I reached for my head and felt only hair. "It must've come off in the shaft. Where's yours?"

He patted his head and sighed. "Are we leaving fifty thousand dollars' worth of night vision and helmets with these Italian dudes?"

Before I could answer, a beam of light panned across the sky, and I followed it back to a pair of men climbing a ladder fifty feet behind us.

"Go, go, go!" I ordered, and Shawn slid over the edge of the raised elevator shaft. I eased the hatch closed and followed him over the side, then we slid to the deck below and stepped across the rail. Before we let go, I said, "CIC, Sierra One, we're going into the water, starboard side, amidship."

# Chapter 18
## *Not a SEAL*

I failed to consider the additional height of the ship when I stepped off the upper deck and plummeted to the water below. With our night vision still mounted to our helmets somewhere inside the elevator shaft, we fell into the abyss until our boots hit the water that felt like concrete. The collision sent the air in my lungs exploding from my mouth and nose as my body absorbed the punishing blow.

The concept of direction isn't difficult to grasp when the sun is burning above the surface and casting streams of light into the water, but in the middle of the night, every direction felt down, and that's exactly where we were headed. The weight of our gear far exceeded the buoyancy of our bodies, and although we escaped the ship, with every passing second, we were farther away from the safety and security of the RHIB somewhere overhead.

"Panic is the killer, not the water." That's the mantra they drilled into my head at The Ranch when I spent two weeks learning to control my mind and operate in the most hostile environment on Earth—the ocean. Remaining calm when the world collapsed into chaos was the critical skill, and every second of that training poured through my head as I descended beneath the *Desert Star* and into the depths of the Atlantic.

*Don't panic, Chase.*

I didn't have time to work on that one, so I moved on.

*Dump the gear, Chase*

I found the three releases and felt my chest rig and gun belt fall away.

*Don't dump the sat-phone, Chase.*

Too late. It was already on its way to the bottom while still securely attached to my belt.

*Determine direction, Chase.*

I stopped kicking and cupped my hand around my mouth while exhaling the minuscule amount of breath that remained in my lungs. The bubbles hit my fingertips instead of my palm, so I had to be on my right side with my body parallel to the surface to my left.

*Swim for the surface, Chase.*

I waved my right arm once to orient myself into a head-up position and resumed kicking. There was no way to know how far away the surface was, but I had a greater concern than just my distance to breathable air.

*Avoid the propellers, Chase.*

If the *Desert Star* were still overhead and motoring, somewhere above me a pair of massive propellers spun like the blades of a food processor. I didn't know how long I'd been in the water and if the ship could've motored clear in that length of time. I could hear the faint rumbling of engines and propellers, and they seemed to decrease in volume with every passing second, so clear of the ship or not, I had to surface to stay alive.

*Ignore the burn, Chase.*

A raging inferno bellowed inside my lungs. My body demanded oxygen, and my lungs were the sirens screaming the mortal demand. I wanted to exhale another bubble, but there was nothing left. I was out of breath, lost in utter darkness, and no longer certain about which direction I was moving. My muscles joined my lungs in their desperate cry for oxygen, but I had nothing to offer other than determination, grit, and will to live.

*Don't drop your light, Chase.*

My brain added insult to injury as I thought about the only signaling device I could use to help Disco find me, added to the list of gear now approaching the bottom of the Atlantic. If I made the surface and gave my brain and body the air it demanded, I'd likely be lost and afloat on the mighty ocean with six hours remaining before the sun filled the sky again. I lingered on the verge of believing I'd seen the last sunrise of my life.

I stroked again with both arms, driving with every ounce of force I could muster, but the ocean didn't resist as I finally stroked against nothing but air. My lungs made the realization long before my brain caught up, and they filled themselves with glorious, precious, salt air.

I made the surface, and I was alive, but where was Shawn?

Spinning in a circle, I begged my eyes to adjust to the absence of light. When I finally stopped gasping, I called, "Shawn! Shawn!"

My ears rang so violently that my desperate calls were little more than muffled moans. That's when it occurred to me that the roaring inside my head wasn't my brain's attempt to force my ears to work; it was the growl of the twin rotors of the Boeing Vertol hovering overhead.

Relief overtook me, but I couldn't silence the agony of not knowing where Shawn was. I remember leaving the ship, side by side, in freefall, but in the eternity that passed between that moment and this one, I hadn't seen, heard, or felt him beside me. No one was more capable of surviving in the ocean than a seasoned SEAL, but even that couldn't assuage my fear.

The team was operating the Vertol in blackout configuration to remain invisible from the *Desert Star*, but I wanted to scream for them to light up the ocean like a Broadway stage. In that moment, nothing was more important than finding Shawn and plucking him from the ocean.

I continued turning in slow revolutions and squinting to catch any hint of my partner's silhouette on the surface. On the chopper was where I wanted to be, but I'd follow my gear to the desolate bottom of the ocean if it would save Shawn's life. As the fear and anguish collided in a terrible flash of lightning inside my head, I felt a hand against my shoulder.

"Hey, brother. I found your light, and I thought you might want it back."

I spun to see my partner with his light in one hand and mine in the other.

He said, "I thought I'd lost you for a minute. Are you all right?"

I grabbed a handful of his collar. "I am now."

After taking the infrared light from his hand, I switched it on and waved it over my head. Disco pulled beside us and dropped the access ladder into the water, and I followed Shawn over the tube and onto the deck of the RHIB.

Disco took a knee beside us. "You two refuse to do anything the easy way, don't you?"

I rolled onto my back and looked up. "Where's the fun in that?"

* * *

The crane operator hauled us over the rail and deposited the RHIB onto her cradle. Dr. Shadrack insisted on conducting an exam to make sure all of our big pieces were still attached. They were, and we headed for the CIC to debrief and replan.

On the way up, I asked, "How did you find my light?"

He chuckled. "You dropped your gear right on top of me, and I figured since you're not a SEAL, you were probably panicking and dropping everything you could get your hands on."

"I didn't know you were beneath me."

He said, "I didn't know you were above me 'til your rifle hit me in the head."

"So, you weren't afraid?"

He gave me a shove. "I'm not smart enough to be afraid. I'm just a frogman with salt water for blood."

Inside the CIC, we laid out the few things that had gone right and the plethora of things that went wrong aboard the *Desert Star*.

Mongo asked, "So, do you think it was the congressman who almost busted you?"

"I never saw him," Shawn said, "but the voice was the same."

"Same for me," I said. "It was the strong, commanding voice of a man who's accustomed to being in charge. I'd say it's better than a fifty-fifty shot it was him."

"And he didn't appear to be in danger?" Skipper asked.

I said, "It seemed like a peaceful night aboard a cruise ship. Nothing about it felt hostile."

Clark stared at the ceiling and ran his hands through his hair. "What's going on over there? This thing keeps getting weirder."

"There's another wrinkle," I said. "We lost our helmets and NODs in the elevator shaft."

Clark let out a long sigh. "In the elevator or the shaft?"

"In the shaft. We were on top of the elevator car."

Shawn said, "With any luck, they're still on top of the car. If they fell down the shaft, they could've gotten caught on a piece of equipment and screwed up the whole system."

Clark said, "Let's hope nobody ever knows they're there. Best case would be they're never discovered, but even if they are, what's the real harm?"

I said, "It depends on what's really happening on the ship. If somebody finds the helmets, they'll know we were aboard. Right now, they just suspect we were there. If it's a hostile situation, it'll make them more vigilant. If it's a sinister situation, it'll make them nervous."

Clark narrowed his gaze. "Sinister? What do you mean?"

I said, "That boat isn't damaged. She's motoring and making electricity. By all appearances, the ship is fine, minus her radar and AIS broadcast. And there were no armed men holding the congressman hostage."

Clark clicked his tongue against his teeth. "So, what's our next move?"

I drummed my fingers against my thigh. "What's stopping us from boarding her in full force, taking command, and wringing the truth out of whoever's on board?"

Clark huffed. "Other than the textbook definition of piracy, nothing."

"The Board authorized piracy," I said.

He laughed. "The Board doesn't have the authority to sanction piracy. If we get busted, they'll hang us out to dry."

Shawn said, "I've done it before. When I was with the Teams, we hit a private yacht that was suspected of having kidnapped girls aboard. We hit that boat like a Mack truck with fourteen SEALs. There weren't any kidnap victims on board, but we found over a ton of heroin."

Clark said, "That's a little different than this, and you had presidential authorization for that mission."

Shawn shrugged. "It may not be signed, sealed, and delivered, but Chase has had two conversations with the President, specifically about this mission."

The room was silent for a moment until Gator spoke up. "Maybe I'm being naïve, but why can't we pull alongside her, roll the cameras, and show the world the *Desert Star* is still safely afloat? I mean, we all saw the newscast about her sinking, right?"

Skipper cocked her head as if considering the idea. "You're not wrong, but we don't have to come alongside her. We already have drone video with date, time, and location stamps, and we can get more anytime we want."

"Hang on a minute," I said. "Let's not get carried away before we understand what's going on. Sharing our video and what we know could put the congressman in more danger than he's already in . . . if he's in any. I think we have to discuss it with the Board and let them make the call. Whatever this thing is, it's so far over my head that I doubt I'll ever understand it."

Clark nodded. "Agreed. Let's not leap before we laugh last."

I quivered in my seat. "I think I just went blind in my left ear. What are you talking about?"

"You know what I mean," he said. "Let's get some more information and direction before we do anything that could jeopardize us or the congressman. I, for one, don't want the world to know anything about us, our equipment, or our capabilities. Once the *Lori Danielle* is on the evening news, she's lost her cover, and that's her greatest asset."

"Now, *that* I understand, and I agree. Let's make the call."

"Not so fast," Skipper said. "We've got company."

# Chapter 19
## *Independence Queen*

The overhead monitor flashed, and the screen filled with a satellite image of a ship approaching from the southeast. The low-light capability of the satellite's cameras wasn't perfect, but it gave us a relatively clean silhouette of the approaching vessel.

"Can you identify her?" I asked.

Skipper's fingers flew across the keys. "I'm working on it, but she's not transmitting an AIS signal."

"What's her range?" Clark asked.

Skipper said, "She's at thirty-one miles and making sixteen knots on an intercepting course with the *Star*."

I worked out the geometry. "That means we've got less than eighty minutes before they rendezvous."

I picked up the direct line to the bridge, and the first officer answered, "Bridge."

"Is the captain still awake?"

"Affirmative, but he's off the bridge and headed to the CIC."

"Thank you. Make ready for high-speed operations."

He said, "I need the captain's—"

I cut him off. "Make ready, and the captain will be on the line the second he gets here."

"Very well," he said.

Captain Sprayberry stepped through the hatch, and I handed the phone to him. "The bridge needs authorization for high-speed ops to the southeast."

He took the handset and barked into the receiver. "Make ready for high-speed ops to the southeast, on command from the CIC."

I didn't have to hear the first officer's reply to know it was only two words. "Aye, sir."

He tossed the receiver onto the console. "Brief me."

I pointed to the overhead monitor. "Skipper's tracking an unidentified inbound vessel on a course to rendezvous with the *Desert Star* in seventy-five minutes. She's running dark and not broadcasting AIS. I need eyes on her to ID her before she makes the intercept."

The captain checked his watch. "You're never going to let me sleep, are you?"

"The first officer can fly the boat," I said.

"Yeah, but then I'd miss all the fun. Are you and Shawn okay after your little adventure?"

I said, "I am, but he's a little soft, so he'll probably need his mommy to kiss it and make it better."

The captain rolled his eyes. "It never ends with you guys. I'm glad you're all right. I'll be awake and on the bridge if you need me."

Skipper glanced across her shoulder at me when the captain left. "What was that about? He never comes up here."

"I guess he needed a reason to go for a walk. Send the coordinates of the inbound ship to the bridge."

"Already done. This ain't my first rodeo."

I leaned down and whispered, "Maybe not, but you can still get bucked off."

"Cute. I guess you want me to get the drones ready to fly."

"You're getting good at this rodeo stuff. Yes, let's get at least two in the air as soon as we get within range. We need to know who and what that vessel is ASAP."

The ship shuddered and rose out of the water onto her foils, and our whole world turned into the smoothest ride on the ocean. It took eighteen minutes to be within the drone's operation range, and the captain retracted the foils. We were once again a conventional ship.

"Drones are ready to fly," Skipper said.

"Send them."

Two minutes later, the high-speed drones were zipping across the water at eighty knots. The feed from their infrared night-vision cameras raced across the monitor, and the inbound ship came into view."

"There she is," I said. "Get her name."

Skipper groaned. "Yeah, I know the mission. Give me a minute. I'm trying to fly two drones at eighty knots, six feet above the water, in the middle of the night."

With the flying machines under control, Skipper parked the first in overwatch above the ship while continuing to maneuver number two. She flew the bird toward the bow and sidestepped just in time to avoid colliding with the prow. The camera focused on the anchor hawser hole and then the name painted on the hull—*Independence Queen*.

Skipper said, "Mongo, take the drone. I'm digging into the registration."

The big man stepped around me and took control of the drone. He kept it just above the waterline, out of sight of the officers on the bridge.

He flew the length of the ship, circled around the stern, and centered the camera on the registry. The same name, *Independence Queen*, appeared on the stern, and beneath the name, the country of registry appeared—*Côte d'Ivoire*.

I shot Clark a glance, and he shrugged.

Mongo said, "Am I the only one who took world geography? Côte d'Ivoire is Ivory Coast. It's on the western coast of Africa between Liberia and Ghana."

"I'm on it," Skipper said as her fingers continued drumming the keys. She leaned toward the screen and groaned. "Come on . . . come on."

Mongo backed away from the ship to get the whole vessel on camera.

Skipper continued her sounds of displeasure. "What's going on here? What's taking so long?" Barely above a whisper, she said, "There's a GPS tracker on drone one if you want to plant it."

Mongo continued manipulating drone two until he captured hi-def video of every inch of the ship, then he parked the second drone in a high orbit before flying the first drone toward the superstructure. We watched as he skillfully approached the highest reaches of the ship. He made the work look easy, but the concentration on his face said it was far more challenging than he made it look.

As he maneuvered closer to the rack supporting the radar and communication antennas, his movements became barely noticeable. Working with the precision of a surgeon, he operated the mechanical arm to affix the GPS tracking device to the steel rack.

With the tracker in place, he backed the drone away from the ship but kept the camera fixed on the device. "Will that do?"

Skipper looked up and studied Mongo's handiwork. "That's perfect. Now, get out of there."

The image from the camera changed from a close-up of the device he'd just planted to a wider angle as he moved the drone farther from the ship. Soon, drone number two joined the first in formation, and Mongo relaxed. "They're coming home on autopilot. What did you learn about the ship?"

Skipper shook her head. "I learned she doesn't exist. There's no ship with that name registered anywhere in the world. The closest thing I could find was a tourist boat in Philadelphia. I don't understand it."

I asked, "Can you search the registry in Ivory Coast for ships matching her size?"

"I'm running that search now, but so far, nothing's popping up. It's obviously a cover, but it looked authentic on the video. I'll study the paint job later and see how it matches the background. Maybe somebody did a paint job name change. If they left any sign of the real name, maybe I can pick it up."

"How long will the tracker's battery last?"

She said, "About forty-five days. It only reports its position every half hour, so the battery life is excellent."

I said, "If this thing isn't over in forty-five days, we need to look for a new line of work."

Clark said, "It's decision time. Are we going to let this ship hook up with the *Desert Star*, or are we going to stop her?"

"How would we stop her?" I asked.

Clark huffed. "A dozen operators with machine guns oughta do it."

I grabbed the handset to the bridge.

"Bridge, Captain."

"It's Chase. Let's play hypothetical for a minute. If I wanted to stop that ship without boarding her, what would you recommend?"

The captain said, "A torpedo at the waterline would do it."

"Let's say I don't want to sink her."

"Oh, sure. Now you're putting parameters on the thing. We could drag a cable."

"I'm not following. What does that mean?"

He said, "You landlubbers sure don't know much about life at sea. Dragging a cable is an old World War Two trick. We'd take a length of cable and rig some floats to it. Cable is heavy, so you have to use a lot of floats or stick with a short piece of cable. Anyway, you drag it across the course of the ship and wait for him to run into it. With any luck, it'll foul the prop or the rudder, sometimes both. It can do a lot of damage when it gets wrapped up in a screw, but even if it misses the prop and just snags the rudder, she'll have to stop and send a diver overboard."

"Do we have cable on board?"

"Sure we do, but I don't know how much. The hard part is finding something to make the floats out of."

I asked, "Have you ever done it?"

"I watched Captain Stinnett do it with the original *Lori Danielle*. We tore up a heavy gunboat off the Falkland Islands. I'll have to tell you that story over a glass of something old sometime."

"I look forward to it. Let's change the game from hypothetical to let's do it. How long would it take to set it up?"

He said, "Meet me down in engineering. We'll have to drag Big Bob out of the sack."

Captain Sprayberry left the ship in the competent hands of his first officer, and I dragged Mongo from the CIC. Big Bob, the chief engineer, wasn't happy about being yanked out of bed, but when we told him what we wanted to do, his whole demeanor changed.

"We're gonna drag a cable? Hot dog! I ain't done this in twenty years."

The captain said, "What do we have for cable inventory?"

Bob said, "I've got a thousand feet of two-inch, and four thousand feet of inch-and-a-half. What are we trying to stop?"

I said, "It's about a three-hundred-foot workboat."

"Not a tug?"

"No, it looks like an oilfield tender."

Bob scratched his unshaven chin. "You got a picture of her?"

I pulled my phone from my pocket, and seconds later, Skipper shot me a picture. I held it up for Big Bob.

He studied it. "Yep, she's a stout-looking thing. Inch-and-a-half ain't gonna do it. I'd double up on two-inch and hope it gets the rudder. That thing's got enough beans in its butt to chew up 'bout anything we throw under her."

The captain asked, "Can we float a thousand feet of cable?"

Bob sniffed the air. "Smell that?"

Soon, all three of us were sniffing the air, but I couldn't smell a thing.

Finally, Bob said, "One of us don't smell so good. I reckon it's prolly me. Anyhow, yeah, we can float it. The cable weighs seven pounds per foot, so that's seven thousand pounds. I've got a bunch of five-hundred-pound lift bags. We can double up the cable and put a five-hundred-pounder every thirty feet. That'll put seventeen bags in the water and make eighty-five hundred pounds of flotation."

Big Bob looked like he couldn't count his fingers without help, but he'd rattled off some of the fastest calculations I'd ever seen anybody do, so I shot Mongo a glance just to confirm the arithmetic. He nodded, and I said, "Let's make it happen."

Big Bob closed one eye and stared up at me with the other. "I don't work for him. I work for the captain."

Barry gave Big Bob the same look the engineer had given me and said, "You're right, Bob. You do work for me, but I work for him. So, wake up some welders."

"Aye, Cap'n. It'll take us a couple of hours."

Barry checked the clock on the wall behind Big Bob and said, "You've got forty minutes."

# Chapter 20
## *Patience*

The weather deck of the RV *Lori Danielle* became the scene of what could only be described as well-choreographed chaos, and Chief Engineer Big Bob was the maestro. Judging by the sparks, helmets, and gloves of half a dozen welders, the scene could've been mistaken for a steel mill.

When Captain Sprayberry gave the engineers forty minutes, I believed the plan was destined to fail. I was convinced there was no way to roll out a thousand feet of two-inch steel cable, fold it in half, and attach seventeen lift bags in less than an hour. But just like everyone else aboard our ship, the engineers were masters of their trade, and they had the rig ready to splash in half an hour.

Big Bob sidled up beside me. "She's ready. Are you sending your divers or mine?"

A marine lift bag is similar in construction to a miniature hot air balloon. It's a large sack with an opening at the bottom that allows compressed air to blow into the bag to inflate it, and it has a valve at the top to allow air to escape when necessary. The bottom of the bag has no closure since it will always be below the surface of the water. Typically, a diver inflates the lift bag by releasing compressed air from his scuba tank, using his alternate air source, but seventeen bags capable of lifting five hundred pounds each would quickly exhaust a scuba tank. We would fill the lift bags from compressed air hoses lowered over the side of the ship.

I said, "Let's use your divers. We may need all the shooters we can get if this thing goes south."

Bob laughed. "Oh, she's going south, all right. This'll never work."

"What do you mean?"

He pulled a pipe from his pocket and lit the bowl. "I reckon I shouldn't have said it won't work. It'll stop that ship, but not how you and the captain think."

I said, "We're getting low on time, Bob. I'd really appreciate it if you'd tell me exactly what you mean."

He studied his pipe and took a long draw. "Ah, it don't matter how it works, just so long as it works, right? Somebody oughta tell the captain we're ready to get this contraption wet."

Conversation with the chief engineer felt a lot like trying to pet a porcupine, so I abandoned the pursuit and called the bridge. "Captain, the cable is rigged and ready to hit the water."

He said, "Good. I'll put us in front of the *Independence Queen* and let you know when to splash the rig."

"Make the call to Big Bob," I said. "I'm going to get the team ready to fight if something goes wrong."

To my surprise, the captain echoed Bob's sentiment. "You can bet something will go wrong, so gearing up for a fight is a good plan."

"Why does everybody keep saying that?" I asked without realizing I'd said it out loud.

"Think about it," Barry said. "We're going to drag a five-hundred-foot cable across the bow of a three-hundred-foot ship, hoping she'll catch the cable just right to foul the prop or rudder. I have to drag the cable with another hawser cable and cut it loose at exactly the right instant for the *Independence* to hit it just right."

"Keep talking," I said.

He continued. "There's no way for us to *push* that cable. We can only pull it. That means I have to judge wind, current, momentum, and sea monsters when I guess where to release the thing. This is the naval equivalent of spike strips across a road to stop a car, but in our case, the road is ten thousand miles wide and constantly moving, and our bad guy can change speed and direction at any minute. We're playing the ultimate game of pin the tail on the donkey and hoping that donkey doesn't kick us in the face when we do it."

No longer convinced our scheme had better than a ten percent chance of working, I readied the team. "Singer, I need you up high and ready to kill the lift bags if this thing goes wrong. We can't have that cable floating around in the open ocean if we don't catch our prey with it. If we miss, shoot out enough bags to send that thing to the bottom."

He nodded. "No problem."

"The rest of us are going to split into two teams. I want Disco and Shawn in the RHIB. Mongo, Gator, Kodiak, and Anya and I will stand by on the helipad, ready to fly." I scanned the team. "Where's Ronda?"

She stuck up a hand from the back. "I'm here."

"Good. I need you on the gun. Hopefully, the cable trick will work, and it won't be necessary for us to assault the ship, but we have to be prepared, and your Minigun makes us a little harder to shoot down."

The ship slowed and drifted to a stop beneath our boots.

Skipper said, "That must mean we're in position."

"Bring up the weather deck camera," I said.

She pulled up the feed and sent it to the overhead monitor. Both cranes were running, and the operators were slowly lifting the cable overboard.

Skipper brought up the stern camera, and we watched two divers fill the lift bags as they hit the water. The five hundred feet of cable slithered astern like a massive python prowling her territory.

I watched closely as a pair of deckhands connected a tether to the end of the cable and rigged a cutaway between the hawser and the cable designed to stop the ship. The cutaway would allow the captain to tow the cable into position and disconnect it from the hawser so we could recover the hawser.

The more I thought about the plan, the crazier it felt, but the tiny corner of my brain where my pirate spirit lives loved every minute of it.

Skipper said, "We're underway again. It looks like it's showtime."

Shawn and Disco headed for the RHIB while the rest of us climbed the ladders to the helipad.

The sun was still ninety minutes from cracking the eastern horizon, so the clock was running, but we weren't under the gun . . . yet.

Our ship was no longer the agile warship she had been. She'd become a locomotive for a two-thousand-foot-long freight train. Her own length, plus the thousand-foot hawser and five-hundred-foot trap cable made her slow, lumbering, and a challenge to maneuver.

Captain Sprayberry made it look easy, but his turns were two-mile affairs instead of the crisp maneuvers he typically commanded from the bridge.

From our position on the helipad, we couldn't see either ship, but our course made it clear that we were between the two and heading northwest, perpendicular to the intersecting course the *Independence Queen* was sailing.

We slowed until we were barely moving through the water. The captain was no doubt gauging his release to position the trap cable directly off the bow of the approaching ship. Even though we had our radar absorption and jamming systems operating at full force, there was still a slight possibility of a sharp-eyed lookout on our target ship catching a glimpse of us in the dark.

We couldn't know how well armed they were, but regardless of their complement, we had them outgunned, and they'd never match our speed if the nautical insanity we were attempting turned into a race. We would escape, but our cover would be blown, and whatever the congressman's captors were planning would devolve into a mighty train wreck at sea.

Slowly, the ship picked up speed, and the vibration of the hawser windlass rattled through the deck. The captain had released his trap, and the thousand-foot hawser line was on her way back aboard the ship. There was nothing left to do except watch and wait.

Skipper said, "Attention all Sierra elements. I'm sending the satellite and radar feeds to your tablets."

I pulled the hardened tablet from my cargo pants and watched the *Independence Queen* motor toward our trap. The cable was invisible to the satellite and radar, but the best intelligence analyst in the business had the engineers place GPS trackers on the two lift bags at opposite ends of the cable.

The scene unfolding on our tablets was like watching a slow-motion replay of a collision. The lines looked good. The angle appeared to be perfect. The *Queen* would definitely strike the cable. The only question was how close to the center. If she clipped one end, the cable could slide across the bow with no effect on the ship. The closer to the center her bow contacted the trap, the higher probability of success we had.

We watched in silence as the ship closed on the trap. With every passing second, the intercept looked better until the bow struck the cable within inches of its center. The GPS trackers vanished as the lift bags were dragged alongside the ship until they failed, allowing the cable to sink beneath the keel.

I tried to imagine what the crew on the bridge of the *Queen* felt as the seven-thousand-pound cable laced itself beneath their ship, but my real fascination lay below the waterline. The instant the cable contacted the propeller or rudder, the result would be violent and obvious, but two minutes after contact, the ship hadn't appeared to change course or speed.

I called the bridge. "It looked like she caught the cable, so why hasn't she stopped?"

The captain said, "We estimated the *Independence Queen* to be three hundred feet in length, right?"

"Yes, that's Skipper's estimate."

"So, if she struck the five-hundred-foot cable in the center, she's trailing two hundred fifty feet down each side, and that's not enough to contact the propeller or rudder."

My heart sank. "Does that mean . . . ?"

He said, "Patience, Chase. The crew knows they hit something. According to radar, they slowed from sixteen knots to thirteen. Give them two more minutes."

Patience had never been my strong suit, but I never took my eyes off the screen as the saga played out. I couldn't let the *Independence Queen* rendezvous with the *Desert Star*, so as the minutes ticked away, I grew more anxious. The coming sunrise would end our ability to hide beneath the cover of darkness, and if the two ships reached each other, whatever the plan was would be one step closer to happening.

I couldn't wait another second, so I gave the order. "Splash the RHIB and fire up the helo."

The crane hoisted Disco and Shawn over the rail in the RHIB, and the twin turbines of the Vertol whistled to life.

I called the bridge. "We're out of time. We're hitting the ship."

Barry's calm tone should've eased my concern, but it had the opposite effect.

"Patience. Give it two more minutes."

"We don't have two more minutes." I ordered, "Mount the helo."

We climbed aboard and took our positions. Ronda strapped into her harness behind the Minigun, and Barbie pulled on her helmet.

I desperately wanted Barry to be right, but the scene on my tablet wasn't changing. The *Queen* was still steaming on the same course, and it was still my responsibility to stop her.

"Bridge, Sierra One. We'll be airborne in thirty seconds."

I stowed my tablet, and Barbie stared across her shoulder, waiting for my signal. I gave the thumbs-up, and the rotors came up to speed. She pulled pitch, and the Vertol's landing gear left the helipad.

We climbed away into the darkness and banked to the south toward our target.

Both Skipper's and Barbie's voices exploded inside my comms simultaneously.

The pilot said, "Target vessel in sight, and she's coming about to port."

Skipper said, "She's turning to port!"

Captain Sprayberry's voice was next. "I told you to be patient, kid."

# Chapter 21
## *To Render Aid*

A thousand possibilities flashed before me. Chief among them was the fear that I had just attacked a civilian vessel on the high seas with no solid connection to any criminal activity. Although the ship should've been broadcasting her AIS signal, its not doing so didn't justify me causing hundreds of thousands of dollars in damage to an innocent vessel. Every piece of information we had on the *Independence Queen* told me she was on her way to rendezvous with the *Desert Star*, but evidence doesn't always point its fickle finger toward the guilty. My letter of marque and reprisal from my president, although weighty, lacked the heft to exempt me from a pirate's fate if my fears became my reality.

Barbie banked the Vertol away from the *Independence Queen* and pointed our nose back toward the *Lori Danielle* at the same moment I thought of a way to ease my troubled mind.

I grabbed the headset from the hook above my seat and pulled off my helmet. With the headset in place, I positioned the microphone in front of my lips. "Unless there's an operational need for us to be back on deck, I want you to put us in visual range of the *Desert Star*."

Barbie said, "Roger," and continued banking to the left.

Although I couldn't see the altimeter from my seat in the cabin, we climbed at least a few hundred feet as we turned to the northeast.

Eight minutes later, Barbie said, "There she is."

I leaned into the cockpit. "Is she turning for the *Queen*?"

She shook her head and pointed toward the radar. "She's actually in a gradual turn to the north."

"Why would she turn away if they were steaming to rendezvous with the *Queen*?"

"You're the smart one," Barbie said. "I'm just the overpaid bus driver."

"CIC, Sierra One."

Skipper said, "Go for CIC."

I asked, "Do you show the *Desert Star* in a turn to the north?"

"Affirmative. She's definitely in a turn."

"Say condition of the *Independence Queen*."

She said, "Her bow is in the wind, and she's adrift."

My heart fell into the pit of my stomach. "Roger. We're coming home. Keep tracking the *Star*, and have the captain put us bow to bow with the *Independence Queen* at first light."

The ten-minute flight back to the *L.D.* was the longest ride of my life. Everything was falling apart, and I was about to look the captain of the *Queen* in the eye and pretend I had no idea what happened to his ship.

The old adage about hindsight being twenty-twenty is horribly wrong. Hindsight, in my world, is an electron microscope. Every minute detail of the past is blown up larger than life to either reward a commander's brilliance on the battlefield or drive a white-hot sword through his failing heart. I was tasting the sword as I handed off my gear to the deckhand before dragging myself to the navigation bridge.

"Permiss—"

Captain Sprayberry growled, "Get in here."

I stepped through the hatch, but he didn't wait to start the speech. "Bow to bow, huh?"

I said, "I don't want them to get a good look at our profile, and if they continue to maintain radio silence, I want to be able to communicate with them. We have one of those flashy light things, don't we?"

"It's called a signal lamp, and we've got one, but I'm the only one on board who's old enough to know how to use it."

"Have they made a distress call?" I asked.

"Not yet. They're probably waiting for daylight to send a diver overboard."

My heart leapt from my stomach to back where it belonged. "How much time do we have before sunup?"

He checked his watch. "Forty minutes."

"I need to splash the SEAL Delivery Vehicle."

He said, "Make it happen. Do you still want me nose to nose with her? I can be on her stern in ten minutes or on her bow in eighteen to twenty."

"Stick me on her stern and make it tight."

He threw up a mock salute, and I sprinted from the bridge.

Shawn, Disco, and I made it to the CIC at the same time, and the SEAL said, "We figured you wanted us back on board."

"I do," I said, "but not for long. Suit up. We're going for a dive."

The crew had the SDV ready to hit the water by the time the three of us made it to the belly of the ship, where the moonpool had been before the *L.D.* went through her refit to relocate marine mammals. Launching and recovering the SEAL Delivery Vehicle was a relatively simple task before the refit, but the complex system of cranes and cabling after the conversion slowed the process by several minutes.

We pulled on our dry suits and rebreathers and climbed into the motorized metal tube—called an SDV—which is designed to covertly move a team of Navy SEALs beneath the waves at seven knots while making very little noise. I didn't have any reason to believe the *Independence Queen* had a sonar system capable of hearing us approach, but the work we'd do beneath her keel would make enough noise for a deaf dead guy to hear anywhere inside the ship.

The crane operator lifted us from the cradle and slowly moved us through the maze of turns until we were situated just above the waterline in the belly of our ship.

I called the bridge. "We're in position. How long until we're on target?"

Barry said, "Thirty seconds. Splash at will."

I gave the signal to lower us into the waiting ocean, and the man on the crane deposited us into the water as if laying his baby down to sleep.

When the hooks and the cable left us, we were an autonomous ship and only minutes away from trying to erase our fingerprints from beneath the *Independence Queen*.

Sound travels through water four times as quickly as it travels through the air. That's just one of the dozens of reasons the ocean is on the same planet but in a different world. On land, our brains identify the direction sound is coming from because it reaches one ear before reaching the other. Underwater, the increased speed of sound erases that advantage of situational awareness. We could hear four things that morning as we motored toward the *Independence Queen* at seven knots in our torpedo—the sound of the *Lori Danielle*'s engines diminishing behind us, the whisper of our electric motor and propeller, the gentle hum of the *Queen*'s engines running but not her propeller spinning, and our own breathing. Aside from the volume changes of those sounds, we couldn't determine the direction of any of the mechanical noise in our environment. Fortunately, the SEAL Delivery Vehicle wasn't limited by the weakness of our human ears.

Mongo and Dr. Mankiller outfitted the SDV with a suite of electronics that gave us not only the ability to magnetically detect huge steel ships in our area, but also precision sonar unlike anything the commercial seagoing world had ever seen. At periscope depth, we could see in every direction, but the high-tech gadgetry erased the necessity to rise near the surface where we could easily be seen. What we needed to see on that morning wasn't something we'd spy with the periscope. It would be what remained of the propeller and rudder of the *Independence Queen*.

Although the sun may have been approaching the eastern horizon, darkness still reigned supreme beneath the docile waters of the eastern

Atlantic. Unlike sound, light travels quite poorly through water, and it tends to find its way to the surface, where prying eyes are drawn like moths to the watery flame. One of the benefits of being surrounded by people smarter than me was that I had a practically endless supply of new toys at my disposal. At that moment, the handiest of those toys came in the form of dive masks fitted with waterproof night-vision goggles.

Disco brought the SDV to a hover beside the propeller and rudder, and we donned our magic eyes. Although the lift bags were destroyed in the initial collision, the massive steel cable had done precisely what the contraption was meant to do. It was wrapped around the shaft of the propeller and twisted like jungle vines around the rudder and post.

Disco held the SDV in position while Shawn and I swam toward the mangled collection of cable, bronze, and steel. We inspected the damage inch by inch until I'd committed the puzzle to memory.

"What do you think?" I asked through the distorting comms of our dive gear.

"I'm no naval architect," he said, "but I don't see much damage. It's a nasty knot, but everything is intact."

"My thoughts exactly. Can you cut the cable away?"

He spun and studied the conglomeration for another minute before waving for Disco to bring the gear.

After parking the SDV a few feet from the rudder, Disco held the sub motionless while Shawn deployed the underwater cutting torch. Our SEAL moved with confidence as if he'd cut a thousand miles of steel cable from beneath ships at sea, and I tried to stay out of his way.

Shawn said, "Move behind me. I don't want this cable to spring away and knock you all the way to Bermuda."

I swam behind him and watched across his shoulder as he worked. The arcing fire from the end of his torch cast eerie, pulsing streams of light from the strands of cable as if the underwater version of the aurora borealis were putting on a private show just for me.

Shawn worked for a minute or so before the first strand of massive steel cable pulled away from the rudder and fell into the abyss. He swam away as the cable fell so he could protect himself from anything that might try to drag him to the bottom.

Apparently confident the danger was over, he moved in and continued cutting. When the last strand finally surrendered to his torch, the bulk of the cable vanished into the darkness, and I instantly understood why Shawn had been so cautious about positioning me away from the cut. The remaining cable, still twisted around the propeller shaft, turned into a coiled spring and lashed like a whip through the water as the weight of the remainder of the cable fell away. If a human had been in the way, the slicing cable would've left him drawn and quartered.

When the pulsating remains of the cable finally came to rest, Shawn motioned for Disco to move the SDV forward a few feet. The SEAL and the torch made short work of the remnants of the cable still twisted around the shaft. After a couple of minutes, all that remained of the evidence of our sabotage were the scars in the barnacles and marine growth on the hull of the *Independence Queen*.

We repacked our tools and motored back toward our waterborne home, retracing our steps through the opening in the bottom of our ship, onto the crane, and finally into the SDV's cradle. We peeled ourselves from our dry suits and headed for the bridge.

Captain Sprayberry met us in the corridor. "There you are. What took you so long?"

My attention shot to my watch, and I couldn't believe an hour had passed since I left the bridge. "I guess that means the sun is up."

Barry huffed. "Yeah, it's up, and I was beginning to think you wouldn't be back on board to see it set."

"We made it," I said. "Have you had any luck getting in touch with the *Queen*'s captain?"

"Haven't tried," he said. "I didn't want to risk starting a conversation while you were messing around underneath her belly. How did it look down there?"

"I was surprised how little damage the cable did. Shawn cut it away, and other than a few scrapes and scratches, it looked ready to run."

The captain said, "It may have looked good on the outside, but that amount of stress on the propulsion system could do a lot of damage you wouldn't be able to see from the outside."

"You're the expert," I said. "I just blow stuff up. Why don't we see if they'll answer the phone?"

We followed the captain onto the bridge, where he made repeated attempts on the marine radio with no response. He tossed the mic onto the console. "Well, that was a waste of time, but I expected that. Let's try the loud hailer."

"Why not the signal lamp?"

He laid a hand on my shoulder and spun me toward the bow. "Do you see anybody on that ship who'd see our signal lamp if we turned it on?"

The loud hailer system is essentially a rock concert without the guitars and drums. Four high-powered, directional speakers mounted on the outside of the superstructure of the *Lori Danielle* had enough power to deafen anybody directly in front of them.

Barry activated the forward-facing speaker and keyed his microphone. "Ahoy, *Independence Queen*. Do you require assistance?"

He repeated the thundering call twice more, with the same absence of any reply, so he laid down the mic. "We're required to render aid, but we're not required to force them to accept it. I'm comfortable reporting the ship's position to the Portuguese authorities and moving on. How about you?"

I stared through the glass at the drifting vessel that could pass for a ghost ship. "We've got a GPS locator on her stack. Let's put a hold on that call to the authorities and get out of here. Skipper can keep tabs on this one while we chase down the *Desert Star*. I've had enough of this game. It's time to change the rules."

# Chapter 22

## *Do It*

Captain Sprayberry rarely barked orders, but when he spoke, he left no doubt about who was in command of the *Lori Danielle*. "Helm, lay us astern of the *Desert Star*, beyond visual range."

The young officer at the helm answered as if he were aboard an American warship. "Aye, sir. Lay us astern the *Desert Star* BVR."

Barry turned back to me, but the helmsman seized the captain's attention. "Uh, sir. I think there may be a problem."

Always a teacher, Barry strolled toward the helm without expressing concern. "Can you be a little more specific?"

The young officer said, "I think we may be chasing the wrong ship."

"Not likely," the captain said. "Show me what you see."

The helmsman laid a finger against the small radar display at his station. "That's the same target we've been calling the *Desert Star* for several days, but she's broadcasting AIS now."

Barry leaned toward the screen and laid his hand across the roller ball. After a few clicks and a sigh, he said, "So it is . . . Interesting. Belay my order to stay beyond visual range. Lay me alongside at pistol shot."

"Pistol shot, sir?"

Barry grunted. "Please tell me you've read Patrick O'Brian."

"Who's that, sir?"

The captain's displeasure grew more apparent. "Get over here, Chase."

I approached with caution, and he said, "Chase, you have the helm. Mr. Connor, you're relieved."

Panic overtook the helmsman's face as he stepped away from his station. "Did I do something wrong, sir?"

Barry said, "You certainly didn't do something right. March your butt into my cabin and pull *Master and Commander* from the bookshelf. Read it and return it before your next shift."

Connor swallowed hard. "Uh . . . yes, sir."

The only person on the bridge who was more nervous than Connor was me. "Captain, I have no idea how to run the helm."

"Then it's high time that you learn."

My class was a crash course in applied physics, and I believed I was doing well until Captain Sprayberry said, "Please tell me you realize the ship is on autopilot."

I lifted my hands from the controls. "You play these games just to amuse yourself, don't you?"

"It's lonely at the top," he said. "A guy's gotta do something to keep his sanity. What do you think is going on with the AIS?"

I said, "I have a theory, but we'll have to get a lot closer to test it."

Barry said, "Not if Skipper still has control of the satellites."

I stepped around him. "You have the controls. I'm going somewhere I won't be abused."

He chuckled. "If you think Skipper won't abuse you, you're in for quite the rude awakening, my friend."

"Touché."

I found Skipper in the combat information center, stuffing a breakfast burrito into her face. "Hungry much?"

She mumbled something, but I ignored whatever it was.

"Do you still have the satellites?"

Still chewing the clump of burrito, she shook her head, "Hm-uh."

"Would you swallow that so we can have a non-caveman conversation?"

She took a long swallow of whatever was in her mug. "No, I don't have the satellites anymore, but I have access to one over the coast."

"What does access mean?"

"It means I can see what it sees, but I can't direct it."

"That's good enough," I said. "I need to know if the *Desert Star* is one ship or two."

She cocked her head in that confused puppy look. "What?"

"The ship we thought was the *Desert Star* is broadcasting the AIS signal of another ship."

Her fingers hit the keyboard. "Ooh, that's not good." She typed and clicked and made noises I couldn't define until she leaned back in her chair and ran her hands through her hair. "Uh, it's the same footprint, but the AIS definitely isn't the *Desert Star*. It claims to be the *Falling Moon*, and guess where it's registered."

"Ivory Coast?"

She rang an imaginary bell. "Ding! We have a winner!"

I leaned toward her monitor. "Look for other ships in the area with similar footprints."

She pointed toward the screen. "There's the *Star*—or the *Moon*—and this is us. The *Independence Queen* is still adrift behind us, and there are a few freighters scattered around. Nothing else out here looks like the *Star*."

"Can you zoom in?" I asked.

"Sure. What do you want to see?"

"Zoom in as tight as you can on the *Independence Queen*."

The disabled vessel soon filled the monitor, and Skipper gasped. "Oh my God! She's sinking."

"She sure is. Ring the bridge."

An instant later, Captain Sprayberry answered. "Go for bridge."

I said, "Get us back to the *Independence Queen* as quickly as we can move. I'm on my way up."

Without hesitation, he said, "Helm, come about on a reciprocal course, and make ready to fly the boat."

Skipper cut the line, and I said, "Spool everybody up, and get the chopper on the pad."

In a rare moment of obedience, Skipper said, "Yes, sir."

The curious part of my brain wanted to investigate her sudden, unquestioning compliance, but the tactical side won the battle. I was on the bridge in forty-five seconds. "She's sinking."

The captain furrowed his brow. "Sinking? I thought you said she wasn't badly damaged."

I replayed the video of the *Queen*'s keel in my head. "There wasn't anything that indicated a compromise in the hull."

Barry scratched his head. "You must've missed it. The only explanation is the through-hull fitting at the prop shaft or the rudder post."

"I could've missed it," I said, "but Shawn wouldn't have."

"Get him up here."

I pulled the phone from my pocket and thumbed in the speed dial for our SEAL. "Come to the bridge double-quick."

"On my way."

In seconds, Shawn was standing at the hatch. "Permission to come aboard the bridge?"

"Get in here," Barry said. "Describe what you saw on the through-hulls under the *Queen*."

Shawn closed his eyes momentarily, as if replaying his mental video. "I didn't see any damage at the prop shaft or rudder post. She was solid."

"Apparently not," Barry said. "She's going down."

Shawn grimaced. "Impossible."

The GPS showed our speed at fifty-six knots, and I stared through the glass until a speck appeared dead ahead. "There she is."

Barry checked the radar. "That's her, but there's no distress call and no EPIRB signals."

I lifted a pair of binoculars from their cradle and pressed the rubber cups to my eyes. We were still too far away to see details, even with the binoculars, but Barry gave the order to secure from flight. Our hull settled back into the water as the foils retracted, and our speed was cut in half.

Shawn lifted a second pair of binoculars to his face. "Are the lifeboats on deck?"

"That's what I'm looking for," I said. "We should be able to see them any minute."

I traded my binoculars for the handset of the ship's internal comms, and Skipper said, "CIC."

"Are you still zoomed in on the *Queen*?"

"Yes, and the answer to your next question is I can't tell if a lifeboat is missing. The angle of the satellite is no good."

I said, "Have them rig the Vertol for fast-rope ops, and send the whole team to the helipad."

"Consider it done," she said. "I'm also continuing to track the *Queen*, and I won't lose her."

I laid down the handset, and Barry said, "You're going to board her?"

"We sure are."

By the time I climbed the ladder to the helipad, The team was already geared up in full battle rattle, and the rotors were spinning.

We mounted the helo, and I gave the orders. "Pair off in teams of two and clear the ship. Shawn, you're with me. We're starting in the engine room. I want Anya and Mongo to work top down. The rest of you start at the weather deck and work toward Mongo and Anya or Shawn and me. We should be able to clear it in fifteen minutes or less."

Disco stuck a finger in the air. "ROE?"

"Rules of engagement are simple. This is a rescue mission with caution. Suppress aggression with minimal force, and move anybody you find to the weather deck."

I stuck my head into the cockpit and watched the *Independence Queen* grow closer by the second. She had taken on enough water to bring her into a bow-high attitude of at least fifteen degrees.

I tapped Barbie on the elbow. "Put us on the bow and hold overhead to recover anybody we find on board."

"You got it, but there's no need to fast-rope. I can stick the ramp on the bow, and you guys can walk off."

"Make it happen." I turned back into the cabin and pulled my water-activated life jacket over my head. "Everybody ready?"

Everyone press-checked their rifles and sidearms, tightened their life jackets, and gave the thumbs-up. Mongo lowered the rear ramp and pulled his headset in place. Barbie listened as the big man directed her every move while lying facedown on the ramp. She slowly descended until the tip of the ramp rested on the bow of the *Independence Queen*, and I gave the order. "Go, go, go!"

We filed out in two-man teams and hit the deck of the sinking ship as if we were storming the beach, and the memory of Don Wood's story of that fateful day in Normandy played through my mind.

Shawn and I were last off the bird, and Barbie climbed away. She moved into a holding pattern above the dying ship while the rest of us went to work.

All sinking ships have two things in common—they're slowly becoming just as wet inside as they are outside, and if people are aboard, they're running for the driest spot they can find. I was quickly coming to believe the only people aboard the *Independence Queen* were on my payroll, but I was minutes away from discovering how wrong I could be.

Shawn and I descended the stairs cautiously at first, but the farther we progressed into the belly of the ship, the more uneasy I became. I felt nothing about the situation was what it appeared to be.

"I don't like this," I said.

Shawn huffed. "If you don't like it now, you're really going to hate your next step."

Instead of the ring of boots on steel when I took the next stride, the sound of sloshing water reverberated from my heel. "I guess we found the waterline."

"I guess we did," the SEAL said. "We've gotta be close to the engine room."

I shone my light on the hatch in front of us, proving Shawn correct. He placed a palm against the hatch, just above the water, and slowly slid his hand upward. "It's cold, so there's at least three feet of water in there."

"That's a watertight hatch," I said.

He took a deep breath. "This is going to be exciting. Tell me when you're ready."

I gripped the ladder rail as if my life depended on it. "Do it."

# Chapter 23
## *Augmented Reality*

Standing outside the engine room hatch with a wall of seawater waiting on the other side should've frightened me, but that wasn't the emotion I experienced. I was confounded. "Wait a minute. Let's see if we can figure this out before we baptize ourselves."

Shawn said, "What do you mean? Somebody sealed the watertight hatch when the engine room started taking on water. That's just good seamanship."

"I agree, but why did they abandon ship once they had the engine room sealed off and the flooding controlled?"

He twisted his mouth into contortions. "Maybe they thought they were still sinking."

"There's no way they didn't hear our loud hailer. The bridge crew had to know we were a few hundred feet astern."

"Maybe they had already abandoned ship by the time we showed up."

"Maybe," I admitted, "but why are the lifeboats still on board? And if they had a launch of some kind, why didn't they motor toward us and take our offer to rescue them?"

He pulled his hand from the hatch. "Maybe they're taking on water from somewhere other than the engine room, so they believed sinking was inevitable."

I chewed on his idea. "Okay, that's the best answer so far, but it's still not the action of a crew of professional mariners."

We stood in silence until Shawn laid his hand back against the hatch. "The water is rising inside. If we wait much longer, we may not be able to close it again once it's open."

"You know how to swim, don't you?"

He gave the door a punch. "Find something to hold on to, boss. Here comes the wave."

I gripped the railing, and he muscled the hatch until it surrendered. The wave Shawn predicted became a tsunami. It hit us like a liquid freight train, knocking both of us from any frail grip we believed we had on anything solid.

I spent more than ten years of my life learning to crouch behind home plate and let ambitious runners from third plow into me in their determination to reach the plate that I considered to be my home. By the time I reached Foley Field at the University of Georgia, I was fearless, and I begged every runner on the field to challenge me. I wanted the collision. I craved the elation of hearing the air leave a runner's lungs as he plowed into me and my suit of armor at the plate. They might have the speed and momentum to put me on my back, but nobody could hit me hard enough to dislodge the ball from my mitt.

When the hatch exploded open, I expected a couple of feet of water to rush through the opening like river rapids, but I never dreamed it would hit me harder than anything or anyone ever had. A black wall of water detonated into an airborne beast, filling the air and crushing me against the ladder I'd descended only minutes earlier.

The roar of the crash deafened me, and the concussion emptied my lungs. My helmet's chin strap sliced into my neck, acting like an anchor dragging me backward. The more I grasped for anything, the less control I seemed to have. I was completely at the mercy of the rushing water, with no idea which way was up or down. All I could do was ignore the burn in my desperate lungs and pray I didn't collide with anything that would send me through death's darkened, flooded door.

When I finally came to rest against a bulkhead, I shoved my boots back to what I hoped was the deck as I lunged upward to gather my first breath. My guess was right, but the breath came wrapped in filthy salt water. I coughed, gagged, and convulsed until most of the water came back up through my nose and mouth, and I finally grasped the dry air my body so desperately needed. I was armpit-deep, confused, and lost, but I wasn't alone. My rifle and its rail-mounted light were somewhere downstream, and my backup light was crushed. The darkness only served to further disorient me as I reached for anything I could recognize. The first object I felt was unmistakable: a lifeless human arm.

I grabbed the elbow and bicep, pulling Shawn against me. He was limp and unresponsive, so I fumbled for his neck, begging God for the feel of a pulse. I found none, and my mind fought in desperation to locate a solid foundation where I could start CPR. Without having him lying on his back on something hard, there was no way to perform chest compressions.

As I squinted and blinked in wasted attempts to regain any vision, I felt a second body drift against me. It was smaller than Shawn, but there was no question it was a body—a corpse with no breath or pulse. I returned my attention to my partner and explored his body for anything that might generate a light. A few seconds into my search, I discovered that his gear was missing . . . all of it. His arms lacked the muscles of Shawn's. His shoes weren't the boots every member of my team wore. The body I so badly wanted to resuscitate wasn't Shawn at all. It was someone else—someone who had floated from inside the engine room.

*If two bodies drifted into me, how many more could there be? Had they drowned? Did someone trap them inside the engine room while trying to save the ship and the lives of everyone else on board? Who were they? And if neither body is Shawn, where is he?*

Dead bodies were meaningful, and I wouldn't leave them behind if I survived the remainder of my time aboard the *Independence Queen*, but there was nothing I wanted more than to find Shawn alive.

The rushing water lost most of its energy as it reached equilibrium, but it was still a formidable foe. The five feet of water, coupled with the darkness, left me grasping around like a blind man in a well. Everything I learned about the layout of the deck before Shawn opened the hatch was gone. I couldn't remember or devise direction, nothing seemed rational, and everything was in utter disarray.

I slid a finger between my chin strap and my flesh, hoping I wouldn't discover my throat open and gushing blood. Thankfully, the only liquid I detected was salt water, and my skin appeared intact. Resituating my helmet into its proper position, I discovered my NODs still in place. As I lowered them into position in front of my eyes, I sent up a silent prayer they had survived the torrent of moments before.

The void of endless black slowly morphed into shades of green and partially identifiable shapes as my eyes adjusted to the augmented reality.

I found the open hatch to the engine room and immediately wished I hadn't. Two bodies lay wedged together in the opening, with arms and legs sprawled unnaturally in every direction. Dead bodies didn't sicken me, but drowned bodies that had once belonged to innocent humans ignited a raging fire in my soul. There was nothing I could do for either of the newly discovered bodies, but I clung to hope as I searched downstream for Shawn.

I drew an imaginary line from the engine room hatch through the place where our SEAL had been standing when he released the hatch. The line extended down a long corridor with nothing resembling Shawn or anyone else in sight. I sloshed my way down the hallway, pulling myself into every opening to the left and right until I came to an intersection with corridors leading away to port and starboard. There was no rational way to make the choice, so I arbitrarily turned right. With my hearing at least partially restored, I thought I detected sounds of movement that water couldn't do on its own.

I increased my pace and forced my legs against the ever-decreasing depth as I trekked farther from the engine room. My heart leapt when I saw one hand, and then a second, protruding from a hatchway.

"Shawn!"

His winded answer came. "Yeah . . . in here!"

My slow progression morphed into stomping as I forced myself toward his voice as fast as my legs could propel me. I rounded the hatch and fell to my knees just as Shawn pulled himself back to his feet.

I said, "Are you all right?"

He shook his head as if shaking off a punch. "What a ride! Let's do it again."

"I'm good," I said. "Once was enough for me. Did you see the bodies?"

"What bodies?"

I pointed toward the engine room. "I found four bodies floating from the hatch. I'm pretty sure they drowned."

He shook the water from his body like a dog. "Let's go check it out."

We waded our way back to the engine room, with the water growing deeper with every stride.

Shawn slapped the water with his palm. "There's no way we did enough damage to let this much water in. There has to be another breach somewhere."

"Right now, I'm more interested in who the bodies are."

We made our way into the flooded engine room after pushing the pair of corpses aside, and the breach Shawn predicted practically raised its hand and waved at us. The fountain of water sprayed from the port side about forty feet into the massive space. The roar of the pulsing water made it impossible to hear each other, but talking wasn't necessary.

Shawn motioned toward his ankle, and I gripped his boot as if his life depended on it. A second later, he plunged himself into the roaring water with outstretched arms. He pulled himself forward against the stream with his hands while I drove him like a wheelbarrow. Slowly, the coursing water lost its strength and finally halted. Shawn pulled his foot from my grasp and stood.

After catching his breath, he said, "We didn't cause that. It's an intentional breach from the inside. I closed the valve. It was a severed raw water intake."

I tried to make sense of the new information, but I couldn't put it together. "Why?"

"Somebody is intentionally sinking this ship."

My gears were churning, but the more I learned, the less I understood.

Shawn said, "That means the bodies you found didn't drown. If they were engine room crew, they would've known how to close the valve just like I did."

We pulled ourselves through the water until reaching the pair of bodies by the hatch. Shawn rolled the first one facedown and sighed. He cradled the man's head in one hand and pointed to the small-caliber entry wound behind his right ear. "Looks like a twenty-two."

I examined the second body and found a similar wound near the base of his skull. While searching for the two remaining bodies, we found three, all with pencil-sized headwounds.

I leaned against the bulkhead and groaned. "The only shooters I know who put twenty-two rounds in people's heads are Mossad."

Shawn wiped his face. "Or killers trying to make it look like Mossad."

"This thing is out of control. Let's get the bodies up on deck and get off this tub. Whoever did this isn't aboard anymore."

He hefted the larger of the two bodies across his shoulder. "You're right about that. Do you have any functioning comms?"

"No. They washed away in the blast."

He headed toward the ladder with his corpse. "Looks like we need to find the rest of our team."

I followed him up the ladder, and I was thankful he grabbed the larger load. My guy was heavy enough to set my legs on fire a minute into our climb. We found all four of our remaining teammates three decks above and paused to catch our breath.

Anya cocked her head and stared at the bodies over our shoulders. "Why would you kill people and then carry them to us?"

"We didn't kill them," I said. "And there's at least three more to go. Somebody put small-caliber rounds into their skulls and locked them in the flooding engine room."

Shawn continued the story. "We shut off a through-hull valve and stopped the flooding."

Mongo, Gator, and Kodiak headed down the ladders. We reconvened on the bow, and Disco called the chopper. Three minutes later, everyone, including the corpses, were aboard, and we were heading back to the *Lori Danielle*.

To my surprise, Captain Sprayberry met us on the helipad.

"What did you find?" he yelled.

I pointed back into the helo. "Five dead guys shot in the head and an open valve flooding the engine room."

"I know what that means," he said. "I'll catch the *Desert Star* in less than ninety minutes."

# Chapter 24
## *Who on Earth?*

Shawn and I escorted the bodies into Dr. Shadrack's capable hands, where the cause of their deaths would be determined without the need for full autopsies, and the corpses would be preserved in cold storage until we could identify and return them to their families for a proper burial. Thankfully, our bodies weren't among the deceased, and in the RV *Lori Danielle*'s sick bay, the living always took priority.

We had abused our bodies for decades, but the doctor examined both of us for signs of head injuries and general damage following our battle against the only earthly enemy who never loses. Water always wins, but fortunately for us, we bore no new injuries from our brush with weaponized agua.

By the time I pulled on a backup prosthetic that hadn't spent an hour submerged in salt water, Captain Sprayberry had the *Lori Danielle* flying on her foils as we gave chase in an effort to catch the *Desert Star*.

The team reconvened in the CIC, and I kicked off the discussion. "It's time to put an end to this whole ordeal. Nobody understands what's happening, but whatever it is has to stop. We've collected five dead bodies, and I'm convinced there will be more. Something far beyond sinister is happening aboard that ship, and I intend to drive a stake through its black heart. Does anyone have anything to add before we brief the strike?"

No one volunteered to open up, but the looks on their faces said they had something on their minds.

"Come on. We don't keep things from each other, so give it to me."

I should've known it would be Mongo who opened up first. "I don't know about everybody else, but I'm having doubts that Congressman Landon Herd is still alive. Are we certain that none of the bodies down in the morgue is his?"

I settled onto my chair. "That never entered my mind."

Skipper said, "I didn't think of it, either, but we're running DNA and fingerprint analysis to try and identify all five of them."

"What do you have so far?"

She turned a monitor to face me. "At this point, all we have are a bunch of questions. The one set of prints that came back already makes this whole ordeal even more mysterious."

I glared down at my analyst. "We have prints back and you didn't tell me?"

"No, Chase. I'd never do that. They came in while you were giving the brief. Well, they didn't really come in at all."

I stepped closer. "What are you talking about?"

She motioned toward the screen. "See for yourself."

I read the two words on the screen and couldn't believe my eyes. "Restricted access? What does that mean?"

Skipper huffed. "It means the U.S. government is protecting whoever owns those fingerprints."

"But you can get around it, right?"

"I can try, but this one may require a call to your buddy on Pennsylvania Avenue."

"Start with the Board," I said. "If they can't get it done, I'll make the call."

"It's already done. I'm waiting to hear back from them."

Mongo stepped from the semicircle. "What about the other prints? Are any of them restricted?"

Skipper said, "We don't know yet . . . Oh, wait."

Her screen flashed, and she typed a long string of numbers and letters that were gibberish to me, but when she hit the enter key, the message was impossible to misunderstand: Access Denied.

"Denied?" Skipper scoffed. "What do they mean, denied?"

Mongo turned his knowing gaze on me. "This is starting to feel like some CIA crap."

I lifted the receiver from its cradle on the console, and Barry said, "Bridge, Captain."

"How long before we intercept the *Desert Star*?"

He said, "Twenty-two minutes."

"Lay us in her wake beyond visual range, and match her speed. I need a little time."

"Consider it done. Anything else?"

"That's all for now. I'll brief you as soon as I can."

"I don't need a briefing," he said. "You're the boss. I'm just the driver."

I dropped the handset back into its cradle. "Anything from the Board?"

She pointed to the overhead monitor. "Speak of the devil, and the devil appears."

I took a step back and looked into the faces of seven of the most stern-faced people I'd ever seen.

The man closest to the camera—somewhere in Virginia—said, "Everyone except Elizabeth and Chase, give us the room."

The team turned to leave the CIC, but I said, "Negative. Everybody stays. This thing has just turned into a national security train wreck, and I need every brain cell we can muster on this one."

My team froze and turned back to face me, and the faces on the screen turned even more stern.

Their spokesman cleared his throat. "Fine, but the Russian has to go."

I said, "Raise your hand if you've got an American passport."

Everyone's hands went into the air, including Anastasia Burinkova's.

"There you have it. We don't have any Russians in the room, so let's hear it."

The only woman on the Board leaned toward the camera. "This is no time for posturing, Chase. This is serious."

I chuckled. "Posturing, ma'am? Pardon my insubordination, but my team and I just pulled five dead bodies off a sinking ship and risked our lives doing so. Now we're being notified that our access to the identities of these men is denied. If you think this is posturing, I suggest you strap on a sidearm and join us next time we go over the rail, ma'am."

She patted the air with her palm. "There's no reason for hostility, Chase. We fear we've made a poor decision in sending you, or anyone, to intercede in this situation."

"Are you calling us off?"

"It's not that simple," she said. "There are forces at work here that we couldn't have anticipated."

I shoved a finger through the air. "Twenty miles in front of us is the ship on which Congressman Landon David Herd was last seen. It didn't sink in the Med like the mainstream media is reporting. It's very much afloat and underway."

"The congressman is not on that ship, Chase."

"How do you know?"

She glanced at each of her colleagues. "Well, we believe the most prudent step forward is to discontinue pursuit of the ship and return to the United States."

"Most prudent? Are you serious? My team and I are out here pursuing that ship for the purpose of determining if a sitting U.S. Congressman is alive, and if he's not, we will apprehend the perpetrators of his murder."

The first gentleman reclaimed the floor. "You see, Chase—"

"Cut it out," I ordered. "And tell me who those five men in my morgue are."

"I'm afraid we can't do that," he said.

I pulled my sat-phone from my cargo pocket and shook it in front of the camera beneath the overhead monitor. "Two buttons. Just two, and the next voice I hear will be the voice of the President of the United States. Tell me exactly what's happening out here, or you get to hear his voice as well."

He said, "Chase, it's time for calmer heads to prevail in this thing."

"I'm calm," I said, "but I'm also the most dangerous man in the room who's backed by the most powerful man on the planet. The bell has been rung, sir, and it cannot be unrung. I'm going to board that ship, and I'm going to find Congressman Herd, dead or alive. If he's dead, I'll start stacking bodies until somebody spits out the truth. It would be of enormous value to the security of my team if *you* started doing exactly that."

He licked his lips and took a long, deep breath. "The truth isn't very simple with this one, and it's even more difficult to express. The short of it is, we made a mistake. There was already a mission underway to rescue Congressman Herd."

I felt like someone had just dropped a building on top of me. "Are you telling me that the bodies in my morgue are American operators?"

He closed his eyes as if trying to decide what he could tell me, so I said, "If you're about to spit out some garbage about 'need to know,' let me stop you right there. Who on earth has a greater 'need to know' than the people in this room? Who on earth is more qualified to end this thing? And perhaps most importantly, who on earth is more capable of making sure that the world never knows the truth of what's happening out here, in the middle of the ocean, than the people in this room?"

Silence filled the air until the woman spoke again. "Are you suggesting you can make this go away?"

"Ma'am, that's exactly what we do. When was the last time you saw our faces or heard our names on the six o'clock news? We do your nasty little bidding, and then we crawl back inside our hole. Just tell us the truth, and let us do what we do better than anybody else."

The screen went dark, and I asked, "Did they just hang up on us?"

Skipper's fingers hit the keys, and she sighed. "No, they're still with us. They just silenced their mics and paused their video feed. They're probably trying to decide their next move."

"Don't you mean *our* next move?"

"Yeah, I guess that's more accurate."

"Can they still hear us?"

Skipper said, "No, I killed our mic, but they can still see us."

I turned to the team with my back to the camera. "Does anybody want out?"

That got a good laugh, and I said, "Is there anything the Board could say next that would make any of you want out?"

Anya spoke for the team. "This is ridiculous thing for you to ask. We are team and family, and we all want to know truth of situation."

When I turned around, the screen came back to life, and the woman said, "Okay, Chase. Don't say we didn't give you a way out. If we brief you, you're committed. Understand?"

I narrowed my gaze. "We were committed the minute we stepped on this ship."

"Indeed," she said. "Here it is. Congressman Herd serves on the House Permanent Select Committee on Intelligence. His position on that committee gives him unparalleled access to the intelligence community of the United States. We believe he has become a traitor."

My jaw fell. "Are you telling me he's a spy?"

"I'm telling you that is what we suspect."

"Who are the dead guys in the belly of my ship?"

To my surprise, she didn't look away. "They are most likely civilian contractors of the Central Intelligence Agency."

"What was their mission?"

She said, "Honestly, we don't know yet, but we're working on it. Our theory at this point is that they were charged with boarding the *Desert Star*, determining the status of the congressman, and if that status included the divulgence of national security information, they were to ensure that information never left that boat."

I scratched my head. "The CIA doesn't hit sitting congressmen."

"The CIA doesn't hit suspected spies, either, but the men in your morgue are contractors, not officers of the Central Intelligence Agency."

As the weight of her words melted its way through my skull, I felt as if I'd been kicked in the gut by an elephant. When I finally overcame the nausea, I said, "Ma'am, I need to know if this is a hostage rescue or a mission to erase a potential black mark before the ink has time to dry."

She leaned toward the camera. "Dr. Fulton, it's highly probable that it's both."

# Chapter 25
## *Terminal Velocity*

"This changes things. Take a seat, and let's talk through it," I said after ending the video conference with the Board.

Skipper spun away from her monitor to join us, and she was the first to speak. "I think you should call the President."

"You beat me to it," I said. "It sounds like the Board doesn't really know what's going on, and they want to make sure their hands are as clean as possible when we end this thing."

Skipper nodded. "That's exactly why I think you should call D.C. The Board was way too vague about what they want us to do."

I said, "Oh, what they want is clear to me. They want this whole mess to go away. It's just a matter of determining if the congressman is alive before we start pulling triggers."

Kodiak grunted. "I know I'm the wild card here, but it sounded to me like they were hoping he wasn't among the living anymore."

Singer nodded. "I got the same impression."

Gator's face turned pale. "We're not going to kill a sitting U.S. congressman, are we?"

"Not unless he tries to kill us first," I said. "We're not assassins."

Anya cleared her throat. "This is not entirely true."

I chuckled. "Okay, maybe not, but we're not gunning for the congressman. Our first objective has to be determining if he's alive and on board the *Desert Star*."

Mongo said, "There's only one way to do that."

"Exactly," I said. "We have to board her, search her, and stay alive. I'd rather not do that while the sun is shining. What are your thoughts?"

Mongo said, "I agree. Too much can go wrong way too fast in daylight, but when the sun goes down, we own the night."

"Does anybody disagree?" I asked, but no one flinched. I said, "I always say this isn't a democracy, but I do want your input on this one."

Mongo said, "Nobody disagrees. Hitting them well after dark is the only thing that makes sense. Now we have to decide how we're getting aboard. You and Shawn didn't exactly hit a home run on your last trip over the rail."

Shawn palmed his chest. "That's hurtful. We came out alive, didn't we?"

Mongo rolled his eyes. "Yeah, but you didn't exactly bring back any usable intel."

Shawn chewed his lip for a moment. "I've never jumped with you guys. How good are you at HALO insertion?"

Gator spoke up quickly. "Not good at all."

Singer threw an arm around his protégé. "Relax, kid. You're better than you think, and I won't let you miss the boat."

"We're not bad," I said, "but it's been a while, so we'd need to knock off the rust."

Shawn said, "We're matching the *Desert Star*'s speed right now. Why not give it a shot? We can stay out of their sight and make a couple of practice jumps onto the *Lori Danielle*. If we miss, we're easy enough to pluck out of the water."

Gator turned sharply to Singer. "Is he serious?"

The sniper said, "He's a SEAL. He's never serious."

"I like it," I said. "Climbing the ladder with the whole team makes us vulnerable on the way up, and fast-roping makes us impossible to miss. If we jump in, we can show up in silence without anybody on board the *Star* knowing we're there. That gives us an enormous advantage."

Everyone stood except Skipper and Gator.

Singer hooked a hand beneath Gator's arm and pulled him to his feet. "Come on. Don't chicken out in front of your girlfriend."

"She's not my—"

Shawn grabbed Gator in a playful headlock. "And she never will be if you're scared to jump out of a helicopter and land on a postage-stamp-sized ship in the middle of the night."

Gator pulled free of Shawn's arm and eyed Skipper.

She gave him a wink and said, "I'll go with you and hold your hand if you want."

That stopped me in my tracks. I turned to the best analyst in the business. "You wanna come?"

She said, "I mean . . . yeah. Not tonight, but I'd love to do it now if you're serious."

"Unlike Shawn," I said, "I'm always serious."

While the rest of the team headed for the armory to collect their jump gear, I made my way to the bridge and explained our plan to Captain Sprayberry.

He shook his head. "You're insane. You and that whole team of psychos are completely insane."

I stuck out my chest. "Thank you! That's a huge compliment coming from you. We're going to do a couple workup jumps onto our stern deck while the sun's shining."

"Fine. Do it. I suppose you want me to launch a recovery boat for those who miss, huh?"

"That would be mighty nice of you."

He waved me off with the back of his hand. "Just go. And try not to get anyone killed, okay? We've already got more dead bodies on board than I want."

"You got it. Oh, there's just one more thing."

He sighed. "What is it?"

"We want you to jump with us."

He hurled an unrecognizable object through the air at my head, but I made my exit before becoming a victim of his unidentified missile.

When I reached the helipad, Singer had Gator lying on his belly with his arms and legs outstretched. I couldn't tell if his flying lessons were sinking in, but we'd know soon enough.

We ran a buddy check on everyone's parachutes and double-tied our boots before climbing aboard the Vertol. Mongo took his position as jumpmaster, and Barbie pulled us from the pad.

We climbed in a huge ascending circle, and the *Lori Danielle* grew smaller with every passing minute.

"This is insane," Gator said.

I gave him a firm pat on the back. "Yes, it is, but you can never say your job is boring."

"Oh, that's for sure."

I tightened the chest strap on his rig. "Listen. You'll go out behind Shawn. Singer will be right behind you, and he'll talk you through the maneuver to hit the ship. Just do what he tells you, and you'll be fine."

"What if I miss the ship?"

"You won't," I said. "But if something goes wrong and you think you're going to hit the water, remember to cut away your chute just before you splash in. You don't want to get wrapped up in that canopy in the water."

"Got it. What about Skipper?"

"Don't worry about her. She's got a couple hundred jumps under her belt. She'll go out first, and let me tell you, you'll never live it down if she sticks the landing and you go in the drink."

"That's exactly what I needed," Gator said. "More pressure."

Barbie's voice came over the comms. "Passing twelve thousand for twelve-five. We're one mile ahead of the ship with wind from three-one-zero at fifteen knots."

Mongo opened the ramp and lay down with his head and shoulders outside the helicopter. He threw a weighted streamer to double-check Barbie's wind call, and after watching the streamer fall, he pulled his microphone to his lips. "Give me fifteen degrees left for thirty seconds."

Barbie made the correction, and Mongo timed the maneuver.

He said, "Good. Now, parallel the ship's course and hold this speed."

The chopper banked slightly right and resumed the original course.

Mongo pulled off his headset and yelled, "On your feet!"

We stood and made our way to the ramp with Skipper at the head of the stack.

Mongo made one final pass to inspect each of our rigs before calling, "You should be under a good canopy no lower than two thousand feet. Got it?"

Everyone yelled, "Got it!"

He grabbed Gator by the arm. "You good, kid?"

"Yes, sir. Let's do this!"

The big man moved back to his position at the edge of the ramp and locked eyes with Skipper. She nodded, and he yelled, "Go!"

Everyone stepped from the ramp three seconds behind the previous jumper to give us plenty of time and separation to avoid landing on top of each other when we hit the ship. I followed Singer into the air, and the sky wrapped me in her loving arms.

Accelerating through the air with nothing except the sound of rushing wind in my ears, I'd forgotten how much I loved falling through the sky at terminal velocity. I was less than two minutes away from certain death if at least one of my two parachutes didn't blossom into a beautiful, billowing canopy above my head, but that thought never entered my mind. If only for a minute, I was alone and flying through the air as if I were a bird of prey streaking toward my unsuspecting victim. Birds of prey were exactly what the team and I would become in a few hours after the sun had dissolved into the Atlantic.

The altimeter on my wrist spun past five thousand feet, and I watched Skipper's canopy unfold into the air three thousand feet beneath me. Disco's chute was next, with Shawn three seconds behind him. Gator was in perfect position when he tossed his pilot chute into the slipstream beside him. The bag containing his main chute exited the carrier on his back, and the lines pulled themselves free of the rubber bands holding them in perfect order. The bag separated from the chute, but the blooming canopy I expected didn't make its appearance. Instead, a streaming mess of nylon pointed skyward as Gator plummeted toward the Atlantic Ocean faster than anyone could survive a collision with the surface. The malfunctioning chute did almost nothing to slow his descent, and I prayed he had the composure to cut it away and deploy his reserve before it was too late.

A glance back at my altimeter showed twenty-eight hundred feet, but I couldn't focus on anything except watching for Gator's reserve to leap from his pack.

If I didn't get a canopy in the air above my head in the coming seconds, I wouldn't have time to pull my reserve in the event of a failure, and I'd be forced to ride whatever I had all the way to the water.

Two thousand feet flashed, and I yanked my pilot chute from its enclosure. My feet fell beneath me, and the familiar *whomp* of the nylon canopy doing exactly what it was designed to do filled my ears. I pulled my toggles free of their Velcro binding and buried the right one as hard as I could pull. That turned me to the southwest, where I watched the streamer above Gator's head drift away and a perfectly formed reserve canopy fill the air. He didn't have the altitude to fly himself and the reserve to the ship, but he was alive, and barring a shark attack, he would remain so.

Skipper touched down like a ballerina, and Anya did the same. Gator splashed in, and the RHIB darted away from the ship to collect him. The rest of the team landed without incident within ten feet of our target, and I was rewarded with the rare sound of Singer laughing like a child when he collected his parachute.

"Did you see the streamer?"

I stepped beside him with my canopy wadded into a ball in my arms. "Oh, I saw it. How bad do you think it scared him?"

Singer continued laughing. "Whoever does his laundry will know how scared he was."

The crane hoisted our young, sopping-wet operator over the rail, and the second his feet hit the deck, he yelled, "Okay, that was not cool at all! We're doing it again, and I'm packing my own chute next time."

We repacked, reloaded onto the Vertol, and did two more jumps, with everyone hitting the mark as if it were a Sunday afternoon walk in the park. We didn't have any more streamers, and Gator was rewarded with a kiss on his cheek and a sincere, "I'm proud of you."

Instead of expressing his gratitude and appreciation for Singer's affection, he shoved the sniper away. "If you ever kiss me again, I swear I'll shoot you in the foot."

# Chapter 26
## *The Best Seat in the House*

With our solid black parachutes packed and poised for deployment when nightfall made her entrance, we staged our gear outside the armory and headed for chow. Meals with the team felt more like family reunions than eating with coworkers. On that evening, though, the typical laughter and playful jabs that often punctuated our time breaking bread together didn't come. Instead, everyone looked somber, as if focusing on the upcoming night jump.

I broke the silence. "How many night jumps do you have, Gator?"

He wiped his mouth, laid his fork on the edge of his plate, and stuck his finger in the air as if working out a math problem. "Counting the one we're about to do, it'll be . . . let's see . . . Carry the two . . . Oh, yeah. It'll be one."

"Don't worry," I said. "It's exactly like jumping in daylight, except there's no visible horizon, everything except the stars is black in every direction, and the ground rush will make you throw up. Other than that, it's easy peasy. Just remember, don't go in the water with a canopy attached to your body. Your night vision won't do you any good if you're wrapped in a nylon burial cloth in the North Atlantic."

He poked at his mashed potatoes with his fork. "Thanks. That makes me feel a lot better."

"I'm just messing with you. We'll be under NODs the whole time, and there's enough ambient light to see relatively well. The ground rush will be surprising because your depth perception won't be great.

Just don't flare too early or you'll drift off the back of the ship. We need you on deck."

Singer had a quiet conversation with Gator as the meal continued, and by the time we shoved our plates back through the stainless-steel window and into the galley, the look on Gator's face turned from discomfort to that of a seasoned, airborne warrior.

As we left the mess hall, Skipper sidled up beside me. "Are you going to call the President?"

"That's where I'm headed now."

She weaved her hand inside my elbow. "Don't let Gator get hurt tonight, okay?"

I stopped in my tracks. "Why does that fall on me? Aren't you coming with us?"

She squeezed my arm. "Funny. Somebody has to keep an eye on you boys, so you know you want me in the CIC."

"I do, but it's not just us boys tonight. Anya's coming with us."

"Oh, I know," she said. "At this point, I think of her as one of the boys."

"She'd like that."

She looked up at me. "She'd like a lot of things she can't have. I'm proud of you for treating her—*and* looking at her—like a teammate instead of your next meal."

"I've never looked at her like she was—"

Skipper cut me off. "Don't lie to yourself or me. We both know better. Now, call the President."

"Yes, ma'am."

Once inside the CIC, I made the call, and the most powerful man on Earth answered on the third ring. "These calls are becoming more frequent. We're not buddies, Chase. What is it now?"

"I'm sorry, Mr. President, but I'm confident you'll agree that this one is essential."

"Let's have it. I'm a busy man."

"Yes, sir, I know. I'll keep it brief. We stopped the ship that was on its way to rendezvous with the *Desert Star*. When we boarded her, we found her flooding with five dead bodies locked in the flooded engine room."

I expected impatience from the President, but instead, I got curiosity.

"Slow down. You stopped the ship. How exactly did you accomplish that?"

"It's a long story, sir, but suffice it to say, we laid a little trap for the *Independence Queen* and she stumbled into it."

"We may need to come back and discuss that in a little more detail before this is over, but carry on."

"As I said, we boarded her and thoroughly searched the vessel. When we opened the hatch to the engine room, we discovered the bodies."

He cleared his throat. "And these bodies . . . What did you do with them?"

"We brought them back to our ship for identification, and that's when we hit the roadblock, which is the reason for this call."

"What roadblock?"

"When we ran their prints and DNA, we learned their identities were restricted."

"Restricted?" he said in disbelief. "Restricted to you? I thought you had the highest access of anyone outside my cabinet."

"I thought the same, sir, but in this case, I was wrong. After speaking with the Board, we learned that the five bodies belonged to a team of contractors who were likely dispatched to find Congressman Herd."

He cut in. "Hold on a minute. Dispatched by whom?"

"I don't know, and the Board appeared intentionally vague about it. Ultimately, we were instructed to board the *Desert Star*, determine if the congressman is still alive, and rescue him from any peril."

"Is that precisely what the Board instructed you to do?" he asked.

"Well, not word for word, but it felt like the general guidance. There's one thing that makes me a little uncomfortable, though."

He huffed. "I can't wait to hear this. You boarded a sinking ship and recovered five bodies you can't identify—even with the highest access imaginable—and *that* isn't the part that makes you uncomfortable?"

"No, sir. Dead bodies aren't exactly a rarity in my line of work. The thing that makes me uncomfortable is that I get the feeling the Board wants this whole ordeal to go away, no matter what it takes to make that happen."

He lowered his voice. "Are you suggesting . . ."

I stopped him before he could say it out loud. "We're not assassins, Mr. President. We're paramilitary operators who directly serve the best interest of the United States. I'm not trying to put you on the spot, sir, but I need to know if I'm a life raft or an eraser."

The sound of the President walking filled my ear for a moment before he said, "Chase, you're both. If Congressman Herd is alive, keep him that way and erase everything else. Is that clear enough for you?"

"It is, sir. I just want to make sure the Board—"

He cut me off again. "Do you want a permission slip from Daddy so you don't get in trouble with your schoolmarm? If so, you're out of luck. My fingerprints aren't on this thing—at least not yet—and I'm counting on you to keep it that way. If you bring the congressman home, I'll make some vague reference to a team of brave Americans, but there won't be any photo ops in the Rose Garden with you and your band of merrymen."

"Anonymity is our greatest asset," I said.

"No, Chase. The skill set of your team, coupled with *your* brain, are your greatest assets, and having that combination available at my fingertips is something every president should be so lucky to have. Go do your job, and then forget about it. I've got a dozen more projects waiting for you when you clean this one up."

"Thank you, sir. I've got one more question, if you wouldn't mind."

The President said, "I don't have time, Chase. Get to work."

I pocketed my sat-phone, and Skipper raised an eyebrow. "Well? What did he say?"

"He said for us to do our job."

She huffed. "We always do that. What, specifically, did he say?"

"He told me to bring the congressman home and erase everything else."

She seemed to chew on that nugget for a moment before asking, "Is that what you're going to do?"

"What choice do I have?"

She planted her hands on her hips. "You always have a choice. Doing what's right and following vague orders are sometimes mutually exclusive."

I checked the room to find that Skipper and I were alone. "What do you think we'll find on that ship?"

She settled into her chair. "I think you'll find no evidence that Congressman Herd was ever aboard. I think you'll find officers and crew who will claim they've never heard of him, and I think we'll never know what really happened to him."

"I hope you're wrong, but five dead bodies with small-caliber bullets in their skulls write a pretty damning prologue for the rest of the story."

She took my hands in hers. "Call Penny before you go."

"What would I do without you?"

She laughed. "You'd make the Russian your next meal and screw up the best marriage a guy could ever have."

I left the CIC and headed for my cabin so I could talk with my wife while enjoying a little privacy. As I rounded a corner in the corridor, I came face-to-face with Don Wood, the WWII vet I'd almost forgotten was aboard. "Oh, hey, Don. Are you doing all right? I didn't mean to ignore you over the last couple of days."

He said, "I'm doing great. This is a grand adventure for an old man."

"You're not old. You're just experienced."

He waved off the compliment. "That youngster of yours had quite an adventure of his own this afternoon, didn't he?"

"That'd be Gator," I said. "That was his first parachute malfunction. I would've liked for him to cut it away a little sooner, but he did okay."

He examined the ceiling above my head. "I underestimated that office girl you've got working for you."

"The first jumper?"

"Yeah, that's the one. I thought she was a clerk or something, but she obviously keeps her jump wings polished."

"Skipper's no clerk," I said. "She's our intelligence analyst. She runs most of our ops either from the combat information center on the ship or our operation center back on the East Coast."

He said, "It sounds like you've got quite the squad under your command. Tonight's the big night, isn't it?"

I tried not to smile, but it was impossible. "You might say that. If everything goes well, we'll bring this thing to an end before sunrise."

He took a step closer and whispered, "If you need an extra shooter, I've still got the rifle you issued me."

Inside his head, he was likely still the eighteen-year-old soldier who stormed the most famous war-torn beach in history.

"I'll keep that in mind, Don. With any luck, our starters will be our closers tonight."

"I hate I'll have to miss it."

I said, "I just had an idea. Come with me, and we'll see about getting you a ticket to the best seat in the house."

I led Don to the bridge and introduced him to the captain. They shook hands, and Don stood two steps away while Barry and I talked through the coming night's mission.

I said, "I want you dead astern the *Desert Star* at a mile when we step out of the helo."

Barry nodded. "No problem. What about when you hit the deck?"

"The first priority will be picking up anybody who misses the boat."

He said, "Nobody's going to miss, but I'll have the RHIB in the water, just in case."

"After you collect the stragglers, if there are any, I want you along-side and ready to sink that ship if things fall apart."

Mr. Connor, the helmsman, turned when I said *alongside*, and the captain noticed. "Go ahead, Mr. Connor. Ask your question."

With the captain's permission, the helmsman asked, "Alongside as pistol shot or rifle shot, sir?"

I laughed. "I see you've caught up on your Patrick O'Brian reading."

"I have."

Turning back to the captain, I said, "Set the distance you're comfortable with in case we need to put her on the bottom."

He said, "I'll lay off three to five hundred yards as a show of force, but we'll be able to peel off and have a torpedo in the water in less than two minutes if you give the order."

"That's perfect," I said. "And it brings me to my next request. I want to put Sergeant Wood on the bridge wing so he'll have a front-row seat to the action."

Barry eyed the nonagenarian. "If he's going to be that close, I recommend a flak jacket and a good rifle."

Don's eyes lit up as if he'd just turned twenty-one again, and I said, "I think we can find a spare vest, and he's already been issued a rifle."

Barry said, "Then it sounds like we're ready to strike."

I checked my watch. "Zero hour is twenty-three hundred local."

# Chapter 27
## *Snake Bites*

Operators deal with the hours leading up to the launch of an offensive in as many different ways as there are operators. I always preferred silent contemplation leading up to ultimate focus, but my preference was not to be my reality on that night. Instead, I questioned every decision I'd made to that point in time and pondered the possibility of how political the coming night would turn out to be. If Congressman Herd had seen his last sunrise, somebody would carry the blame, and a team of covert operatives on a ship in the middle of the ocean was as likely a scapegoat as anyone else. I wouldn't let my team bear that burden. If the Board and the President were unwilling to give us direction beyond a general instruction to solve the problem, I would do everything possible to protect my team from the fallout of what we were about to do.

As I pondered every minuscule detail of the coming night's mission, I kept returning to the one directive I didn't fear: Skipper's order to call my wife.

"Hey there," Penny said. "I've been hoping you'd call. How's it going?"

The sound of her voice brushed away every fear and doubt I'd allowed my brain to create in the previous hours and days.

"Sorry it took so long. Things have been a little hectic."

She sighed. "I get it. Can you tell me what's going on?"

I considered her question, and I did exactly the wrong thing as far as everyone else on the planet was concerned, but between Penny and me, I got it right, and I told her every detail.

When I finished briefing her on what I planned to do when the clock struck eleven p.m., she asked precisely the question I expected.

"Is Gator okay after hitting the water?"

That's why Penny Fulton was my anchor in the most tumultuous seas. She didn't care about the political implications of every single bullet we would unleash before midnight. She didn't care who would get elected next and who'd be uncovered as an immoral subhuman in the coming hours. But she did care about a member of our family who'd danced with the reaper and came out ready to dance again. She'd always be the best of me. She'd always be the steadfast rock that never wavered, and every man should be so fortunate to call such a place his home. When I sought the place where I was most complete—the place I could truly rest and believe every truth—that place was always my Texas girl with the wildest hair and brightest smile.

"Gator's fine," I said. "The only thing hurt was his pride—especially since Skipper stuck the landing and he didn't."

"Do they have some sort of rivalry going?" she asked.

"I wouldn't call it a rivalry. It's more of an irrational need for each to impress the other."

"Oh, really? I guess I haven't been home enough to pick up on that. Interesting. How do you feel about those two doing the South Texas tango?"

I laughed. "I don't even know what that means."

She chuckled. "I just made it up, but you're a bright boy. You can probably piece it together."

"I'm okay with it as long as it doesn't interfere with the operation of the team."

I didn't know if it was intentional or just convenient, but Penny changed the subject, turning the conversation on a dime. "Speaking of team disruptions, is Anya still shaking her tush at you every chance she gets?"

"Come on," I said. "If a snake bites you often enough, you start to develop an immunity to that particular venom."

She blew out a raspberry. "Immunity, huh? Is that what you're selling today?"

I thrust my point a little further. "When a man's got a Bentley at home, he's not tempted by a Toyota on the road."

"Baby, I'll be your Bentley anytime you want to take me for a spin."

"You're a funny girl, you know that?"

"It sounded like you could use a little chuckle. I can always tell when you're inside the pressure cooker, and I like being the one who gets to help you let off a little steam."

"How's the life of luxury aboard the *Freedom Four*?"

"It's magnificent," she said. "I never want it to end."

"It doesn't have to. We can retire and move aboard."

"Yeah, right, Chase Fulton. You'll never retire. You'd pull your hair out if you didn't get to catch grenades and throw 'em back."

"Maybe you're right," I admitted, "but I don't see you walking away from Hollywood any time soon, either."

"Birds of a feather, baby. Birds of a feather . . ."

"I have to run. I've got a congressman to rescue and a ship to sink. I love you. I'll call you in the morning."

She said, "Sounds like just another Thursday night for you. Have fun. I love you, too. Oh, and Chase . . . If that snake bites you again, come on home to Momma and I'll suck the venom out."

\* \* \*

Eleven o'clock rolled around, and Barbie rolled on the throttle and pulled us clear of the helipad. Ronda No-H lifted the retention pins from her favorite toy, and the M134 Minigun swung freely in front of her. I'd watched grungy, bearded men press triggers all over the world, but I'd never seen anyone turn it into a magnificent ballet the way our beautiful, bean-counting, purser turned door gunner did. With her eagle eye and surgeon's touch on that gun, she'd saved my life and the lives of my teammates on beaches and cliffs all over the planet.

Before me, seven battle-hardened warriors sat with rifles poised between their knees and parachutes strapped to their backs. Every face told the same story: The outcome was assured. All that remained was the fire and brimstone we'd wade through to grind our way to that predestined finale.

Singer closed his eyes and whispered to the heavens. Shawn strummed an imaginary guitar against his leg. Mongo subconsciously scanned everyone's jump gear. Kodiak silently sang the Bob Seger classic, "Mainstreet," and I wondered if Shawn was playing the same song. Gator sat motionless, staring into nothing as if a billion thoughts were pouring through his head. Although I hoped I was wrong, I suspected at least a few of those thoughts included walking with Skipper on a forgotten beach a thousand miles from everywhere. Disco touched the tips of each of his fingers to his thumb in a mindless rhythm as he, no doubt, pictured himself playing a young man's game. Finally, Anya sat coiled and ready to strike, leaving me suddenly unsure if I were as immune to her venom as I so badly needed to believe.

Barbie's voice broke my trance. "Twelve thousand five hundred."

I pressed the small button on the side of my headset and said, "Hold here until the *Lori Danielle* is in position."

Our pilot said, "She's a mile in trail of the *Desert Star* and closing fast."

Skipper's voice was next. "We'll be in position in thirty seconds. Jump at will."

Mongo sprang from his seat. "On your feet!"

He lowered the ramp, and everyone shuffled into position with our chests pressed against the parachutes of the knuckle-dragger in front of us.

We press-checked our weapons and pulled our night vision into position. An eerie green glow emanated from the NODs, making us look like a team of aliens readying to descend on our unsuspecting earthly victims.

Mongo walked the line of jumpers, giving each pack one final check before sending us into the darkened sky. As he touched every rig, he activated the infrared light each of us carried so we'd be easily identifiable as a friendly when the obsidian night absorbed us. Finally, he let his eyes meet mine, and I gave the nod the oversized jumpmaster expected. "Go . . . go . . . go!"

Just as we'd done a few hours before, each of us stepped from the Vertol three seconds in trail of the jumper in front of us. The difference wasn't what we saw, but how we saw it. As good as the night-vision optics were, they would never display the world truthfully. Our narrow swath of vision required that we continually sweep left and right, filling the missing areas of peripheral vision.

A little over a minute into the free fall, Anya's parachute bloomed from its container and slowed her descent from a hundred miles per hour to twelve. I watched the stream of parachutes fill the air behind hers as each of my brothers-in-arms ended their plummet to the earth beneath the lifesaving wing of nylon. I deployed my chute and joined the slithering snake as it prowled through the darkness toward the *Desert Star*. A glance behind me gave me a view of Mongo's oversized parachute working a little harder than everyone else's. Less than thirty seconds after Anya's boots kissed the deck of the *Desert Star*, Mongo touched down just as gently, and my team was reunited and complete.

I reported, "All hands safely on deck."

Skipper said, "Roger."

We doffed our rigs and tossed the gear overboard. As valuable as the parachutes and harnesses were, in that moment, they were nothing more than liabilities for the remainder of the mission.

I glanced at the *Lori Danielle* in our wake as she sidestepped to avoid fouling her Azipods with the stray parachutes. Our ship was running dark, but my NODs painted her ghostly form on the background of sea and stars. Knowing she was there reassured me that we had the ultimate lifeboat waiting only seconds away if it became necessary for us to abandon the ship we'd just boarded. Although I can't quote the law, I was convinced that we had perfectly fulfilled the textbook definition of *modern-day pirates*.

We set our radios to open-channel comms, and I made the first call of the night. "CIC, Sierra One. We are feet-dry and operational. Commencing search."

Skipper answered promptly. "Roger, Sierra One. Happy hunting."

It was time to repenetrate the interior of the *Star*, as Shawn and I had done before getting trapped in the elevator shaft. We split into two-man teams. Shawn and Anya moved to the port side with Singer and Gator close in trail. Disco and Mongo followed Kodiak and me to the starboard side.

Before pulling open the first hatch, I said, "We are proactive, not reactive on this one. Preemptive hostility is authorized. If they are armed, capable, and intent on harming you, do not wait for incoming fire. Suppress aggression before it becomes deadly."

A chorus of "Roger" came through my bone conduction receiver glued to my mandible, just as it did through everyone else's on the team.

I called the CIC again. "Start the clock. We're going in."

We made covert entry through the first hatch. Yanking open the door and running into the corridor like berserkers with our hair on fire would only serve to provide our adversary advanced warning of our arrival. Disco pulled the hatch, and I was first through the opening with my rifle shouldered and ready. Kodiak moved beside me, mirroring my position. By the time Mongo and Disco stepped behind us and raised their rifles, confusion and disbelief had already filled my head.

Mongo whispered, "What is that?"

As if we'd moved in unison, Shawn said, "Uh, we've got a situation over here. This place looks like a Hollywood soundstage. There's cameras, lights, and position marks on the deck."

"We've got the same over here," I said. "If the cameras are rolling, they know we're here, so let's cut 'em down."

The sound of two suppressed rounds from Shawn's rifle hissed through the radio, and I followed suit, putting two .300 Blackout hollow points through the lens of the camera aimed directly at me and my team.

# Chapter 28

## *Brand-New Boots*

When Shawn and I were aboard the *Desert Star* the first time, we probed the cabins by feeding a flexible lens beneath the doors, but there was no time for such meticulous work on our current quest. Mule kicks served as master keys, and we searched every room in seconds as we progressed through the ship. We made enough noise to arouse suspicion on each deck, but I doubted the sound could climb stairwells. The eight of us could suppress any aggression we were likely to meet, so the speed we enjoyed justified the noise we created.

"Corner left," I called as we approached the end of the corridor.

Having drilled close-quarters battle for endless hours, my team moved as one. I paused only an instant before stepping into the corridor with my weapon leveled and my trigger finger poised. Kodiak took a knee to my left and directed the muzzle of his rifle down the length of the short hallway.

I said, "No doors. Corner right."

We gave a repeat performance of our previous assault on the bend in the hallway, but turning the opposite direction put Kodiak in the danger zone first. I moved before his boots stopped, and I rounded the ninety-degree bend, painting the next space with my vigilant eye. "Clear."

We advanced just as we had in the first corridor and continued clearing the ship. Kodiak positioned himself to plant a heel beside the first doorknob when a distant crack rang out.

I grabbed Kodiak's shoulder. "Hold. I think that was a gunshot."

Mongo said, "It was definitely a gunshot."

I called our SEAL. "Shawn, was that your shot?"

"Negative, but we heard it, too. It was at least one deck above us."

Leaving uncleared spaces behind us was a tactical sin, but moving toward gunfire was almost instinctual for us. As I battled the decision, a second shot sounded from above, and a flurry of full-auto fire broke out. The decision was made for me, and I ordered, "Move to contact. Call the stairs."

Shawn said, "Roger. Moving to contact. Stairs in three seconds."

"Same for us," I said. "Call the top."

Knowing the position of the team following Shawn would keep us from putting ourselves in their line of fire and vice-versa. If any of us took a bullet that night, I didn't want it to be a friendly round.

Shawn called, "Top of stairs and holding."

Two more brief flurries of automatic gunfire sounded, and Shawn's theory was proven correct.

I said, "The gunfire is on this deck. We're moving aft."

Shawn said, "Roger. We're paralleling you down the opposite corridor."

The same back-to-back, ninety-degree turns in the hallway waited ahead, identical to the deck below. We rounded the S-turn without pausing and stepped into the strangest gunfight I'd ever seen.

Well-equipped hooded figures wielded short-barreled rifles with their muzzles trained away from us. They were assaulting nothing, but they were doing it like soldiers. Their movement was precise and practiced, and their muzzle discipline was impeccable. We were dealing with pros, and just like any seasoned operative would do, the last man in the stack would soon turn to check his six and discover four commandos poised behind him and ready to kill.

I raised my hand and signaled for the team to retreat. We moved silently back around the first corner, taking cover behind the bend.

"Who are they shooting at?" I whispered.

Kodiak whispered, "I think I saw another camera rig at the other end."

"Is there another team like us trying to rescue the congressman? They looked like they knew what they were doing."

Disco said, "The soles of their boots weren't worn."

I shook my head. "What?"

"Their boots," he said. "They're new. I can understand one guy having new boots, but all four?"

I called for a sitrep from Shawn's team, and he said, "All clear."

I said, "Roger. We made contact with a four-man team, but they're working away from us."

"Were they the ones doing the shooting?"

"Affirmative."

He said, "They must be pursuing somebody."

"Move your team to cover and hold. We're going to push the team of shooters to your side of the boat."

Shawn said, "Roger. We'll be in position in twenty seconds."

I lay on my belly and whispered, "I'm going to kill that camera before we move."

Mongo planted his massive foot beneath mine, giving me something solid to push against. I used the anchor and slid my head and shoulders barely far enough around the corner to bring my rifle to bear on the lens. The more I thought about the cameras, the less I understood them, but no matter how the rest of the night played out, I didn't need footage of my team shooting up the crew of a ship at sea. With one press of the trigger, the camera fell into dozens of pieces, and Mongo yanked me back by my ankle.

I said, "Easy, big guy. That's my prosthetic. You almost ripped it off."

"I'd rather have you back here reattaching your leg than dead with your brains shot all over that hallway."

"Point taken," I said. "Let's press 'em."

Back on my feet, I led my team down the corridor, ready for anything they might throw at us. We covered the two hundred feet in seconds and rounded the corner, ready for a fight. And that's exactly what we got.

In spite of my command to lower their weapons, they moved as if they hadn't heard a word I said. Rifles came to shoulders, and flashes of orange flames exploded from the muzzles of their rifles. We were in a corridor barely five feet wide, and I had started a war. Somebody was about to die, and I had waited a microsecond too long to be the first to press my trigger. But just because I was late to the party didn't mean I couldn't dance.

The recoil of my rifle against my shoulder told me I was still on my feet and fighting instead of lying on my back and bleeding out. A thousand pieces of information flooded my brain in that instant. My team hadn't moved an inch. We were solidly in position and returning fire. That had to mean we had just won the gunfight lottery. Four fighters pulled their triggers first, but my team and I remained standing with our blood still coursing through our bodies instead of puddling at our feet.

Shout-outs come in two varieties: those that last hours upon countless hours, and those that are over before the echo of the first shot stops thundering through the air. I had a preference, and the universe had granted my wish. The four shooters whose rifle barrels were too hot to touch lay in a pile of bodies, and the good guys kept breathing.

"Is anybody hit?" I asked as I stepped forward with my rifle still trained on the aggressors.

Three reports of "Negative" came simultaneously, and Kodiak said, "I guess they weren't the pros we thought they were. How do you miss a hallway full of shooters?"

The closer we moved to our victims, the clearer it became that their shooting days had come to an end. There were no pulses and not the first sign of breathing.

Mongo grabbed a handful of one of the dead guys' body armor. "It's empty."

I pressed my palm against another man's chest. "You're right. It's good gear, but there aren't any plates inside the carriers. Why do you assault a ship without real body armor?"

Disco said, "Maybe they weren't expecting any resistance."

I said, "If that's the case, we ruined their expectations."

Shawn's voice filled my ear. "Sitrep?"

"Four down. No friendly casualties, and we're moving to your position."

We pressed on until the remainder of our team came into sight.

"Are you certain you are not injured?" Anya asked as we took a knee.

I brushed a hand across my plate carrier. "Yeah, we're good. We must've surprised them hard enough to make them throw their shots. It was crazy, but we're fine."

Skipper said, "I've been monitoring the frequency, but I just want to make sure I understand what's happening over there. Nobody's hurt, right?"

"That's right," I said. "We're fine, but we put down four of them. They were wearing new boots and empty plate carriers."

She said, "They sound like amateurs to me. What made you think they were hardcore?"

"The way they moved," I said. "Somebody taught them to move like us, but they should've taken some shooting lessons."

"Did you find any identification on them?"

"We'll deal with that later. Our first priority is safeguarding or extracting the congressman."

Almost before I finished my sentence, the rattle of high-speed machine gun fire exploded far too close for comfort. We broke for cover and took up the best defensive positions our environment would allow. The gunfire grew closer, and my gut told me it was time to retreat.

I gave the order. "Fall back and cover our six. We need to put some steel between us and that shooter."

We moved in unison, with one of us always watching behind us.

The burp and roar of the weapon came again, but this time, it was joined by a friend. A second weapon of the same type added its lead to the party.

"That's a pair of submachine guns," Mongo said. "If we don't get out of the corridor, they'll mow us down before we can put up a fight."

I scanned the hallway in front of me for the best exit and saw a hatch adjacent to a crossing hall leading left. I commanded, "Door right, going right. Plug left."

Kodiak relayed my command and said, "I'm plugging left."

I hit the hatch at a sprint, sending it flying open to the catwalk outside. Kodiak fulfilled his role and stepped into the hallway opposite the hatch to provide security for the rest of the team to clear the door. Disco, the last man in our stack, cleared the door at the same instant the pair of submachine gunners stepped into the corridor, directing their fire down the long, narrow opening.

Gator said, "Kodiak's trapped. We've gotta get him out of there."

Kodiak came over the comms. "Hold your position, kid. I'm good for now. I'm crossing to the starboard side."

I said, "Shawn, Anya, Singer, and Gator, get over there and cover Kodiak's retreat on the starboard side. We'll flank the shooters when they pass."

Without a word, the four sprinted toward the stern deck to make the crossing to the opposite side of the ship. If Kodiak was lucky enough to get through an opening, the gunners would be tight on his tail, and I intended for my team to make them pay.

I pressed myself against the bulkhead and peered through the small glass porthole in the hatch. The steel door would stop the pistol-caliber rounds from the submachine gun, allowing me to catch a glimpse of the shooters when they passed. I waited impatiently with my rifle on auto and my finger hovering just outside the trigger well. Kodiak would need four seconds to escape the fatal funnel he was in, and I intended to manage the clock to perfection.

"Report clear of the corridor," I said.

Kodiak spoke barely loud enough to hear. "I'm working on it, but I took a bad fall and went down hard. Some covering fire would be nice."

"Are you hit?" I asked, but the sound of the burp guns drowned out his answer.

They were close, and my brother was down and hurt. There was only one right move, but our giant seized my arm before I could yank open the hatch and step back into the hell inside that corridor of death.

# Chapter 29

## *The American*

"Hang on, Chase. Don't open that door," Mongo said as he pulled me away from the hatch.

Resisting the strength of a man the size of a walking wrecking ball was futile, but arguing my point couldn't hurt.

"Kodiak's pinned down and hurt. We don't have time to discuss tactics here."

The instant I finished my ridiculous statement, a flurry of rounds struck the heavy steel door from the inside.

The big man motioned toward the hatch with an enormous Vanna White–style, outstretched palm. "That's why I didn't let you open the hatch. Kodiak may be on the deck and hurt, but as long as he's alive, he'll keep pulling that trigger."

I focused my attention back on my man alone inside. "Kodiak, we're coming in. Hold your fire."

His calm, confident reply made Mongo's point even more powerful. "Come on in, but be careful not to step in the blood. There are a couple of dead bodies between you and me."

Mongo pulled open the hatch, and I checked both directions inside the corridor before stepping inside. The scene was gruesome by any description. Two gunmen with submachine guns I couldn't identify lay sprawled against the bulkhead. Checking for pulses was a waste of time, so I stepped across them and called to the team. "Everybody, collapse on the cross corridor amidships and set security in every direction. Kodiak is down."

The burly man I'd come to love like a true brother rested on his right side with his rifle in one hand and his sidearm in the other. His leg lay unnaturally beneath him with a tourniquet affixed to his thigh and his foot facing a direction it should never point.

I said, "Stay down. We're closing on you. We'll get you out of here."

Mongo pushed me aside as he thundered past and took a knee beside Kodiak. Seconds into his examination, he turned his head back toward me. "Get the helo in here. It's bad. Multiple gunshot wounds and significant bleeding."

I called Skipper. "CIC, get Barbie down here ASAP, and put the *Lori Danielle* on our starboard rail. This thing just became force on force."

Instead of Skipper's voice, Barbie answered the call. "I'll be on the portside rail in twenty seconds."

Mongo yanked Kodiak from the deck like a rag doll and headed back for the exterior of the ship. I moved aside because I had no interest in a collision with that freight train. As they passed, Mongo held his pistol in his left hand, covering the converging corridor, while Kodiak pressed his rifle to his shoulder, focusing on the opposite direction in spite of his demolished ankle. The remainder of the team covered the evacuation as I followed our three-hundred-pound human ambulance through the door.

When we stepped onto the deck, Barbie had the Vertol hovering in perfect position with the ramp open and almost touching the rail. Ronda No-H lay on her stomach with outstretched arms, and Mongo planted Kodiak on the edge of the ramp. Ronda pulled him fully inside as Barbie climbed away.

I sprinted to the stern deck to see the *Lori Danielle* gaining on the *Desert Star* at an astonishing rate. The motion of the ship didn't prevent Barbie from planting the chopper on the helipad only seconds after flying away.

Two medics and Dr. Shadrack pulled Kodiak from the helo and headed for sick bay. An instant later, Barbie and Ronda were airborne and racing ahead.

Barbie said, "Sierra One, verify you want to stop the ship."

"Affirmative. We're going to war."

Barbie rounded the bow of the *Desert Star*, and Ronda did what she does better than anyone alive. She poured a wall of lead into the water only inches ahead of the bow. A glowing stream of tracer rounds looked like thousands of thirty-caliber meteors streaking through the sky.

The helmsman of the *Star* threw the rudder hard over, sending the ship violently departing her original course to the left, but the *Desert Star* didn't slow.

Barbie obviously needed to make a stronger impression, so she maneuvered the helo directly in front of the navigation bridge windows with Ronda's Minigun trained on the glass. Two short bursts of tracer fire, left and right of the bridge, turned out to be exactly what the helmsman needed to come around to our way of thinking.

If the fire-breathing dragon hovering in their face wasn't enough, Captain Sprayberry brought the *Lori Danielle* within inches of the starboard bow and flooded the *Star* with every light she could shine. The sun herself couldn't have lit up the foredeck of the *Desert Star* any brighter. Our covert operation vanished like the darkness and was immediately transformed into a full-blown seizure at sea.

Just as I believed our show of force had reached its crescendo, Weps opened up with both close-in weapons systems, sending a pair of crisscrossing streams of 20mm M61 Vulcan Gatling gun rounds across the bow between our Vertol and the bridge. With nine thousand rounds per second piercing the sky, our captain and weapons systems officer made it crystal clear who was in charge.

I yelled into my comms. "Shawn, Anya, secure the bridge."

Barbie backed away, but she kept Ronda and her Minigun well within range to part the helmsman's hair if it became necessary. With the rotors of the Vertol at a greater distance, we had a quieter environment for us to work, and it gave Captain Sprayberry a chance to further strengthen his—and our—position.

Barry spoke over the loud hailer in a booming voice. "*Desert Star*, you will heave to and hold position. Any failure to do so will be considered hostile action on your part, and I will not hesitate to send you to the bottom."

Stopping a ship the size of the *Desert Star* isn't a simple task, but her bridge crew should've made it into the *Guinness Book of World Records* for the speed at which they brought their ship to a halt.

Barry continued his commands over the loud hailer. "All armed individuals aboard your ship will be considered hostile and will be eliminated with extreme prejudice by our boarding party. If you are holding a weapon, put it down immediately if you value your life. You are outnumbered and outgunned."

Anya said, "Bridge is secure, Sierra One. We have captain and three officers."

"Well done," I said. "Have the captain make an announcement over the ship's intercom that all passengers and crew are to immediately report to muster stations."

"Roger."

Seconds later, the captain of the *Desert Star* made the announcement, and the interior lights of the ship came to life.

Anya said, "Is very curious. Captain says we are not supposed to do it this way."

"I'm not looking for his approval," I said, "but what does he mean?"

"I do not know. Perhaps you should come to bridge, or I can throw him over catwalk onto deck with you."

I liked her idea, but I said, "Please don't throw him over the rail yet. I'm on my way up."

I ordered, "The rest of the team, clear the interior and find the congressman. Eliminate all viable threats."

I made my way to the navigation bridge and didn't ask for permission to step inside.

Anya grabbed a handful of a man's hair and directed his face toward me. "This is man who *was* captain."

I stepped uncomfortably close to the kneeling man who was wearing the epaulettes of a sea captain. "How's your English?"

He looked up at me with a cocktail of fear and disdain in his eyes. "My English is good, but this is not how you are supposed to do this."

"What are you talking about?"

"This was never the plan," he said. "You were supposed to stay on the lower decks and do all of the shooting down there. He's going to be very upset."

"Who's going to be upset?" I said.

The captain's look turned from hostility to bewilderment. "The man you work for."

"I don't think you understand who I work for," I said. "I need you to break this down for me. What were you expecting to happen?"

Confusion seemed to explode behind his eyes. "Aren't you the people who are supposed to pretend to take the ship and threaten the American congressman?"

"We took your ship, but we're not here to threaten anyone who doesn't resist. Where's the congressman?"

The captain scanned the room as if trying to make sense of what was happening around him. "He is supposed to be on deck number five."

I relayed the information to the team, and Singer answered. "Roger. Deck five."

"One more thing," I said. "Something's not right. The captain's telling a story about a fake takeover of his ship. Are we certain the shooters we put down were firing live ammo?"

Mongo answered instead of Singer. "The holes in Kodiak's leg didn't come from blanks. Those rounds were just as live as ours."

"What about the first team we put down? They made a lot of noise, but I don't remember any bullet holes in anything."

Singer reclaimed the floor. "Nobody understands being shot at better than us, and we were under fire."

A rotten feeling festered in my gut, but I had too much to do to let the past half hour of my life stop me from completing the mission. "Thanks, guys. Now, find the congressman."

I turned away from the captain and pulled two chairs from the back of the bridge. "Cut his hands free."

Anya produced a knife as if out of thin air and sliced the flex-cuffs from the captain's wrists. Still holding him by his hair, she "encouraged" him to have the seat I slid beside him. Her encouragement worked, and he slid onto the seat while rubbing both wrists.

I sat on the edge of my chair and leaned toward him, but I gave him a little more space than before. "Tell me what's happening on your ship right now."

He stared down at his irritated wrists and continued rubbing. "I have lost my ship to you, whoever you are, but this is not at all what I was told would happen."

"Who I am isn't important at the moment, but we might get to that in time. You're clearly unsure what's happening on your ship, so let's deal with that for now. What were you told was going to happen?"

"I was told there would be filming of an assault, but no one would really get hurt. That's everything I know."

I furrowed my brow. "And your cruise line was okay with that?"

"I don't know. I haven't been allowed to speak with them for several days."

I leaned back. "Okay, this is getting weirder by the second. Is there an American congressman on this ship?"

"Yes," he said. "His suite is on deck five. It's the most luxurious suite on the ship. I didn't know he was a politician until we were already steaming for the Strait of Gibraltar."

I stared at the ceiling for a moment, trying to piece together what little I knew. Unable to make sense of any of it, I asked, "Where is your second-in-command?"

Singer called, "Hey, One, we've got a situation down here. There are people everywhere who want to get the lifeboats in the water."

I grabbed the handset from the console and handed it to the captain. "Tell everyone the ship is not sinking, but they are to stand fast at their muster stations until they receive further instructions from you."

He made the announcement, and a commotion rose from the doorway. I turned to see what was happening, and Shawn had an obviously terrified man pinned to the wall.

The captain tossed the handset back to the console and motioned toward Shawn's trembling prisoner. "You asked about the first officer. Here he is."

"Bring him in," I said.

Shawn frog-marched the man to the center of the bridge and put him on his knees.

I said, "Nobody's going to hurt you as long as you give us the information we need. Do you understand?"

His Greek accent was magnified by his obvious fear. "Captain, are you all right?"

*Oh, I like this guy*, I thought. *His first move was to check on his captain.*

I leaned toward the second-in-command. "How much were you paid to allow this to happen on your ship?"

His eyes darted from mine to the captain, and Shawn read my mind. He slapped the younger officer in the face and pointed at me. "Answer his question. We already know the captain's answer. We're about to find out which one of you was paid more."

The first officer blinked rapidly and swallowed hard but didn't offer a response, so Shawn unleashed a little encouragement of his own. The tendons of the man's wrist stretched beyond their natural length as our SEAL applied enough pressure to capture the man's attention.

I asked again, "How much?"

He cast his eyes to the deck. "Half a million euros."

The captain exploded from his chair and lunged for his first officer. "You son of a bitch!"

Anya threw a perfectly placed uppercut, sending the master and commander of the *Desert Star* to the deck in an instant.

The first officer recoiled against Shawn. "He got one million. I know this to be truth. I am not guilty alone."

I pounced on that golden opportunity. "Guilty of what?"

Shawn shook the man. "Answer him."

"I don't know! I don't know!"

I took a knee in front of him. "You said you weren't guilty alone. I want to know what you and the captain are guilty of doing. This is your final chance to come clean. Otherwise, you can take your chances swimming to Portugal."

"No . . . I mean, yes. We are guilty, but I do not know the exact name of the law."

I grabbed his shirt and moved my face within inches of his. "Tell me what you agreed to do for the half million euros."

He shuddered and continued blinking. "I . . . uh, we agreed to allow ship—our ship—this one to be used without questions. And uh . . ."

I backed off. "Take a breath, and tell me what else."

He didn't relax. "We had to agree to no AIS and no communication with anyone who was not on this ship."

I glanced up at Shawn, and his face bore the same look as mine.

The captain stirred, and Anya dragged him back onto his chair. She slapped him several times until he jerked away, and then she squeezed his face between her hands and stared into his eyes. "Is good. You are now awake. Do not make me do this again to you. I am pacifist and detest violence. I am very good at it, but I hate it."

I tried not to chuckle, but I had to admit our Russian's sense of humor was coming along nicely.

I shoved the captain's knee. "Hey. Can you understand me?"

He rubbed his neck and chin where our Eastern Bloc "pacifist" clocked him. He said, "Yes, I understand you."

"Good. I'm going to ask you and the first officer one question, and the first one of you who answers honestly gets to live. Who gave you the money?"

As if they'd practiced the routine a thousand times, both men spoke in unison. "The American."

# Chapter 30
## *I'm the Only One*

I glared at the two highest-ranking officers. "You'll need to be a little more specific. There are over three hundred million of us who qualify as Americans."

Anya jumped in with her trademark quip. "I am also American girl, but I am certain I did not give to you one point five million dollars."

I wanted to shut her up, but part of me liked her keeping our detainees uncertain of just how crazy my team and I were.

"Which American?" I demanded.

The captain and first officer stared at each other until Anya stepped between them.

The headache from her uppercut turned the captain into a chatterbox. "He's on the ship, but I'm not certain of his name. Some of the other guests called him Mr. Beller."

Skipper said, "I'm on it."

One of the distinct advantages of open-channel comms is having our analyst listen in on every interrogation. I didn't need to respond for her to know I appreciated her vigilance.

"Describe him," I said.

The first officer looked away, but the captain said, "Maybe fifty. Graying hair. Maybe one point eight meters. Perhaps eighty-five or ninety kilos."

Skipper showed up in my ear again. "Conrad Beller is Congressman Herd's chief of staff. He ran his campaign for Congress. Undergrad in poli-sci from Georgetown and MBA from Pitt. It looks like he's been a political hanger-on most of his adult life. Environmental lobbyist for a while, but it doesn't look like that lasted long. He's got a couple of DUIs, but other than that, no serious criminal record. Twice divorced. Two adult daughters. Net worth around one point three."

I said, "Roger," and leaned toward the captain. "Tell me how you want this to end."

His eyes widened. "Please don't kill me."

What little respect I had for the captain went out the window, so I turned to the first officer. "What about you? How do you want all of this to end?"

He locked eyes with me. "I want to see the people responsible for whatever this is arrested and convicted. I want the innocents left aboard unharmed, and I want our ship back."

Anya read my mind and slipped the razor-sharp blade of her knife beneath the captain's epaulettes, slicing the button free. She removed the captain's rank and tossed it onto the deck in front of the first officer.

I pointed toward the gold bars embroidered on the former captain's epaulettes. "If I eliminate the threat of violence from this ship, can you take her back home?"

He didn't take his eyes from mine, and he nodded slowly.

"In that case, the ship is yours," I said. "I'm taking the former captain with me, and the rest of my team is clearing the ship as we speak."

Mongo's voice stopped me cold. "Uh, One, we've got an escalation down here. You probably want to come down to five and see for yourself."

Anya and Shawn heard Mongo and perked up as if anxious for what was next to come out of my mouth, so I didn't make them wait. "Get the former captain onto our ship, and lock him down. Check in with me when that's done."

They didn't hesitate, and the former master of the *Desert Star* was on his way to my brig.

Turning to the new captain, I said. "Get on your feet, and don't leave the bridge until this thing is over. If you move this boat an inch, I'll pour so much lead through those windows that you and everything in sight will look like Swiss cheese. Trust me, you do not want to test my resolve. I've got a job to do, and in a few minutes, you'll have a ship full of innocent people who need to get home. Understood?"

"Understood. How will I know when I can turn for home?"

I pointed out the window. "See that giant hunk of floating steel? When it leaves, you can leave, but not a second before."

He stood and took a long, deep breath. "What's going to happen to the captain?"

I couldn't tell the man we had no authority to hold his former captain, and I certainly couldn't say I had no idea what I was going to do with him. I needed the younger officer to believe the fate of his captain was something far more horrific than he could imagine, so I told him something that wasn't quite a lie. "You don't want to know. Just do your job and stop asking questions."

He nodded, and I headed for deck number five.

When I arrived, my team was standing vigil in the corridor outside of what I assumed was the congressman's suite. "What's going on in there?"

Mongo stuck a small monitor in my hand. "That's him. He's threatening to kill himself if we come through the door."

I studied the image on the device that was receiving its signal from the fiberoptic lens threaded beneath the congressman's door. "He's well-armed. Is he alone?"

Mongo said, "No. There's a woman and the chief of staff guy in the other room. There's no exterior door to that room, so we don't have visual, but I watched them go in there. They've got the curtains drawn, so we don't have any visibility from the veranda, either."

I took a step toward the door. "Maybe I can talk him down."

"Be my guest," the big man said. "We didn't have any luck."

I knocked softly on the door. "Congressman Herd, my name is Daniel, and I'm here to take you home safely. Do you understand?"

"Here's what I understand!" he yelled from inside. "You people have no authority here. I will personally see that you spend the rest of your lives in prison."

I said, "I'm a little confused, Congressman. I was told you threatened to kill yourself if we came in. Was I misinformed?"

He continued yelling, growing more agitated with every word. "If any of you come through that door, you'll be guilty of murdering a sitting U.S. congressman, and I don't think you want that hanging around your neck, Daniel . . . or whatever your real name is."

"Take it easy, Landon. You're under a great deal of stress, but you're no longer in danger. We're Americans, and we're here to take you home safely."

His voice grew louder and even more volatile. "You have no idea what you've gotten yourself into, whoever you are. The whole system is rigged. There's no democracy left. You're destroying your own country, and you don't even know it. I'm the only one who can fix it. I'm the only one who can restore our country back to what it was supposed to be in the first place. Me! I'm the one! I'm the only one!"

I whispered to Mongo, "What's he talking about?"

"I've got no idea, but he's clearly out of his mind."

"Do we have any gas?" I asked.

Mongo shook his head. "Not enough. That room is too big. We could pump what we have in there, but at most, it would make them sleep. It wouldn't put them out."

"Do we believe the chief of staff or the woman is a threat?"

He said, "Until we know differently, we have to assume so."

I ran a hand through my hair. "Okay, give me a minute to think." I paced the corridor, running through scenarios and desperately searching for a way to end this without having the corpse of a congressman on my hands. I said, "Skipper, get a team into Herd's office and his residence. We have to know what's going on here."

She said, "Way ahead of you, boss. I have a team inside his house right now, and Ginger's poring over the contents of his hard drives from the office as we speak."

"Keep me posted," I said. "I'm going to work on keeping the congressman alive. It sounds like he's unraveling."

"That's not good," Skipper said. "I'll let you know as soon as we find anything interesting."

I continued pacing and talking to myself in my schizophrenic-style conversation. *Why is he afraid of us? Why doesn't he believe we're here to rescue him?*

That's when the President's direction hit me squarely in the chest.

*If Congressman Herd is alive, keep him that way and erase everything else. Is that clear enough for you?*

I turned to continue my through-the-door conversation with a man who'd potentially gone completely mad, but before I could take a step, I stopped myself and called the CIC. "Skipper, we need to search the chief of staff's office and home."

"I'm on it," she said, "but we've only got so many irons we can throw into the fire."

I said, "Pull off of the congressman's house, and get on the chief of staff. I think he's the one pulling the strings. Find me something, and do it fast. At best, we're minutes away from this thing exploding in our face."

She sighed. "Okay, I'm on it."

"Show me the video feed," I said as I passed Mongo.

He stuck the device back in my hand, and the scene only fortified my new theory. "Look at him. He's falling apart."

Mongo looked over my shoulder at the screen to see Congressman Herd lying over the couch with both hands in his hair and his legs extended. Mongo said, "We've got to do something, quick. There's enough firepower in that room to start a pretty good fight, and I, for one, don't want to be on the receiving end of any of it."

I said, "I've got an idea. Give me something to write on."

He pulled a small pad from his pocket and stuck it in my hand.

I wrote:

*I have proof that your chief of staff is behind all of this. I can get you out of there and make sure he gets what he deserves. If you want me to get you out, fold this note in half and slide it back to me.*

Mongo furrowed his brow. "Do you really think it's the chief of staff?"

"I don't know, but it doesn't matter. If it's not him, the congressman will see this as a way to escape his own trap and pin it on somebody else. Maybe that's all he wants. We can sort out the details once we have everyone in our hands."

Mongo said, "I think I like it, but how are we going to pull it off?"

"I haven't gotten that far yet," I said. "Let's see if he takes the bait, then we'll figure out how to pull it off."

The giant chuckled. "There's nothing like operating by the seat of your pants."

I motioned for Disco to pull the fiberoptic lens from beneath the door, and I took a knee beside him. He withdrew the camera, and I spoke softly. "Listen to me, Landon. Look at the bottom of your door."

I slid the slip of paper through the threshold and waited. The sound of footsteps approaching grew louder with every step until I saw the corner of the paper disappear. Holding my breath, I waited to see it return. Instead of the paper coming back folded in half, the footsteps walked away.

I groaned, angry with myself for wasting time and possibly making things worse. Everything inside me wanted to kick the door down and dogpile the congressman, but if my hunch was right, it was the man in the other room who was the real threat. If Herd showed the note to his COS, I just made everything exponentially worse.

I motioned for Disco to bring the fiberoptic lens back into place so I could see what Herd was doing inside that room.

Disco laid a palm against the deck and carefully threaded the tiny line toward the threshold. Just as the tip slipped beneath the door, a whisper came from the other side. "What kind of proof?"

I pressed my palm against Disco's hand, stopping the advance of the lens. "Irrefutable."

Herd whispered, "How do I know I can trust you?"

Instead of answering his question, I redirected. "I need you to back away from the door, and tell me where you'll be inside the room when we come through. I'll put two operators on you, and I'll personally cover your extrication."

"No!" he said in a voice louder than I wanted to hear.

Establishing non-hostile communication was an enormous leap forward, but if the COS or the woman discovered what was going on, the gig would be up, and we'd have no choice but to make a dynamic entry. I needed to lower the tone.

"Quiet, sir. I need you to—"

He whispered, "You can't come through the door. It's rigged with explosives."

I looked up at my team and gave the universal hand signal for explosives. A collective sigh returned, and my brain shifted gears.

"Okay," I said. "We can't risk breaching through explosives, but we can blow the door from the outside. That might set off the explosives on your side, as well, so I need to get you someplace safe. Do you understand?"

He said, "Yes, but where?"

"The bathtub," I said. "Can you get to the bathtub without the others knowing?"

"Yes. There's a bathroom on the right side of the suite opposite the bedroom. I can go to that one."

I said, "Don't just go to the bathroom. Get inside the tub, and get as much of your body as possible below the top edge. Got it?"

He said, "And you're certain you've got Conrad dead to rights?"

"I do, but my primary concern is getting you out of there safely and back on American soil." I glanced down to see the slip of paper neatly folded in half, returning beneath the door.

He said, "I'm heading to the bathroom now. How long before you come in?"

"We need time to rig our breaching charges. Give us at least ten minutes." I stood and motioned for my team to back up.

Gator said, "So, we're going to blow the door?"

I said, "Not a chance. I just want him to believe that's what we're doing."

# Chapter 31
## *Dirty Dishes*

The clock was ticking, and I had a lot of assets to move before my ten minutes expired. Before I abandoned the congressman's door, though, I had to know if he was telling the truth about the entry being wired with explosives.

I said to Disco, "Twist the lens to give me as much of the inside of the door as possible."

He slid the fiberoptic as far into the room as he could and turned the dial to orient the lens upward. The pneumatic closer at the top of the door came into focus, but instead of the bare metal it should've been, the arm had a passenger.

"That looks a lot like C-Four to me," I said.

Mongo peered over my shoulder. "No doubt about it. Anybody opening this door is in for quite a ride."

"How much do you see?"

He said, "Enough to blow a hole through the wall behind me."

"Can you build a countercharge?"

"I'll need three minutes."

"Get on it," I said as I backed away.

I called Anya and Shawn. "Meet us on the exterior of deck five, and bring two breaching charges."

Shawn answered, "Roger. We're on our way. The captain is locked up nice and tight."

Leaving Mongo behind to rig the outside of the congressman's door, the rest of us sprinted for the exterior of the ship. Shawn and Anya arrived at the same time the rest of us stopped outside what had become the congressional suite.

I said, "Wire both windows to blow simultaneously. Mongo's rigging the interior door. We've got less than five minutes."

Anya pressed the shaped charge against the larger window into the main salon of the suite while Singer worked on the smaller window into the bedroom.

They stepped away from the windows less than a minute later, and I assigned teams. "Shawn and Gator, you're with me on the main window. We're going in fully dynamic. The congressman should be in the small bathroom off the main room to the left. He's our primary. We're going to get him out of that bathtub and down the corridor as fast as we can move. Shawn, you'll cover our exfil and fall in on Team Two when we're clear. Got it?"

The youngster and the SEAL nodded, and I said, "The rest of you are to take down the two individuals in the bedroom. It should be a man and a woman. The man is Conrad Beller, the congressman's chief of staff. The woman is an unknown, but I want them both alive."

The rest of the team acknowledged, and Mongo's voice came over the comms. "Wired and ready inside. My clock says two minutes."

I said, "Roger. Stand by to breach."

The exterior team and I pressed ourselves against the walls, away from the windows that were only seconds away from disintegrating, and I'm certain Mongo did the same inside the ship.

I said, "Breach on my mark. Three . . . two . . . one . . . execute!"

All three charges blew simultaneously, but the massive lump of C-4 on the door closer didn't go off. If it had, it would've felt like an earthquake, but I didn't have time to concern myself with unexploded ordnance at that moment. Getting Congressman Herd out of that room was my singular focus.

Shawn led the charge, bursting through the opening with dust, smoke, and debris still billowing through the air. He broke right as he stepped through the opening, and Gator and I turned left. I couldn't see the bedroom team, but I trusted them to do their job to perfection.

I kicked open the bathroom door, and the barrel of my rifle led the way into the small room. Just as I had instructed, Congressman Herd was lying facedown in the bathtub with his feet protruding from one end.

"Get up!" I yelled as I yanked him from the tub.

He landed roughly on his feet, and I threw an arm over his head and shoulders, forcing him into a bowing position as I dragged him from the room.

I called, "Coming out," and Shawn answered, "Clear to move."

"Moving!"

As soon as Herd and I were clear of the bathroom door, Gator stepped behind me and covered the congressman's opposite side. We moved through the space where the front door had been only seconds before and turned toward the stern of the vessel.

I ordered, "Cover down" as we passed Mongo, and the big man joined Shawn on the interior.

We continued covering Herd as we ran him down the hallway. A pair of small-caliber rounds cracked off behind us, and I turned to cover our six. No one was there, so I had to assume the shots were fired from inside the room. The cracks weren't answered by rifle fire, so my team wasn't in a full-blown gunfight, but somebody was shooting.

We plowed through the hatch and onto the stern deck, where I shot a glance into the sky. "Barbie, get down here on the stern rail, double-quick."

The thunder of the approaching rotor blades answered before she could. Seconds later, the ramp was open and resting over the rail. I shoved Herd onto it and said, "Go with him, and keep his head down. Treat any wounds, but consider him hostile for now."

Gator leapt onto the ramp and grabbed Herd's arm. "Yes, sir."

I sprinted back through the interior corridor and into the debris field that had been a luxury suite before my team and I made our grand entrance. I found Mongo and Shawn pulling security in the main salon and asked, "Is everybody good?"

They both nodded, and I continued through the suite. I yelled, "Coming in!" as I stepped through the bedroom door.

Anya and Singer answered in unison. "Clear!"

The smoke and dust had settled, and the scene in front of me looked like a master class in less-than-lethal takedown procedures. Anya had the woman flex-cuffed and facedown on the bed, and Singer and Disco were subduing the chief of staff against his impressive resistance. They made short work of cuffing him and bringing him into compliance with their will.

I took a knee in front of the prisoner and stared into his face. "It's over, Conrad. And you've got a lot of explaining to do."

He shook his hair out of his eyes. "You have no idea who you're messing with."

I gave his cheek a gentle slap. "You took the words right out of my mouth."

We marched everyone to the stern deck, and I called home. "CIC, Sierra One. All secure. We'll be inbound with two additional shortly."

Skipper said, "Roger. I've got a treasure trove of intel for you when you get here. You'll want to see what I have before you start questioning anybody."

"That sounds interesting," I said.

"Oh, it is. Are you coming home on the chopper, or do you want the basket?"

"Send over the basket. I'd like to keep Beller and Herd apart."

The crane operator aboard the *Lori Danielle* swung the crew basket across the rail and landed it only feet away from where we stood on the deck of the *Desert Star*.

Anya and Disco stepped inside with the still-unknown woman, and within seconds, they were exiting the basket back aboard our ship.

Nothing made sense yet, but I was beginning to piece together a possible scenario about what we had just stopped. I had the feeling it would take a long time to fully understand the whole scheme, but I was determined to get to the rock bottom of the whole ordeal.

The basket returned, and Singer, Mongo, and COS Conrad Beller stepped inside, leaving Shawn and me behind to clean up any dirty dishes still remaining on the ship.

Just as the crew basket left the deck, a high-caliber rifle shot rang out across the water, and a bullet struck the top of the cage near the cable connection from the crane. The shot was answered by two rapidly fired shots from an M4, but none of us had pulled the trigger.

Mongo threw Beller to the deck and covered him while he scanned the area in search of the two shooters. I dived to the deck and joined the rest of my team in scanning for the aggressor.

I called out, "Somebody find those shooters, and make it quick!"

Ronda No-H said, "I've got both of 'em. The heavy gun is silenced, and the M4 came from the bridge wing of the *Lori Danielle*."

"Bridge wing?" I asked in disbelief. "Who would be firing from our bridge wing?"

Ronda almost laughed over the comms. "It looks like your D-Day buddy, Don Wood, just earned his Expert Marksmanship Badge again."

I raised my head and stared up at the portside of the big, beautiful ship I called my home away from home looming over us, and right where Ronda said he was, I saw Sergeant Don Wood offering a crisp salute. I returned it, but I still couldn't believe it.

I called Ronda again, "Where was the heavy gun?"

"It was on top of a tender about four hundred meters astern. They turned away, but we won't have any trouble catching them."

"A tender? From which vessel?"

She said, "Unknown, but it's headed south and probably making twenty knots."

"Can you sink it without killing everybody on board?"

"Of course I can. Give me thirty seconds." Barbie turned the chopper to the south and lowered the nose in pursuit of the small vessel.

I hopped to my feet and ran to the aft rail to see around the *Lori Danielle*. A dot on the water appeared, but it was too far away for me to see clearly. I raised my rifle and twisted the eyepiece to magnify the object. As it came into focus, a stream of fire pierced the ocean's surface and waved its way across the stern of the vessel. An instant later, the bow of the tender melted away under the 7.62mm fire from Ronda's Minigun. Water poured inside the remains of the boat that was missing both ends, and she began her trip to the bottom. A handful of life jacket–clad people abandoned the sinking boat. If they were hostiles, a few minutes floating on the Atlantic would give them time to reconsider their choice of allies.

We continued the crew basket operation, and the crane operator changed missions. With our prisoners headed for a holding cell until I could interrogate them, the crane lifted our RHIB over the rail and planted her gently on the surface, with Mongo, Singer, and Disco aboard and armed to the teeth. They would collect our floating unknowns while Shawn and I made one final pass through the *Desert Star*.

Believing we had done all we could to secure the ship, we headed for the bridge, where the first officer stood, still wearing his second-in-command rank.

I said, "Your ship is secure, and we're pulling off. Someone will be in touch with your company about the damage to the ship. What you choose to put in your log is your business, but I don't recommend doing any television interviews in the near future—or ever, for that matter."

The man wore an expression full of disappointment. I suspect it was targeted mostly at himself, so I said, "You got caught up in a situation that wasn't yours. You made a bad decision, but one bad decision at this point in your career shouldn't be the end of that career. There's still a mess to clean up, but I'm confident you'll come out the other side."

He nodded. "Is the captain still alive?"

"He is," I said, "but his decision at this point in *his* career is far more detrimental than yours. We're not going to kill him, but he's got a lot of questions to answer before he'll be a free man again."

He said, "I understand. Thank you for . . . well, just thank you."

"Get your boat home," I said. "And call your company and let them know you're safe."

He continued nodding. "I will, but what about the dead bodies on board?"

"We had a crew move them to our ship. We'll sort out who and what they were. At this point, I recommend forgetting that you and I ever met."

He grimaced and said, "Aye-aye, sir."

# Chapter 32
## *Oh, What Tangled Webs*

Barbie planted the Vertol on the helipad, and Gator marched the congressman down the ladder just as Shawn and I stepped from the crew basket and onto the stern deck. As I approached to meet them at the base of the ladder, I hadn't yet decided how I would play with Congressman Herd. I might've gained a slight advantage if I treated him like a VIP, but where's the fun in that?

My decision was made, and I would approach my conversation with the congressman from a position of power, albeit slightly delayed.

I took his arm. "Come with me, sir. We're going to get you someplace safe while we sort all of this out."

He attempted to pull his arm away, so I started the powerplay a little earlier than I thought I would by gripping him hard enough to make it clear that I was the engine and he was just the caboose. "Where are you going?"

He tugged again. "I have to make some calls, so I would appreciate it if you would—"

"About that," I said. "This has become a national security event, so no calls will be made until I lift that restriction."

My grip must've been tight enough to dampen his will to continue pulling, but he wasn't finished playing his VIP card. "Now, you listen to me. I don't know who you think you are, but I am a United States Congressman, and I'm going to make some calls."

I chuckled. "That's cute. On this ship, you're either a protectee or a suspect. Let me explain the difference. Protectees get a chair with a cushion, and prisoners do not." I pushed him back toward Gator. "Put him in the empty cabin beside mine, and station an armed guard on the door. Nobody goes in or out except on my order."

Gator hooked the congressional, self-important arm. "Yes, sir."

The list of places I needed to be was longer than my prosthetic leg, but I wouldn't allow my priorities to be out of place. Sick bay on most ships is a small, relatively clean, but smelly place. The sick bay aboard the *Lori Danielle* was far from typical. Most big-city emergency rooms weren't as well stocked and staffed as our mini-hospital.

"How's the patient?" I asked as I stepped through the curtain and into the treatment area.

Dr. Shadrack looked up with a pair of glasses that could almost pass for night-vision goggles perched on his nose. His gloved hands were bloody and gripping a pair of instruments I didn't want to touch. "He's not feeling any pain right now, but that will change."

Kodiak lay on his back with a breathing tube protruding from his mouth and his eyes taped shut. "How bad is it?"

The doctor said, "It looks a lot worse than it is, and it could've been disastrous. I just pulled the second bullet from his thigh. It's a miracle neither of them struck the femoral artery. He would've bled out before you could get him back to the ship."

"What about the broken leg?"

He stepped aside, allowing me to see the wound. "I'll get to that next. I can only do so much, and making sure these bullets weren't going to kill him is more important than putting an ankle back together."

I said, "I'll get out of your way. I just wanted to make sure he was going to be okay before I start the interrogations."

He turned back to his work. "I'll have somebody find you if anything changes for the worse."

The CIC was next on my to-do list, and I could barely wait to see

240 · CAP DANIELS

what Skipper found. It turned out to be far more than a mere treasure trove. It was an entire gold mine.

Instead of her usual electronic presentation, she had stacks of paper laid out on the conference table when I stepped through the door.

She wasted no time. "Oh, good. You're here. How's Kodiak?"

"He's going to be fine. The doc is pulling bullets out of his leg as we speak."

She grimaced. "That doesn't sound like much fun."

"He's feeling no pain. So, what's all this?"

She sighed. "I really have no idea where to start. I guess this pile is as good as any."

She slid a stack of papers toward me, and I thumbed through them. "Emails?"

"Yes," she said. "Hundreds of them. Those are from a private account used by Congressman Herd. Give the top three a look, and I'll summarize the rest."

I read the short, choppy emails and couldn't believe my eyes. "And you're certain these are from the congressman?"

"Absolutely certain," she said. "Ginger discovered the account back in Silver Spring. I hope you don't mind me calling her in on this one. I was overwhelmed."

"Not at all. You know you have free rein on things like that."

She said, "Thanks. As you can see, our boy Herd was setting up quite the scheme."

"Who's the other person on the email?"

She said, "Other *persons*. All of the emails in that stack are between Herd and two guys in Ivory Coast. They're not exactly Boy Scouts. Ultimately, that whole stack establishes the conspiracy to have a team of actors pretend to assault the *Desert Star*."

"They weren't actors," I said. "Just ask Kodiak."

She groaned. "Give me time. This thing is a mess, but I need you to listen. There are two conspiracies at work here. The first one is the actors pretending to assault the ship. That was supposed to play out with good old Landon David Herd playing the hero and taking them down. The plan was to get it all on camera, establishing Herd as the white knight who saved everybody on board, including himself."

I reclined in my seat. "But—"

She stuck her finger against my lips. "Just listen. I'll probably answer all of your questions as we go."

"Okay, keep talking."

She took the three papers from my hand and returned them to the first stack, then she slid a second stack toward me. "These are sub-part A of conspiracy number one. I told you it's complex. Glance through a few of them, and tell me when you're done."

I scanned the first several pages and held them up. "Who is this Garrison Ledbetter dude?"

She spun to her computer and brought up a picture of a man in his fifties or sixties. "He's a political strategist and campaign manager extraordinaire. He's practically a kingmaker. Clearly, Herd was planning to have Ledbetter run his campaign for president while using the video of the faked attack on the ship as a springboard."

I squeezed my eyelids closed and massaged my temples. "But I thought Conrad Beller, the chief of staff, was Herd's campaign manager."

Skipper raised a finger. "Beller *was* Herd's campaign manager, but based on the email chain in the stack you just read, Herd was leaving Beller and making a bid for the White House under Ledbetter's seasoned hand, and that's our segue into conspiracy number two."

Another stack appeared in front of me. "These are emails between Beller and another guy whose name I can't pronounce in Ivory Coast. There are too many consonants and not enough vowels in his name, but that doesn't matter. What matters is that Beller set up a real hit on his boss because he was pissed about Herd jumping ship, so to speak, and dumping him for Ledbetter."

I kept my eyes closed as I drew the spiderweb, line by line, in my mind. "So, *Independence Queen*—the ship we stopped fifty miles from here and found the dead mercenaries on—that ship was carrying the real hitters who were supposed to kill Herd?"

"No, not exactly. They were carrying a team of private security operators who'd been hired to testify to the heroic work done by the congressman in saving the *Desert Star* from the actors playing assaulters."

"Slow down. I'm not as smart as you. Who were the guys aboard *Desert Star* with live ammo?"

Skipper sighed. "Try to keep up. They were the ones hired by Beller, the chief of staff, to kill his boss, Congressman Herd."

"So, where are the actors?"

She grinned. "I thought you'd never ask."

A third stack of papers landed in front of me.

She said, "This isn't as cut-and-dried as the rest of it, but if you read between the lines, the real shooters probably took out the actors before they ever left Ivory Coast. Most of those are in French and Dyula."

I rattled the paper. "What's Dyula?"

"It's one of the languages spoken in Ivory Coast. It's a Manding language that—"

I waved her off. "Okay, I get it, but I don't speak that or French, so this stack is meaningless to me."

"Chill out," she said. "I'm going to give you the *Readers Digest* version. That country is a mess. Anything you want done has a price tag. Pay the price, and it gets done. That's what happened. The real shooters ended up boarding *Desert Star*, pretending to be actors who planned to pretend to attack the ship."

I squeezed my head between my palms. "So, what was *Independence Queen* doing, and who killed the American mercenaries we found in the flooded engine room?"

She finally sat down. "Don't you get it? *Independence Queen* was the getaway car for the real shooters on *Desert Star*."

I slapped the table, sending Skipper's stacks into disarray. "Oh! That's why the guy on the launch was shooting at us. He was making one final attempt to hit the congressman."

She clapped. "Very good. Now you're catching on."

"We're not finished yet," I said. "Other than the sniper, who was on the launch that Ronda sank?"

"I'll take that one," Disco said as he stepped through the door and into the CIC.

I turned to see him throw up his hands.

He said, "We don't know who they are, but my money is on the crew from *Independence Queen*. No matter how hard we pushed, they either wouldn't or couldn't speak a language any of us knew."

"What did you do with them?" I asked.

"They're down in the lockup for now."

"That puts everybody back on board, right?"

Disco nodded. "We're all back in the nest. How's Kodiak?"

I motioned for the door. "The doc should be almost finished putting him back together. You're welcome to go check on him if you'd like."

He closed the door behind him as he left, and I spun back to Skipper. "I've still got a lot of questions, and the biggest one is, who is the woman?"

"What woman?"

"We nabbed a woman in the suite with Herd and Beller."

She said, "Tall blonde with great cheekbones?"

"That's the one."

She pointed to a short stack of emails. "She's Herd's dirty little secret and conspiracy number three. She's the archnemesis of the current Mrs. Herd."

I stood. "I'll go toe to toe with any man who wants to fight, but I'm not getting in the middle of a pair of women scorned. Give me stack number one. I'm going to have a little chat with soon-to-be former Congressman Landon Herd."

She fastened the stack with a large butterfly clip, and I stuck it beneath my arm.

I found Gator sitting on a stool outside the congressman's temporary quarters. "I didn't mean for you to stand guard. We've got people for that."

He stood. "It's okay. I needed some time to think. I wanted to figure this thing out, and I think I've got it."

I shook the stack of emails at him. "Trust me, you don't have it figured out. As Clark would say, this thing is a conundrum masquerading as an enigma inside a cup of worms."

He furrowed his brow. "Isn't it supposed to be a can of worms?"

"We're talking about Clark," I said.

"Oh, of course he'd call it a cup."

I reached for the knob. "Come on in. You'll like this part."

He followed me through the door, and Herd glared up at us from his seat on the edge of the small bed. "It's about time. I've been kept waiting long enough."

I tossed the stack of papers onto his lap. "Do those look familiar?"

He read a few lines of the first email, flipped the page, and read a few more. The color drained from his face, but his will to fight hadn't been quashed quite yet. He threw the stack of emails to the deck. "I have no idea what any of that is, and I demand to use the telephone."

"Simmer down, Landon David Herd—or Montgomery—whatever you're calling yourself today. All of those emails are legitimate, but you already know that. You wrote them. Our tech team has established a direct tie to you. We know all about the conspiracy and your plan to play the part of the Lone Ranger and save yourself and the *Desert Star* from the big bad killers."

"That's preposterous!"

"Perhaps," I said, "but it was believable enough for your chief of staff and former campaign manager, Conrad Beller, to hire a team of real killers from Ivory Coast to kill the actors you hired."

His expression changed in an instant, and his tone softened. "What are you talking about?"

I abandoned the position of power I had standing over him and sat next to him on the bed. "That's right, Landon. Your chief of staff discovered your plan and concocted one of his own. It turns out that hell may have no fury like a woman scorned, but a campaign manager scorned comes mighty close. The actors you were going to kill weren't going to be quite so easy to put down since they were well-trained soldiers with real bullets and pockets full of blood money."

Herd stared at the deck. "That son of a bitch."

I slapped him on the back. "Stings a little, doesn't it?"

He growled. "I'll see that he spends the rest of his life in a federal prison. Conspiracy to assassinate a sitting U.S. Congressman is—"

I cut him off. "Actually, I've got a better idea. I think it's time you made that phone call you've been harping about, except let's make it a video call to your constituents. You can officially resign as the representative from the first congressional district of Colorado, right now, on a live video feed from right here on my ship. Once that's done, I'll be happy to drop you off in Ivory Coast. Maybe they don't have an extradition treaty with the U.S., but I don't know. That's political stuff, and I don't get involved with that sort of thing. I just travel the world and bust up conspiracies at the behest of the President of the United States."

It's a pitiful sight when a formerly powerful man is reduced to tears, but dethroning the truly corrupt is a reward like none other.

* * *

Landon David Herd resigned on national television from the deck of an unknown research vessel, at an undisclosed location, somewhere on the Atlantic Ocean.

He didn't accept my offer to deliver him to Ivory Coast, but the remainder of the crew from *Independence Queen* did. I'll never know what the officials did with the crew, but my focus remained on the Americans. Since Herd didn't take the African route out of the mess he created, I delivered him, his former Chief of Staff Conrad Beller, and the tall blonde with amazing cheekbones to the United States Marshal's Service, along with approximately fifty pounds of documents detailing the massive, tangled web they weaved when first they practiced to deceive.

# About the Author

**Cap Daniels**

Cap Daniels is a former sailing charter captain, scuba and sailing instructor, pilot, Air Force combat veteran, and civil servant of the U.S. Department of Defense. Raised far from the ocean in rural East Tennessee, his early infatuation with salt water was sparked by the fascinating, and sometimes true, sea stories told by his father, a retired Navy Chief Petty Officer. Those stories of adventure on the high seas sent Cap in search of adventure of his own, which eventually landed him on Florida's Gulf Coast where he spends as much time as possible on, in, and under the waters of the Emerald Coast.

With a headful of larger-than-life characters and their thrilling exploits, Cap pours his love of adventure and passion for the ocean onto the pages of the Chase Fulton Novels and the Avenging Angel - Seven Deadly Sins series.

Visit www.CapDaniels.com to join the mailing list to receive newsletter and release updates.

Connect with Cap Daniels:

Facebook: www.Facebook.com/WriterCapDaniels
Instagram: https://www.instagram.com/authorcapdaniels/
BookBub: https://www.bookbub.com/profile/cap-daniels

# Also by Cap Daniels

**The Chase Fulton Novels Series**

Book One: *The Opening Chase*
Book Two: *The Broken Chase*
Book Three: *The Stronger Chase*
Book Four: *The Unending Chase*
Book Five: *The Distant Chase*
Book Six: *The Entangled Chase*
Book Seven: *The Devil's Chase*
Book Eight: *The Angel's Chase*
Book Nine: *The Forgotten Chase*
Book Ten: *The Emerald Chase*
Book Eleven: *The Polar Chase*
Book Twelve: *The Burning Chase*
Book Thirteen: *The Poison Chase*
Book Fourteen: *The Bitter Chase*
Book Fifteen: *The Blind Chase*
Book Sixteen: *The Smuggler's Chase*
Book Seventeen: *The Hollow Chase*
Book Eighteen: *The Sunken Chase*
Book Nineteen: *The Darker Chase*
Book Twenty: *The Abandoned Chase*
Book Twenty-One: *The Gambler's Chase*
Book Twenty-Two: *The Arctic Chase*
Book Twenty-Three: *The Diamond Chase*
Book Twenty-Four: *The Phantom Chase*
Book Twenty-Five: *The Crimson Chase*
Book Twenty-Six: *The Silent Chase*
Book Twenty-Seven: *The Shepherd's Chase*
Book Twenty-Eight: *The Scorpion's Chase*
Book Twenty-Nine: *The Creole Chase*
Book Thirty: *The Calling Chase*
Book Thirty-One: *The Capitol Chase*
Book Thirty-Two: *The Stolen Chase*

**The Avenging Angel – Seven Deadly Sins Series**
Book One: *The Russian's Pride*
Book Two: *The Russian's Greed*
Book Three: *The Russian's Gluttony*
Book Four: *The Russian's Lust*
Book Five: *The Russian's Sloth*
Book Six: *The Russian's Envy*
Book Seven: *The Russian's Wrath* (2025)

**Stand-Alone Novels**
*We Were Brave*
*Singer – Memoir of a Christian Sniper*

**Novellas**
*The Chase is On*
*I Am Gypsy*

Made in the USA
Columbia, SC
04 June 2025

58920801R00150